Praise for the works of Louise McBain

Claiming Camille

The characters are amazing, the dialogue is perfect, the romance is off the charts, and I laughed multiple times throughout the story. At several points while reading this lovely story I realized my face was hurting from smiling for so long. Not to say that there isn't plenty of drama and intrigue because there is, but overall the story gave off a fun and sexy vibe that was perfect and entertaining. A supremely great read.

-Kris W., *NetGalley*

Maybe Charlotte

Like *Claiming Camille* before, *Maybe Charlotte*—which can be read as a standalone despite being set in the same universe—is a light and sweet read. Both Charlotte and Lily are good people who only want the best for everyone. They have their flaws too, but they act like adults and communicate instead of making assumptions, and that's really refreshing.

There's also a great ensemble of secondary characters, especia[...] romance with very lovable charac[...]. I'm looking forward to more b[...]

-Les Rêveur

With each book McBain's growth as an author and storyteller is unmistakable, and *Maybe Charlotte* is the best proof of it. It is a full-blooded romance with very charming and likable protagonists who have great chemistry together. There are also numerous perfectly done secondary characters who give the story depth and interest. The writing is very good with an interesting plot, nice dialogue and pacing.

Overall, this is a lovely book very well worth reading. I recommend it, and am looking forward to the next romance by this author.

-Pin's Reviews, *goodreads*

Maybe Charlotte by Louise McBain is wonderful! ...one of the most enjoyable reads I've had in awhile.

Charlotte and Lily are both looking for love, but it starts off a little chaotic. The story really explores Charlotte's family and her ex girlfriend Madison, and it turns into this delightful, funny, witty and charming story!

I don't want to give too much away, but the family of Charlotte's twin brother, their great aunt (and her two male friends), just bring so much heart and love to the story.

I highly recommend this book!

-Emma A., *NetGalley*

This is the first time for me reading a Louise McBain book, and I wasn't disappointed. *Maybe Charlotte* is a good read, a romance with some funny moments thrown in. Great story with an added bonus of fantastic secondary characters.

-Cathy W., *NetGalley*

What sets Louise McBain apart for me is that her books are so funny, but it's not artificially hilarious sitcom dialogue funny. She sneaks in random observations that maybe some readers don't notice, but I found myself chuckling several times. Some terms that have completely new meaning now are Madness, Charlie Pie, The Geoffrey Problem, and Laurel Jaguar.

I loved the entire cast of characters—not only the MCs Charlotte and Lily, but Charlotte's twin brother Daniel is really a MC too. Maddie, the obsessed ex, and Wellesley and her two house mates all added interest and depth. This book is set in the same universe as *Claiming Camille*, and although it can totally be read as a standalone I would highly recommend reading Camille first—I loved it so much.

-Karen C., *NetGalley*

This is a lovely romance about two women who have been very unlucky in their past relationships....*Maybe Charlotte* is listed as a sequel to *Claiming Camille* in the blurb, and this book does take place in the same "world" as the former with some of the same characters, but honestly, you could read this book as a standalone if you haven't read the first one yet. However, both are excellent romance novels, and I recommend you read both in order. I certainly enjoyed them both.

-Betty H., *NetGalley*

Astrid Inside/Out

Other Bella Books by Louise McBain

Claiming Camille
Maybe Charlotte

About the Author

Louise McBain lives with her family and pets in Washington, DC.

Astrid Inside/Out

Louise McBain

BELLA
BOOKS
2021

Bella Books, Inc.
P.O. Box 10543
Tallahassee, FL 32302

Printed in the United States of America on acid-free paper.

First Edition - 2021

Editor: Cath Walker
Cover Designer: Heather Honeywell
Photo credit: Matt Mendelsohn

ISBN: 978-1-64247-265-3

PUBLISHER'S NOTE

Acknowledgments

Astrid Inside/Out is dedicated to my sister, Linda. The day I was born she appointed herself my champion and has never once faltered in her mission to offer me unconditional love and friendship. I appreciate this more and more as the decades roll by. May everyone be so fortunate as to have someone who supports them as my beautiful sister has supported me. Thank you for always being there, Linda.

And thank you to my beta readers. Of course, Linda is among them, but Dr. Eliza McGraw and author Stacey Lynn Miller were also of great help. Thank you also to T. Elizabeth Bell, Maggie Menditto, John Menditto, Cade Haddock Strong, Mary Stapp and Christy Ross for your support on this project. Plot walks, transcontinental chats; you all helped keep Astrid on the path.

I'd also like to thank editor Cath Walker. This is my third time working with Cath and having her voice in my head is making my craft better.

Astrid is dear to my heart as her daily life is the most similar to my own. Writing and being in nature are two things I try to do every day. If you are looking to find yourself, I believe this to be a gentle and productive way. It's been an excellent journey so far. Stay tuned.

PROLOGUE

Twelve Years Ago

Bethesda, MD

Warm summer sun slanted through the back porch railings of the Dibello family home, shadowing hatch marks across fourteen-year-old Astrid's bare legs. She'd just dashed up the steep hill from the Potomac River and was still in the tired, one-piece bathing suit she'd worn kayaking. There hadn't been time to change. Her sister, Claire, was going to a party and Astrid wanted to be there to say goodbye. Right now, Claire and her intriguing new friend, Simone Galliano, were inside having a wardrobe consultation. Astrid couldn't wait to see what her beautiful big sister chose to wear. Entering her junior year of high school, Claire Dibello was a rising star at the Washington National Ballet but might be mistaken for a runway model. With perfect posture, a long willowy body and the face of a porcelain doll, Claire decorated any space she was in. She was also Astrid's best friend.

Astrid was two years younger and had just finished middle school. Weeks away from the start of her freshman year, she was in an unclassifiable purgatory that Claire assured her would go away the minute she stepped foot in the high school. She'd invited Astrid along to a party full of upperclassmen that night, but the idea was impossible. Astrid wouldn't go to the party if it was downstairs in her own living room. Her father liked to say she was shy, but Astrid didn't feel this was true. She simply preferred her own company or the company of her cat to most of the kids she met at school. And why bring anyone home when she already shared a room with her best friend?

Tonight, Claire was celebrating maintaining her position in the top tier of the dance company. Every year she went through the same agonizing process of reauditioning for the A1 spot, and every year she made it. But this was Simone's first time in the highest group. Her ascension meant she'd be spending a great deal of time with Claire. For reasons she couldn't explain, Astrid felt happy about this. There was something exciting about Simone, who was the daughter of the Italian ambassador and went to a prestigious girls' boarding school in Virginia where there was an option to bring your horse. But it was more than just her convertible Fiat with light blue diplomat plates and the accent that belonged in a James Bond movie. Of all Claire's friends, Simone was the one Astrid liked best. Maybe one day they could be friends too. But not tonight. Astrid wouldn't ruin Claire's evening by playing the tag-a-long little sister.

"Hey Stinky." The door opened, and Claire walked out in a cloud of strawberry body lotion. Freed from the confines of the perfunctory ballerina's bun, her thick blond hair lay across her shoulders in golden waves of glory. "Are you sure you won't change your mind and come with us? Simone doesn't care. She just said so."

"It's true." Simone shrugged her shoulders and her own glossy hair, which was long, dark and curly, shimmered in the light, catching Astrid's eye. Her Italian accent was very light from years of American boarding school and her English easily understood. "It's a party. Why shouldn't you come? There will be lots of boys." She smiled and a dimple showed in her left cheek.

"No, but thank you," Astrid said, and then for some unexplainable reason felt a blush creep up her neck and settle atop her head in the roots of her own blond hair. She brought her knees to her chest, forming her body into an egg shape, and stared down at her scabbed shins. Why was she still wearing this hideous bathing suit?

"There isn't a drinking age at Simone's house," Claire informed Astrid.

Simone made a tsking noise. "Everyone in the USA thinks this is very important," she said and linked an arm companionably through Claire's.

"Why isn't there a drinking age at your house?" Astrid asked.

"My parents live at the Italian Embassy. Technically, it's not American soil. It belongs to Italy. So, American kids can drink there."

"Don't you love that?" Claire asked, but the sight of Simone's hands on her sister was distracting Astrid in an unfamiliar way. She struggled to stay with the thread of the conversation.

"Um, teenagers can drink at your house?"

"If they like." Simone shrugged again and now Astrid was fixated on her clavicle. What was it about this girl? She lifted her eyes to Simone's lips. Watching her talk, she felt light-headed. "But Italians do not understand the desire to always be so drunk. It is no fun for us to walk into furniture and be sick in the morning."

"Americans don't like that either," Claire assured her, and made a *yikes* face at Astrid. Earlier in the summer the sisters had sampled too much Champagne at their cousin Ashley's wedding and taken turns holding each other's hair back in the dune behind the beach cabana.

"I think it's cool, that the Italian government trusts you to make the choice," Astrid mused and Simone nodded in surprise.

"Your little sister is very smart, Claire."

"Astrid's the brains of the operation," Claire said, smiling. "She's going to be a famous writer one day. Just wait."

"Don't say that," Astrid said crossly. Though confident, she didn't want to be the center of attention in front of Simone.

Claire was defiant. "Well, I'm counting on you to be successful. When my ballet career is over, and I'm a crippled old woman, I may have to live in your basement."

"How will you get down basement stairs if you can't walk?" Simone asked making Claire laugh, but Astrid had an answer.

"I'll carry her," she said, and was rewarded with a smile that sent another surge of heat to her face.

"Your sister is wonderful, Claire."

"My sister is the best."

CHAPTER ONE

Sudden Impact

"Do me a favor? Keep your eye on those girls?" Tara Turkman nodded toward a trio of teenagers rifling through a display of two-thousand-dollar cashmere sweaters in her Georgetown boutique.

Astrid Dibello studied the young women browsing the luxurious merchandise. Dressed in the short tartan skirts, white-collared blouses and blue sweaters of a prestigious Washington, DC girls' academy, they might be considered old-fashioned looking if not for their flat ironed hair and trendy skateboarding sneakers.

"Have they been in before?" Astrid's older sister, Claire, asked.

"Yes, and they only pay if their mothers are along," Tara told them. "When they come in without their moms they steal me blind. Last month someone took a silk jacket worth more than my car."

"No way," Astrid called bullshit. As pricey as Closet Diva's merchandise was, there were no jackets in the store of equal value to Tara's Turkman's Tesla.

"Okay, your car," Tara conceded and they all laughed because there was almost certainly something in the store pricier than Astrid's Volvo station wagon. Twenty-six years old, it had been new when her parents drove her home from the hospital. How the thing was still running was anyone's guess.

"Entitled jerks," Claire said, her big, blue eyes tracking the tallest girl who was now walking toward the back of the store. "I hate them."

"I hate them, too," Astrid echoed her big sister. Hate was a strong word but Tara deserved solidarity. She'd been Claire's best friend since preschool and also, she was smoking hot.

"Right?"

"Definitely." Astrid smiled.

It felt good to be hanging out with Claire again. Her heavy practice schedule with the Washington National Ballet and Astrid's ridiculous pouting had lately kept the sisters from spending quality time. Astrid was ready to get back on track and was happy Claire had included her in the going-away lunch.

Tara raked a manicured hand through her glossy dark hair. "They pull this trick where one girl distracts me by buying something cheap and the others sneak out the door with the good stuff."

"There's nothing cheap in your store." Astrid snorted.

"Sure, there is." Tara picked up a miniscule strip of silver Lycra. "This headband only costs forty dollars."

"Oh. Excuse me," Astrid laughed. "Except for these bargain basement headbands." Pulling one back on her thumb, she flicked it at Claire who caught it and pulled it over her head.

"Nice catch."

"Nice throw."

The sisters smiled at each other.

"Forty dollars isn't expensive," Tara said.

Astrid rolled her eyes but didn't push it. As the granddaughter of DC's most successful retailer, Tara Turkman had a different perspective on money than she and Claire, whose parents were mere commercial real estate agents.

Claire pulled her long blond hair off her face showcasing the perfect symmetry of her features. Looking at her, no one would argue that their mother had been second runner-up in the Miss America Pageant. Astrid looked more like their father, Jerry, whose defining physical trait was a strong Roman nose. Most members of the Dibello family had inherited the prominent facial feature but, besides Astrid and her cousin Adrienne, only the men chose to keep it. Astrid didn't think too much about it and enjoyed being included in the *Cosa Nose-tra* family photos staged each year at Thanksgiving.

"Gwynnie sells these on Goop," Tara informed them. "It really suits you." She lifted a hand to help Claire with the accessory and Astrid knew their friend was switching to sales mode. Claire might be Tara's BFF, but she was also a client and, as a principal dancer for the Washington National Ballet, a walking billboard for the boutique.

"You think so?" Claire looked doubtful.

"Absolutely," Tara plucked at a sliver of fabric trapped beneath the elastic. "Don't you agree, Astrid?"

"It's okay," Astrid said truthfully. The headband was fine but it didn't enhance Claire's looks as much as coexist next to them. Claire would look good with a turtle on her head. This wasn't sisterly prejudice as much as a fact of life. Because Claire was stunning. Next week she was leaving on a national tour, dancing the title role in *The Sleeping Beauty*. After struggling for years with a recurring Achilles injury, Claire was finally realizing her dream. She fit the billing so well they'd used her face in the promotional material.

Tara handed her friend a different colored headband. "It might be nice to have something new when you're on the road. How long is the tour?"

"Two months," Claire said, smiling. "We're doing cities in both the US and Canada and they're giving us time to rest and see the sights. Coty is so excited. I'm having fun watching him make plans. Thanks for looking after Eartha Kitty."

"You're welcome," Astrid and Tara said in unison.

Claire laughed and Tara put a hand on her hip drawing Astrid's attention to her tiny waist. "I thought I was watching Eartha."

"You're both watching Eartha." Claire took off the headband. "She needs lots of attention and you won't be the only people checking in."

"Why didn't you just make Miles do it?" Tara asked. Astrid pulled her eyes away from Tara's ass and considered the question. Tara's brother was the owner-occupant of the historic Dupont Circle mansion where Claire and her boyfriend Coty rented a second-floor apartment. Surely it would have been easier to have him cat sit.

"We asked him, too." Claire handed Tara the headband. "Coty wants to make sure Eartha isn't lonely. And Simone is going to look in as well."

"Simone? When did you see Simone?" Tara pursed her lips. "I didn't think she got into town until next week."

"I haven't," Claire admitted. Pulling out her credit card, she gestured for Tara to wrap up the headband. "We've been texting. I told her I'd leave a key with Astrid."

"When were you going to tell me?" Astrid teased. She was happy to perform any errand Claire required. Her job, writing a popular nature blog, allowed her flexibility of both time and place. If in the right mood, she might even write about cat sitting. Draping an arm around Claire's shoulder she inhaled the familiar scent of strawberries. It felt wonderful to be with her sister again.

"I'm telling you now," Claire said, and pulled a key from her purse. "I'm giving you another apartment key to hand off to Simone. You remember her from ballet?"

Astrid didn't have to think to conjure up an image of the woman she credited with her sexual awakening. It was one of the very few secrets she hadn't shared with her sister and, though it felt great to be reconnecting, she wouldn't tell her now. Especially not in front of Tara who was historically jealous of Claire's friendships that revolved around ballet. "Um, yeah. I remember Simone."

"She emailed me out of the blue, looking for apartments in DC. I told her Miles was renovating the attic space above us and she took it."

"Isn't she really rich?" Astrid asked.

"That's what I said!" Tara shouted, and pointed at Claire. "Simone's family owns half of Milan. Her dad was the ambassador, wasn't he? Why is she taking my brother's filthy little apartment?"

Claire frowned. "Oh, it's not filthy. Miles did a great job. I was up there yesterday. The place is adorable and really reasonable. If Astrid wasn't so happy living with Leigh, I'd have snagged it for her."

"How are things with your sporty dentist?" Tara asked.

Astrid crossed her fingers behind her back. "Fantastic."

Claire gave her a funny look but Tara nodded. "Well, cohabitation certainly agrees with you." She waved a hand up and down Astrid's frame. "You look great. Have you lost weight?"

"Maybe a little?" Astrid said, uncomfortable with the subject. Weight loss was not something she generally thought about. At five foot ten, Astrid's frame was similar to Claire's who sometimes had to worry about being too skinny.

"Leigh had better be feeding you," Claire said playfully, and Astrid was careful to keep her smile fixed in place. Her so-called girlfriend was an ultra-marathon runner with the diet of a rabbit and the economy of a miser. The idea of her feeding Astrid anything, besides a line about why Astrid needed to pay more for utilities because she took longer showers, was laughable. Sadly, the joke was on Astrid.

For four amazing years she and Claire had shared their lives and wardrobes in a Mount Pleasant fairytale castle of a run-down mansion owned by a friend of their father's. Four floors, it had seven bedrooms, three staircases and a screened-in sleeping porch. Astrid and Claire were the only ones on the lease but the other rooms were always in use by wayward dancers. Between companies, between apartments, between lovers, Astrid hadn't asked questions. Happy with the light from these ethereal beings swirling around her, she'd simply absorbed their energy.

It wasn't unlike being in nature. Astrid might still be there now if Claire hadn't met Coty and fallen in love.

Six months ago, when the lease had ended, Claire had moved in with her new boyfriend, and Astrid had moved in with Leigh. Full of resentment at losing a home she truly loved and her roommate in one fell swoop, Astrid had flouted her family's advice and shacked up with the sporty dentist she'd just begun dating. It had been a horrible mistake. Aside from the easy river access, Astrid hated almost everything about living with Leigh, who turned out to be stingy to the core. Astrid had known almost immediately that moving in with her was a bad idea. So far, Dibello pride hadn't allowed her to admit the mistake to her family. In fact, Astrid had been avoiding them, but Claire's departure had succeeded in rousing her out for lunch. It was wonderful to see her sister again, who was graciously pretending nothing was amiss. Currently she was reading Astrid's latest blog out loud to Tara.

Each week on her website *Outside Astrid*, Astrid posted a story linking something in the local area—also known as the DMV for DC, Maryland, and Virginia—to the natural world. She barely made enough money to cover the rent and her student loans, but at fifty thousand subscribers the blog attracted enough sponsors to allow her to quit her copy-editing job and pursue her dream fulltime. She counted this as a victory. Anything worth doing, took doing.

Last week she'd written a piece about a group of menopausal women who'd formed a drumming circle. Every month the Different Drummers collected under the full moon to beat out their frustrations on plastic Costco buckets. Claire had reached the part about the dangers of carpal tunnel syndrome when Astrid made her stop.

"That's enough. You can email Tara the link."

"Fine, but don't forget to read the comments section, too," Claire told her friend. "Some of Astrid's readers are really funny. And I love these Different Drummers." Her eyes sparkled. "Your post makes me want to buy a bucket."

"They have extra," Astrid told her.

She didn't add that hanging out with the feisty percussionists had been the highlight of her week. It wasn't Claire's fault that Astrid had cut herself off from the family over hurt feelings regarding a living arrangement. She hoped to properly apologize when the ballet company returned from the tour. Right now, it was Claire's time to soar. Astrid would not weigh her down with issues that would keep.

Claire handed her the key to her apartment. "Please, take this to Simone next week when you go over for NASCAR?"

"I'm not watching NASCAR with your cat," Astrid said, but put the key into her pocket. She would not mind running into Simone.

"You don't have to watch the actual races, just be there in the room with her." Claire kissed her cheek.

"How about, no?"

"How can you be so mean? You know how she loves the little flags they're always waving. And don't make me list the things I've done for you during your lifetime." Claire arched a perfectly sculpted eyebrow and Astrid's jaw dropped open in surprise. For as long as she could remember, her sister had been trying to master the dramatic move. When had she finally figured it out?

"You're doing the eyebrow thing!"

"Coty taught me." Claire beamed, and did it a few more times.

Tara, totally missing the point, remarked, "Actually, I was just noticing your eyebrows look amazing Claire, perfect really. They're symmetrical but not identical. As my esthetician always says, eyebrows should be sisters, not twins." She beamed at Claire who raised one non-identical eyebrow again as she smirked at Astrid.

"You have an esthetician?"

"Who doesn't?" Tara shrugged. "So, what's the ambassador's daughter up to these days? Does Simone have a boyfriend?" Tara laid the headband down on a piece of sparkly tissue paper.

"I'm not sure she dates guys," Claire said, casually.

"What? When did she tell you that?" Tara asked, clearly shocked by the information. "I thought you hadn't seen Simone in ten years."

"I haven't," Claire said, and Astrid was surprised to hear her sister on the defensive. "And I'm not completely certain she's gay, it's just something I've always suspected."

"Well, you never told me," Tara said, pouting.

"It's just a hunch," Claire told her, and then made a high squeaky noise, Claire-speak that meant something was wrong.

Astrid turned and saw two of the high school girls approaching the counter. One of them was holding a tiny, lace tank top and the other was on her cell phone. The third girl, the tallest of the three, was nowhere to be found.

"Where's the tall girl?" Tara hissed through clenched teeth. Astrid arched her back and saw the tall girl creeping slowly along the other side of the store. Back facing the register, her hands were on the front side of her body and not visible at all.

"On it," Astrid said, and dropped to a crouch.

Claire's eyes widened. "What are you doing?"

"I'm defending Tara's bottom…line," Astrid quipped and army crawled in the direction of the front door.

"Astrid, no," Tara said, but it was too late.

The next thirty seconds happened very quickly. The tall girl saw Astrid coming and made a run for it. Throwing open the heavy plate-glass front door, she hit Astrid squarely in the face. Pain, like nothing she'd felt before, shattered her consciousness. Astrid heard someone scream, and then passed out cold.

* * *

She awoke to someone stroking her hair. "Astrid? Honey? Oh, Jerry, she's waking up." It was her mother's voice. Astrid tried to open her eyes but wasn't able to. What was going on? Why couldn't she see?

"Darling?" her mother asked, hopefully.

"Mom?" Astrid croaked. "What's the matter with my eyes?" She flicked her tongue out and found her bottom lip split open.

Her whole face hurt, her nose in particular, which throbbed like a beating heart and seemed to have a bandage on it.

"Your eyes are swollen shut," another voice boomed. "You look like a prize fighter." Astrid didn't need to be able to see to know her father was in the room.

"Do you remember what happened?" Her mom sounded tentative.

"I was trying to stop a shoplifter," Astrid said. Reaching up, she gently touched her bandaged nose. Pain exploded through her head and she swore, "Shit!"

"Be careful!" her mother yelled, and Astrid lay back against the pillows.

"It really hurts. Can I have some water?"

For some reason, her mother didn't think this was a good idea. "I'm not sure. Let me call the nurse."

"Of course she can have some goddamn water, Katrina," her father pushed back against her mother's caution. "We don't need to get the green light from any nurse. I've got a bottle right here."

"Don't give her any water." Katrina said, sternly.

"Fine."

"Where are we, Dad?"

"We're at Georgetown Hospital," he told her.

"They're taking excellent care of you. You were hit by a Westover." Her mother sounded impressed with the pedigree of Astrid's assailant. "The nurse should be here soon to let us know about the water."

"We can give her water, Katrina," Astrid's father muttered but the argument stopped when another person entered the room.

"Glad to see you're awake," a voice chirped. "My name's Janet and I need to take your vitals."

"Astrid wants some water, is that allowed?" her father asked, immediately. "And an ice pack, how about an ice pack?" He squeezed Astrid's hand.

"The ice, I can do," Janet said brightly. "But it's a no-go on the water until Dr. Coleman takes a look at her."

"Is it true that Senator Westover pulled him off the golf course?" Katrina tried to engage her, but Janet didn't seem interested in gossiping.

"Dr. Coleman will be here as soon as he can."

"It was the senator's granddaughter who hit her." Katrina made another attempt but Janet didn't respond. Even blind and semiconcussed, Astrid could tell the nurse was annoyed with her mother.

"I'll let you know when the doctor arrives. I need to take your daughter's vitals now. If you don't mind?"

Astrid felt Janet's gentle hand on her pulse point. She tried to relax but her mind felt sluggish. Why would water be bad for a broken nose? "I'm really thirsty," she said, and Janet squeezed her wrist.

"You can have some ice chips in just a sec. But you can't have anything else in your system in case Dr. Coleman wants to operate."

"Operate?" Astrid sat up too quickly and the room began to spin. How hard had the door hit her?

"It's going to be fine, sweetie." Her mother was now by her elbow. "We'll need to keep an eye on your concussion but Dr. Coleman is the best plastic surgeon on the east coast. He does all the anchors on the Today Show. People Magazine voted him sexiest doctor last year. After the operation, your nose will be as good as new, maybe better."

"I don't want a new nose," Astrid croaked. She reached for the bandage and her father lay a hand on her shoulder.

"I know, baby. It's going to be okay."

"Dr. Coleman is the best." Her mother assured her. "Now, how can I reach Leigh?"

"Please, don't call her," Astrid said. The last thing she needed was to bring Leigh into this situation.

"Why not?" Her mother sounded surprised. "Won't she care that you've been in an accident?"

"She has surgeries all day," Astrid lied. She'd no idea what Leigh had scheduled for the afternoon but if asked to come she might want to be reimbursed for parking. "I don't want to distract her."

Janet slid the blood pressure monitor up her arm and tightened the cuff. "Mind if we postpone this conversation until after I finish? Would hate to get your blood pressure up and get a false reading." She paused with her hand on the pump.

"Sure." Astrid was happy for any excuse not to talk about Leigh. Like Claire, her parents still thought they were a happy couple. Astrid planned to correct the situation soon. Now did not seem like the best time.

"Your vitals are all fine, considering the trauma you've had," Janet informed them. "Can I get you anything?"

"A cold pack," her father repeated. "And ice chips."

"I'll get the cold pack now," the nurse said and her voice moved toward the door. "The ice chips are down the hall in the kitchen."

"I'll go," her mother said. "I'll send Claire back with them. She's desperate to see you. Tara's in the lobby too."

"Tara's here?" Astrid was surprised. Tara never closed the store unless there was an emergency or a sale at Saks.

"She's been here all afternoon," her father assured her.

"Turns out she knows Celia Westover from Pilates." Her mother sounded thrilled.

Astrid could barely follow her. "Who?"

"Celia Westover is the daughter of Senator Westover and the mother of the girl who hit you with the door. She called in a favor. That's how the world works." Warm, dry lips pressed to Astrid's forehead. "I'll send Claire back with ice chips."

Astrid waited until she heard the door close to address her father.

"Daddy?

"Yeah, sweetheart?"

"How bad is it?"

CHAPTER TWO

Flipping Out

"Need anything at Trader Joe's?" Leigh called from the living room. "I'm going to pick up a few things after my run. You can Venmo me the cash later."

Astrid heard the jingle of keys and knew her so-called girlfriend already had one foot out the door. Though a medical professional, Leigh had been almost nonparticipatory in Astrid's recovery. In training for the Marine Corps Marathon coming up in a couple of weeks, she was more focused on her workout schedule and a new woman on her running team named Shoshana. Astrid had heard the name too many times in the last month to doubt Leigh was working a crush. It was obvious to the point of being absurd.

"Get me some spinach gnocchi?" Astrid requested. The front door of Closet Diva hadn't knocked out any teeth but her lower jaw was still sore. Everything was still sore.

"Sure, no problem," came the reply with a clear note of relief. Astrid had noticed that Leigh seemed happiest these days when she was leaving the apartment. If it wasn't the mysterious Shoshana, it had to be someone else.

"Want to invite the Gowear team over for wine next week? My bandage comes off tomorrow and the swelling should be gone by then. We can introduce everyone to my new face. I want to meet your new friend Shoshanna," Astrid tried. When Leigh didn't respond, she wondered if she'd heard her. "Leigh? Isn't it your turn to host? Have you ever hosted?"

"Can we talk about it later?"

Leigh was still in the living room, so Astrid stepped out of the bathroom to have a proper conversation. The two-bedroom townhome in Georgetown was tiny but immaculate. Leigh's father had purchased the place when Leigh was an undergraduate at American University twenty years before and given it to her when she'd graduated from dental school. In between, she'd painstakingly rehabilitated every square inch to historic Georgetown standards.

"What's wrong with now?" Astrid pushed her. The situation was getting fairly silly. How long could they go pretending things were normal? They slept in the same bed and never had sex. It was the opposite of romantic. Platonic wasn't the right word either. Platonic would be a step up. With Leigh, every night felt like a rejection.

"I'm running late." She put her hand on the mantle of the fireplace that, though functional, was never used because Leigh couldn't abide a mess. It's probably why they'd stopped having sex and had never kissed on the mouth. Who didn't kiss their lover on the mouth? The one time Astrid had mustered enough courage to ask Leigh about it, she'd muttered something cryptic about having seen dark things in dental school and changed the subject. Astrid had let it go, because by that time, she'd known moving in with the sporty dentist was a colossal mistake.

"What time will you be home? I've got to read over my blog, so I might be up a while."

"I thought you said you had several ready to go," Leigh said.

"Yeah, I do have a few finished, I just like to give them another look before I post."

"Don't stay up too late," Leigh said, looking stern. "Lack of sleep could affect your recovery."

"I'll keep that in mind," Astrid said, and couldn't help wondering if Leigh was meeting the mysterious Shoshanna. Did she even care?

"So, I guess I'll see you later?" Astrid asked.

"Um, maybe."

"Are you running other errands?" She gave it one last try.

"I'm not sure. I've really got to go."

Astrid glared at her. Tall and very thin, Leigh had closely cropped red hair and symmetrical features that gave her a clean androgynous appeal. Astrid had once found her very attractive. She now thought she looked like a whippet. They'd met a year ago, through a mutual connection to Gowear. The local outfitter who sponsored Leigh's running club was also the premier sponsor of *Outside Astrid*.

"Okay, then, bye," Astrid said, and the towel slipped down exposing a breast. Eyes glued to her phone, Leigh didn't notice. Was she made of stone? Astrid decided to test her. Maybe the blow to the head had jarred something loose but she was tired of living in this status of nothing. Something had to give. She let the towel fall away completely. The motion caught Leigh's eye and she lifted her head.

"What are you doing?" She gasped.

Her eyes were so full of horror that Astrid felt as if she'd been struck. She scrambled to cover herself. "Nothing, never mind." Stumbling backward, she fumbled with the towel as Leigh looked away pointedly.

"Astrid, I'm sorry. I don't think you're ready for that," she said, in what Astrid imagined was the same voice she used when she told someone they needed a root canal.

"Ready for what?" Astrid asked, and felt her temper begin to boil. The Dibello nose wasn't the only thing she'd inherited from her Italian family. She also had a notoriously short fuse. "What am I not ready for? A hug? A back rub? A kiss on the cheek? You haven't touched me in four months." Holding the towel firmly in place with one hand, she fanned the other in Leigh's face. "Why won't you even look at me?"

"That's not true!" Leigh protested and bright spots of color stained her cheeks in perfect red circles like a Raggedy Ann doll. It always happened when she was feeling a powerful emotion or competing hard in a race. Never once had it happened when they'd had sex. Today the passion spots were flaring in anger. "We spooned last night!" Leigh argued and Astrid exploded.

"You keep a pillow jammed between us. That's not spooning. I've been closer to people on the Metro bus."

"That's just nasty." Leigh looked horrified at the idea of ride-sharing with strangers.

"Riding the bus is not nasty," Astrid yelled, and then began to list all the things Leigh missed by being a germaphobe. Ticking them off on her fingers she let the towel fall to floor. "And neither is swimming in the river, or shopping at thrift stores, or having a pet live inside the house with you, or kissing. Kissing isn't nasty!"

Leigh grew very still. The only things moving were the spots on her face which flashed like a caution signal. Instead of responding to Astrid, she turned on the heel of her high-end Gowear running shoe and walked out of the room. Naked, Astrid charged after her into the entrance hall.

"What are you doing?" Leigh looked as if she thought Astrid might try to follow her out the door.

"Forcing a conversation. My nudity obviously bothers you."

Leigh heaved a heavy sigh. "Can we talk about this later? It's obvious we both have stuff to say."

"Should I wait for you? I'll be up working on the blog."

"No."

Leigh's cheeks spotted again and Astrid decided to let it go. She fingered the splint on her nose. "It's coming off tomorrow."

"Great," Leigh said, but her smile was tenuous and she didn't offer Astrid any words or encouragement. She picked up her keys and walked out the door.

Okay then. They definitely needed to have that talk, sooner rather than later, and Astrid probably needed to move out. She'd been in denial for too long and now it looked like her girlfriend had the hots for someone else.

She picked up the towel and rubbed it against her damp blond hair. The shower had been glorious. Thirty minutes with hot water cascading over her body. Astrid had felt reborn. Showers weren't recommended until after the splint was removed but Astrid had been so desperate for the kind of clean feeling you only got from standing under a hot spray that she'd taken the risk. If she hadn't made the mistake of looking into the water at the last minute, it would have been perfect. Now the bandage was damp and she was worried it might fall off before her appointment tomorrow.

How much would the surgery alter her appearance? Dr. Coleman was confident Astrid would be happy with the outcome. He hadn't been able to give her an exact rendering of what that outcome might be. The shop door had a heavy steel frame and reinforced bulletproof glass—nothing but the best for Tara Turkman—and the impact on Astrid's face had been catastrophic. The headache from the concussion had only just subsided a few days ago and though Astrid could see again, the bruising was still visible around her eyes. She avoided touching her nose but if she bumped it by accident, the pain was severe.

She slipped into her old Georgetown sweatshirt. Right now, she needed to post her blog. She'd written the piece about Potomac mudlarkers the month before, after following a group of scavengers across the debris fields of the river plain. The story of the outing would go over well with her subscribers who loved anything quirky and nature-related. The most vocal people in the comments section had taken to calling themselves The Outsiders, after *Outside Astrid*. They'd forged a community that followed Astrid's every word, then added some of their own.

She searched the documents on her laptop until she found the one titled RFK. Before pulling it up she decided to check the bandage on her nose one more time. The gauze truly felt as if it might fall off. Walking into the bathroom Astrid checked the shelf in the medicine cabinet Leigh had designated for her bathroom supplies. She didn't like Astrid's possessions to commingle with her own because she used fancy skin-care products her mother mail ordered from Paris. Astrid used basic things like soap, water and sunscreen. Segregated products were another problem that would need to be remedied if they decided to go forward. Not that Astrid was holding out much hope.

She took her face lotion and sat down at the vanity station in the bedroom. Leigh was also overtly territorial about the piece of furniture set in the window, and Astrid was careful only to use it when she wasn't in the apartment. Moving into Leigh's space had been tricky. None of Astrid's furniture matched Leigh's carefully chosen arts-and-craft period pieces, so what Claire hadn't wanted she'd stuffed in her parent's basement. Her only contribution was a bird feeder she'd hung on a holly branch outside the kitchen window. So far, it had only attracted squirrels.

She squirted some lotion into her hand and dabbed it on her cheeks and neck. She didn't wear any make-up but was scrupulous about applying sunscreen. Her unblemished skin was the one good turn wrought by her mother's extreme vanity. As children, Claire and Astrid had not been allowed out of the house without first being slathered in lotion. Katrina associated sun-kissed skin with working-class people. Astrid had found the practice beyond annoying when she was younger, and impatient to hit the river. Now it was not only a part of her daily personal practice but part of the sign-off on her blog. Every piece ended with the same directive. *Go outside, leave no trace, take water and sunscreen.*

The phone buzzed in the bedroom and she ran to answer it. She'd rather talk to a cold-caller from a religious cult then look at herself in the mirror for another second. It had never been one of her favorite pastimes. Now that a giant bandage dominated her face, even less so. The call was from her mother. Katrina had been oddly maternal since the accident. Astrid had talked to her more times in the last two weeks than she had in the past year. Normally, her mom was a texter. It wasn't unusual to get twenty-five messages from her in a single day, but she didn't call unless something was urgent. It was a nice distinction, one Astrid had been able to count on, until her world had been turned upside down by a sixteen-year-old heiress in black-watch plaid.

"Mom?"

"All set for the appointment tomorrow? I'm excited for the unveiling." Say what you wanted about the former Miss Connecticut but she didn't beat around the bush. Her mother was acting as if she'd just scored tickets to *Hamilton*.

"It's at noon." Astrid wasn't thrilled her mother was her plus-one at the plastic surgeon's office, but Leigh wasn't an option and Claire was on tour.

"Perfect, I'll do an early barre class and meet you at his office. Are you excited?"

"That's not the word I'd pick. How different do you think I'll look?"

"Oh honey, don't think of it that way. You're going to look fabulous. You saw Dr. Coleman's portfolio. Celia was so nice to call him."

Astrid was positive her mother hadn't spoken with Celia Westover since the hospital waiting room but was now dropping her name like they were old sorority sisters. She let it go. Her mother's realtor business depended on her ability to foster and collect connections. Astrid's father was a whiz with the financials, but Katrina brought in the clients and, more often than not, closed the deal.

"Is Dad coming to lunch?" Astrid asked.

"I told him to meet us at the club."

"I'd rather not go there." Astrid was firm. Chevy Chase Country Club had a lovely dining room but it was sure to be full of Katrina's friends who would all have opinions about Astrid's new nose. It all felt so stupid. People were acting as if something momentous was about to occur when Astrid had just broken her nose. How much could it possibly impact her life? It wasn't as if she were having a baby. Heck, she wasn't even rescuing a dog.

"I already made a reservation," Katrina protested, and Astrid imagined her lips pursed into the tiny pout that necessitated biannual collagen injections.

"Let's try that noodle place in Spring Valley. I heard the Obamas used to eat there all the time," Astrid lied, shamelessly.

"What noodle place?" Katrina perked up. Mentioning a name she could then mention to someone else almost always had this effect. "Is it vegetarian? You know your father won't come if it's vegetarian."

"They have amazing Korean BBQ. Dad will love it."

"I hope it's not too greasy."

"It's fine, Mom," Astrid insisted and rang off after agreeing to meet Katrina the next morning at Dr. Coleman's office. God, she wished Claire was here to go with them. Their mother would still insist on inserting herself into the experience, but Claire would have buffered the impact. The dynamic had been in place since they were children buying dresses at the mall. Astrid loved her mother dearly but didn't place the same value on physical beauty. Probably because no one had ever called Astrid beautiful. The adjective she heard most often in association with her appearance was handsome. It was the Dibello nose.

All the female cousins, except Adrienne, had had theirs fixed at eighteen. They now had cute, little, bobbed buttons and looked like dolls on a shelf. Astrid had opted out of the surgery because the inherited Dibello nose gave her a sense of belonging. As a consequence, Astrid had always felt closer to Adrienne than her other cousins. Adrienne was also gay, which added an additional level of understanding to the relationship. It had been months since they'd had a proper conversation. Astrid was worried if Adrienne asked her about Leigh, she would tell her the truth and she wasn't sure if she wanted to face that conversation quite yet.

She looked at her reflection in the small mirror on the vanity. Still damp from the shower, the bandage hung limp and loose on the splint. What would happen if Astrid removed it early? She teased the corner of the medical tape and then smoothed it down quickly. It would be better to wait another day for Dr. Coleman to do it properly. There could be protocol, some special lotion you had to put on immediately.

Stifling a yawn, she considered a nap. Her sleep pattern was still off. In the two weeks since the surgery Astrid hadn't gotten more than six consecutive hours. Thankfully, this week's blog was almost ready to go and there was nowhere she had to be tomorrow until the doctor's appointment at noon. Pulling up the document, she began to read.

Mudlarking on the Potomac.

Squabbling has broken out amongst the mudlarkers. Someone is angry with Long Haul. So called for her lanky build, she has found a sterling-silver teething ring wedged between two rocks inciting jealously within the crew. From where I'm standing, three feet away from the raging rapids of the mighty Potomac, Long Haul has more than earned her find. Boldly scrambling between giant debris-covered boulders, she's ventured into some gnarly spots, outpacing the others in her zeal to find treasures coughed up by the river. By the time the suggestion was made that she was being greedy, Long Haul had already found an enamel doorknob, a hunting knife and a heart-shaped piece of pink quartz the size of a volleyball. None of these things seem remotely treasure-like to me, but beauty is in the eye of the lark and feathers are clearly ruffled.

For the last decade, Rivers, Finders Keepers, or RFK, have met twice weekly to scour the flood plains of the Potomac river between Locks 6 and 4 of the historic C&O Canal looking for items of historic or prehistoric interest. In England the hobby is known as mudlarking which is an apt description of the what's going on today. This is fun. Squabbling aside, there is a lovely camaraderie among this group of hikers who don't report their finds to any civic or historic organizations, choosing instead to display the objects in a large case at their local recreation center.

"We found a two-hundred-year-old pewter plate a few years ago. If we gave it to the National Park Service, that piece of local history would disappear," a retired map maker, known only as Bear, tells me as he takes a few practice swings with a two-by-four he's using to bat tennis balls into the river. Long Haul lobs a perfect pitch, and he knocks it halfway to Virginia. The duo does a little dance, and we keep walking.

RFK is not about environmental conservation. Thankfully, most of the garbage on their stretch of the river is collected by local scout groups or DC high school kids looking to complete their public service requirements because RFK is not out here to pick up the trash. They are looking for treasure.

"In England you have to have a license to mudlark," Bear says, looking wistful. "They would make Long Haul turn that teething ring in."

A new member, a woman called Coconuts, suggests that items burbling up from the Thames might have greater historical significance and he gently informs her that the native Americans who once fished the Potomac predate the Europeans by a thousand years.

The evidence is at the Palisades Recreation Center.

Hurt feelings over the teething ring resolve a few minutes later when the jealous member finds a beautiful rack of deer antlers. Eight points, they are completely intact and a trophy by anyone's standard. Another larker called Little E takes a photo to document the find on Instagram. Long Haul hands out vitamin C drops and they are all friends again.

To date, the only things RFK has found of interest to the authorities are a rusted-out Glock handgun and bags of underwhelming pharmaceutical prescriptions thrown over the bridge after a drug store heist in McLean. But as long as the river flows, they'll keep looking.

Astrid read the story once, made a few corrections, and then uploaded it to her server. Hiking with RFK had been great fun. Everyone in the group was at least twenty-five years her senior but if they invited her to go again, she planned to say yes. It was pathetic and illustrated just how lonely she was. She was hoping a group of strangers would ask her to go with them to pick garbage.

The piece would go live sometime in the next few minutes and the Outsiders would start commenting right away suggesting that the group had set up alerts. This made Astrid both nervous and proud. It was great to have dedicated readers, just alarming how dedicated some of them were. Astrid had chosen not to engage. She checked in now and then to get their reaction to a particular piece but stayed behind the veil because it was both safer and more professional.

She lay on the bed and closed her eyes. Thirty minutes of sleep and she'd feel like a new person. Her mother called this a beauty nap, though Astrid had also heard it called a power nap. Did the words mean the same thing? Images of her mother from old scrap books floated through Astrid's mind as she drifted to sleep. Katrina competing in the evening-gown competition at the Miss America Pageant, Katrina swimming in the ocean with a B-list movie star. Astrid slept for what felt like an eternity, her limbs becoming impossibly heavy objects, her brain blissfully off. She awoke to her cell phone ringing on the nightstand.

Something felt different. Her head felt wonderfully clear. Maybe that was it. She reached for the phone and smiled when she saw her sister's name on the screen. It was Claire, calling from the tour. After six months of nursing hurt feelings, it felt wonderful to be connected again. Fumbling, Astrid mistakenly activated video chat and Claire's face appeared in front of her. Great. Just what you wanted when you had a splint on your nose: Facetime with Sleeping Beauty.

But Claire looked rough. Beautiful yes, but there were dark circles under her eyes and her hair looked weird, really strange actually. The color was darker and it was a complete mess. And what was she wearing? When did Claire get a Georgetown sweatshirt?

"Flip the picture, sweetie," a voice said, but the face on the screen didn't move.

"Flip what?" Astrid said, and then closed her mouth.

"You're looking at yourself, flip the screen."

"No, way." Astrid couldn't believe what she was seeing. The bandage must have come off during her nap. She wasn't looking at Claire but at herself.

"Flip the screen so I can see you."

"Give me a second." Gingerly, Astrid put a hand to her nose. The surgery had indeed altered her face. But for the circles under her eyes and ratty hair, Astrid now looked exactly like her sister.

CHAPTER THREE

Deviant

Dr. Jasper Coleman's office was on the top floor of a big office building on Wisconsin Avenue. During the course of her lifetime, Astrid had been here too many times to count. Conveniently located across the street from Saks, it was filled with medical professionals of every conceivable focus and one-stop shopping for efficient Bethesda moms. In addition to housing Astrid's childhood pediatrician, the building was also home to the orthodontist who'd fixed her overbite and the gynecologist who'd broken the unfortunate news that lesbians were not exempt from sexually transmitted diseases. There was a pharmacy on the ground floor and somehow also a crystal shop, where Jerry always let Astrid and Claire pick out talismans and trinkets.

Astrid stepped into the elevator where an older woman was holding the hand of a tiny girl. Astrid rarely had an opportunity to spend time with children but loved their candor. Last year, she'd vacationed with her cousin Carrie, whose three preteen daughters had dispensed unsolicited fashion advice like judges on a reality TV show. It had been hilarious. They'd generally provided excellent counsel, though once had gone too hard on Carrie's trendy new rubber slides and made her cry. Carrie had been the first cousin to get her nose fixed. Astrid remembered seeing her after the surgery and thinking she'd gone from looking like Jo, on the old TV show *The Facts of Life*, to Blair. Astrid had always liked Jo better.

"Can you press number fifteen for me?" Astrid smiled at the tiny girl.

The child smiled back revealing missing front teeth. "You're really pretty," she said, matter-of-fact, and reached up to punch the button.

"Oh, thank you," Astrid replied, and felt a weird rush of pleasure. She was used to complete strangers complimenting Claire but the attention had never been directed her way. The older woman gave her a benign smile but didn't contest the assessment. That felt strange, too. Since the bandage came off, the day before, Astrid had only seen Leigh, who'd said some downright hurtful things. It was as if she thought Astrid had chosen to turn herself into a carbon copy of Claire.

"Are you a model?" The girl asked now.

Astrid blinked in surprise. "No, I'm a journalist."

"On TV?"

"I write a nature blog."

"You should be on TV," the girl said.

The elevator stopped and the woman took the girl's hand, leaving Astrid alone with her thoughts. Breakfast had been awful. Leigh wouldn't make eye contact but had gaped openly when she thought Astrid wasn't looking. This had to be strange for her, but how did she think Astrid felt? The face she'd woken up to every day of her life now only existed in photographs.

The elevator opened directly into Dr. Coleman's office and Astrid wondered if he had the whole floor. It was certainly possible. The *People* article her mother had forwarded listed him as the top cosmetic surgeon on the east coast. The fact Astrid had never heard of him meant nothing. The few friends she had were not concerned with altering their physical appearance.

Claire was the only person Astrid hung out with who even wore makeup. This had to be part of why Leigh had been so horrified. Though they'd never discussed it, there'd been an unspoken contract between them that neither worked too hard at being pretty. Astrid could understand that her dramatic facial surgery might be a shock. But Leigh had acted as if Astrid had walked in with false eyelashes and cheek implants instead of a new nose necessitated by an assault that included blunt force trauma to the head. It wasn't fair. Astrid had also suffered a substantial concussion and her eyes had been swollen shut for days. You'd think it might be a mitigating factor.

The lobby was brightly lit and bustling with energy. A long desk ran the length of the room fronted by four women whose looks suggested they may not have been hired solely for their management skills. The redhead who handed Astrid the clipboard had the poreless skin of a newborn baby. It was hard not to stare. Astrid took her sunblock very seriously, but this woman looked like she may have never actually been outside. She handed Astrid a pen.

"New patient?"

"I guess," Astrid hesitated. "My name is Astrid Dibello. I saw Dr. Coleman at Georgetown hospital, but I've never been to this office."

"Then you're in our system," the woman beamed, as if all of Astrid's problems were over. "Have a seat, I'll call you in a minute."

"Thanks," Astrid said, now feeling exposed. The word had hit a nerve. She appreciated Dr. Coleman leaving the golf course to treat her nose, but she didn't want to be part of his system. Astrid had written about body enhancement compulsion in its various forms. Plastic surgery, like tattoos, or body building, was known to be addictive. A wall of pamphlets advertising various elective treatments performed at the practice suggested Dr. Coleman and his team might be enablers.

She took a seat next to a woman who had a trembling canvas dog-carrier at her feet. Astrid peered inside and found an ancient chihuahua looking unduly concerned with the state of the universe. For the first time since the accident, she felt her brain shift to work mode. The term support animal had become so subjective. There were trained working dogs at one end of the spectrum and pocket gerbils at the other. What about a piece on support animals that caused their owners more stress? An idea began to form.

"His name is Arfunkel," the woman offered, and unzipped the carrier to let him out.

The chihuahua stepped timidly from the box and leaned forward on its front paws to stretch its hamstrings. Straightening, it yawned then began shaking again.

"He's adorable," Astrid said. It wouldn't be appropriate to question a woman in a doctor's office, but Astrid could form impressions that might add color to a story already taking shape. The intensity in the dog's eyes made Astrid wish she could offer it solace. The tremulous quivering, which Astrid knew was common in the breed, only added to the effect.

"Arfy's my serenity," the woman explained, and several people in the waiting room looked at them indulgently. Astrid knew that if the woman had pulled out a bigger dog or a giant snake their reactions might have been more guarded. It was impossible to be scared of an old, shivering chihuahua. You wanted to give this dog your coat.

Astrid smiled at her bit of good fortune. It wasn't unethical to talk to a private citizen, even in a doctor's office, if they talked to you first. "Do you take him with you everywhere?"

"Oh, yes," the woman nodded, vigorously. "Dr. Coleman even lets him come to the preop visits but he won't be allowed in the hospital."

"That's too bad," Astrid slipped a card from her purse. "I'm doing a story on comfort pets. Would you be interested in being interviewed?"

The woman studied the card for a moment and then recognition dawned. Astrid's readership was large enough that she was no longer surprised when this happened.

"Are you *Outside Astrid*?" she enthused, and the waiting room eavesdroppers looked up with interest. Arfunkel walked over to sniff her foot.

"Yes, I'm Astrid," she said, and held out her hand. Interacting with the public was not her favorite part of the job, but it was necessary if she wanted to grow her brand. People felt connected to her. It was gratifying, though they sometimes overstepped her comfort level. The Outsiders had once sent her an invitation to hike with them which she'd ignored. She didn't like disappointing people but wouldn't put herself on display. This woman, albeit high-energy, didn't seem threatening in the least.

"You want to do a story on Arfy?" She clapped her hands with delight. "I can't wait to tell my daughter. She loves *Outside Astrid*!"

The woman seemed so thrilled that Astrid hated to have to let her down. She didn't know how a story was going to turn out until she'd done the reporting. Arfy's interview would likely be part of a larger piece. The dog might not wind up in the blog at all.

"What do you want to know about him?" She grew more excited. "He loves riding in the car."

"That's wonderful," Astrid said. *But not interesting at all.* "I'm not actually sure what the focus of my story will be. I'm talking to some other pet owners this week." This was a lie but didn't have to be. Finding people who wanted to talk about their dogs was not a trick one had to learn. It was just as easy as a walk in the park.

The woman didn't seem to hear her. "He turns thirteen next week. We did a photo shoot on the National Mall."

"That's so fun," Astrid said, and hoped the nurse would call one of them back soon. The photo shoot sounded intriguing, but she didn't know how Arfy was going to fit into the story.

"Of course, we're having a bark muttsvah."

Unless Arfy was the story.

"A bark muttsvah?"

"Yes, it's just like a bar mitzvah but for dogs," she explained. "A woman from our temple performs them. The kids love it. You should come."

Astrid kept a straight face. "To Arfy's bark muttsvah?"

"Yes, we're having it at the Castle Resort in Bethesda." She shook the business card at Astrid. "I'll email you an invitation."

"That would be great," Astrid said, her mind racing as it always did when she found a feature topic. She made a mental note to do some research on the ancient Jewish coming-of-age-ceremony. She'd gone to one when she was in middle school and remembered a lot of singing and a boy from her geometry class lecturing them about Leviticus. How would this translate to a dog? It all seemed vaguely sacrilegious. Astrid scratched Arfy's head. The chihuahua leaned into her hand like they were old friends.

"My daughter's going to watch him when I get my eyes lifted."

"You're lucky she's local," Astrid replied and felt guilty for not yet checking in on Eartha Kitty. Claire had released her from the NASCAR commitment, but Astrid wanted to go the extra mile for Claire. They were finally back on track and it was important to make an effort. If Astrid had to choose a comfort animal of her own, it would be her sister.

It certainly wasn't her mother, who was now fifteen minutes late. It was frustrating. Katrina Dibello was never on time but seemed to have an uncanny sense of knowing when things actually happened so never missed anything. Claire said it was because their mother knew how to make an entrance. Astrid found the trait vaguely unsettling and had spent a lot of her life waiting for Katrina to show up. She might be in the waiting room an hour before the nurse called her back, but the minute she did, her mother would walk in the door.

"Astrid!" Or, she might be here, already. "Stand up, and let me see you in the light!"

"Mom, calm down," Astrid said, but did as she was told. Arfunkel yawned and stared up at Katrina who was wearing her barre class outfit of black leggings and a tight-fitting leotard. Astrid's mother possessed an undefinable star quality that made people want to look at her. If she were wearing jodhpurs, you'd say she belonged in a horse film.

"Come to the window."

"Mom, please."

Arfunkel followed them across the room to the wall of windows spanning the back of the lobby. Holding Astrid's chin between her thumb and forefinger, Katrina looked closely at her daughter's face and then began to cry.

"I can't believe this, my beautiful baby," she murmured to herself. "You look so different."

"It's okay Mom," Astrid was touched at her mother's reaction. "It doesn't hurt anymore."

"I'm so glad," Katrina's face transformed into a radiant smile. Astrid could not remember ever seeing her mother this happy. Practically giddy, she gave voice to Astrid's biggest concern. "You look like Claire."

Astrid pulled her face away. "Leigh thinks so, too. Do you think Claire will be mad?"

"Mad?" Katrina dismissed the notion. "Why would Claire be mad? Your beauty is only a positive reflection on her."

"What does that mean?" Astrid asked. "What was I before?"

Katrina shook her head. "You were you, and you still are. Don't worry about Claire, she's your biggest fan."

Fortunately, Astrid knew this to be true. Despite their recent estrangement, which had been entirely Astrid's fault, Claire had always been in her corner. She'd never faltered. When Katrina had lobbied for Astrid to have her nose fixed the summer after her eighteenth birthday, Claire had refused to discuss it beyond declaring her opinion to be whatever Astrid decided. Yesterday, after seeing Astrid's new nose on FaceTime, she'd been positive and supportive. If she was weirded out, she hadn't mentioned it. But Astrid felt weird, and she needed to talk about it.

"It's just strange, Mom. Every time I look in the mirror, I feel like I'm seeing Claire. Leigh doesn't like it at all."

"Oh? What did she say?" Katrina's eyes narrowed. Astrid wasn't sure if it was the ten-year age difference or a mother's sixth sense, but Katrina had never been a fan of the sporty dentist.

"We had a fight," Astrid said, though the word was an understatement for the scene that had played out earlier that morning when Leigh finally saw Astrid's nose without the bandage.

"Tell me what happened," Katrina said, but Astrid shook her head. Now was not the time to tell her mother all the hurtful things Leigh had said to her. Katrina was likely to think the Barbie doll comment a compliment, anyway.

"Can we talk about it at lunch?"

"Of course."

Leigh's tactless reaction had been the catalyst to finally push Astrid out the door. She'd packed a bag and left. Astrid still needed to get her kayak from the shed in the backyard and she needed to tell her parents about the break-up. Especially if she wanted to stay in their basement while she figured out her next move.

"Astrid?" A nurse appeared, rescuing her from further conversation. "Dr. Coleman's ready to see you now." It would have to wait until after the appointment.

They followed the nurse into Dr. Coleman's office and sat down in comfortable chairs facing his desk. To the right, a sleek reclining chair that looked like it belonged in a dentist's office lay beneath examination lights.

"Can I get you anything to drink? Water? Tea? Kombucha?"

"Kombucha, please," Katrina said, as if she'd missed her morning infusion. Astrid was willing to bet she'd ordered it to impress the nurse.

"Nothing for me, thank you," Astrid said, and closed her eyes to channel Claire's counsel. If her sister were here, she'd remind Astrid that Katrina only wanted what was best for her and could be counted on to pay for lunch afterward and Astrid was suddenly ravenous. Cheered, she opened her eyes. "Thanks, for coming with me, Mom."

Katrina looked incredulous. "Are you kidding? I'm thrilled with how the surgery turned out. I love it."

Astrid wanted to ask if Katrina had loved her before the surgery but held her tongue. The plastic surgeon's office wasn't the place to pick a fight with her beauty-queen mother about her lifelong obsession with physical appearances. She looked around the room. In addition to the requisite diplomas from top universities on Dr. Coleman's ego wall, there were pictures of him canoodling with A-list celebrities that Astrid assumed were also patients. She recognized news anchors and politicians, actresses and models. Katrina's assertion that Dr. Coleman only operated on top clients had been an understatement. These people were the tippity-top. It occurred to Astrid that the impact of the Closet Diva door might be more than just physical. It was as if she'd entered a portal into another world.

There was small knock and the nurse returned with Katrina's kombucha. Close at her heels was a tall man a with a thick head of salt and pepper hair and a chiseled jaw line. Astrid's eyes had been swollen shut during their previous encounters, so she hadn't formed an opinion, but it was easy to see why *People Magazine* had put him on their sexiest man list. Astrid did not sleep with men but could not deny he was objectively handsome. Jasper Coleman looked like a matinee idol from the 1930s. Her mother had not missed this detail.

"Dr. Coleman, hello," she purred and Astrid had to stifle an eye roll. Watching Katrina flirt always made her uncomfortable. Her father took it in stride, said it was good for business, but her mother's overt sexuality embarrassed Astrid and offended her feminist sensibilities. Leigh was aghast at her behavior and thought Katrina a complete relic.

"Mrs. Dibello." The doctor nodded, and sat down in the chair behind the desk. He turned to Astrid and squinted at where the splint should be. "Hello, Astrid."

Her hand flew to her nose. "The bandage got wet in the shower yesterday and came off while I was sleeping," she explained, hurriedly, as Katrina began to gush.

"Doesn't she look incredible? You did a wonderful job. There's no swelling at all."

The doctor ignored Katrina. "How do you feel, Astrid?"

"Okay. I mean, no more headaches and my mom's right, the swelling is gone."

"Mind if I have a look?" He gestured to the exam chair.

Astrid got up and walked across the room. On the wall next to the reclining chair was a flat screen television monitor displaying an x-rayed profile of a skull she presumed was her own.

"Is that me?" she asked. Settling into the reclining chair, a story idea occurred to her. The x-ray, though it looked like any ordinary human skull, was literally what she looked like on the inside. Could she spin a play on words for her blog? *Inside Astrid*. It was a cool title but what would she write about? Often, she didn't know until she began. "And if it is, can I have a copy?"

The doctor nodded his handsome head. "If you like. I can email you a file." He rose from the desk to examine the image. "We always radiograph nasal fractures in case the trauma has impacted the sinus cavity." He traced a small white line on the x-ray with his pen. "I don't see anything here that worries me. Let's take a look at how you're healing."

"I think she looks wonderful," Katrina said, and pretended to sip her kombucha.

"So you've said," the doctor murmured. He switched on the fancy light over the examination chair and positioned it over Astrid's face. Taking blue latex gloves from a box on the table he carefully pulled them on. "May I?"

"Of course." Astrid closed her eyes.

He gently touched the slope of her nose. "How does this feel?"

"Fine. Maybe a little numb?"

"That's normal. It could take up to six months for the numbness to subside." He continued prodding for several more seconds and then sat back. "Tell me, are you happy with the way it looks?"

"It looks wonderful!" Katrina said, again.

The doctor ignored the comment. "How do you feel about it, Astrid?"

Astrid swallowed hard. She'd spent the morning debating whether to address her concerns with the doctor. The *People Magazine* article claimed he billed six hundred dollars an hour. It was now or never.

"I know I got hit really hard by that door, and there's only so much you could do." She began searching for the correct words to express her feelings. "But I don't look like myself anymore. I look like my sister, and it's weird."

"That's ridiculous," Katrina protested, and Doctor Coleman held up a hand.

"Mrs. Dibello, please." Smiling gently at Astrid, he turned back to the x-ray. "It wasn't possible to restore your nose to the original shape."

"Why not?"

"As you said, the impact was severe, but you also have a deviated septum. Were you aware of that?"

"I had no idea. What exactly does that mean?"

The doctor pointed to Astrid's x-ray. "The nasal septum is the bone and cartilage that separates your nasal cavity into two nostrils. See? It's right here."

"Okay," Astrid said, following along. She was definitely going to write about this.

"Normally, the septum lies centrally and the nasal passages are symmetrical."

"But not with me?" Astrid asked.

He shook his head. "It's not abnormal. Eighty percent of all people have some deviation and never know about it. You might have been fine if not for the accident."

"Or she might have had problems," Katrina interjected.

The doctor sighed. "It's possible. The condition can result in sinus issues. People also complain of difficulty breathing, headaches, bloody noses. Some have sleeping disorders down the line."

"Does a deviated septum affect the shape of the nose?" Astrid asked.

"It can." The doctor nodded, thoughtfully. "And it doesn't surprise me that you now bear a closer resemblance to your sister. Siblings often have similar skeletal structures."

"They both have blond hair, too," Katrina crowed.

He ignored her. "I think smoothing out your natural bump will make it easier for you to breathe."

"I've never had breathing problems."

"Maybe not yet. But, like I said, these things get worse as you age. Individuals with deviated septa often develop issues with snoring and even sleep apnea."

"But I don't snore."

"And now there's a chance you never will."

"So, the Westover girl did her a favor." Katrina was triumphant. Her eyes caressed Astrid's face in way that felt unfamiliar.

"I wouldn't classify a blunt force head trauma as a favor to your daughter, Mrs. Dibello," Dr. Coleman replied coldly.

"I didn't mean to suggest that," Katrina protested, but Astrid cut her off.

"We know exactly what you meant, Mom."

CHAPTER FOUR

The Getaway

"Astrid, are you still there? Can you hear me?" Claire's voice came softly through the speaker of the cell phone.

When Astrid tried to respond the words came out in a hiccupping cry.

"Stinky! Tell me what's going on. Are you okay? If you can't say it, text it? Okay? Can you text me?"

Astrid sent her sister a heart emoji followed by four words in all caps.

MOM IS A BITCH.

She let out another small sob and lay the phone on the passenger seat of her Volvo station wagon. She hadn't planned to come to the overlook, but here she was, parked in the tiny parking lot across from the Potomac River. Either the car had a homing device or Astrid did.

"God, what did Mom do now?" Claire said. Astrid heard her sigh and knew her sister probably had a hand pressed to her temple. "Is she trying to make you join the Junior League again?"

"I'm never joining the Junior League or the fucking country club," Astrid said, and another hiccup escaped. Her stance on the environmental impact of golf courses was well known. Neither of her parents played golf yet helped finance an unconscionable use of natural resources.

"Oh, hi. There's my sister." Claire responded in her goofiest voice and Astrid smiled in spite of her hurt feelings. "Tell me what's going on. I don't mean to rush you, but I've only got a few minutes."

"Why? What are you doing? Oh, shit!" Astrid felt a wave of guilty adrenaline as she realized Claire was preparing to dance the Saturday matinee in San Francisco. She checked the vintage diver's watch she'd purchased years ago at an estate sale. She'd completely spaced the time difference.

"When do you go on?"

"The show doesn't begin for a half an hour. I'm already dressed and have on my makeup and shoes. I've got five minutes."

"Oh my God. Go! I'll talk to you later," Astrid said. Their mother's reaction weighed heavy on her psyche but she couldn't unload on Claire before a performance. Especially not this show. It wasn't fair.

"I've got time. Tell me what's happening, right now. I know you're really upset," Claire pressed, and Astrid cursed herself. She rarely cried and this episode had been a real gusher. Claire wouldn't let it go without an explanation.

"Mom is just so happy I no longer look like me."

"That's not true," Claire said, but there wasn't much conviction in her voice. Astrid choked back another sob.

"It is, too," she said, sniffing. "Mom has hated my nose since I was a little girl and now that it's gone she's acting like she's won the lottery. It makes me feel worthless."

"Mom won the lottery the day you were born," Claire said, and began the familiar speech she'd often employed in her role as family peacemaker. "Grandma did a number on her with all those beauty pageants. It was like child abuse. You know that."

Astrid allowed her sister to walk down the familiar path that mitigated their mother's behavior. Now wasn't the time to dredge up past hurts or expose fresh wounds, no matter how ghastly they were. Claire needed to be in a peaceful headspace to deliver a good performance. Astrid feared she'd already pushed her big sister off balance. She wouldn't make it worse.

"You're right, I'm just being dramatic. The nose job is a shock. I look so different. It's crazy. You know?"

"Of course," Claire agreed. "Have you thought about seeing a therapist? I can ask Annette for a referral."

"You're my therapist," Astrid said.

"Just until I get back," Claire joked and then her tone grew sober. "Seriously though, have you thought about it?"

"I have actually," Astrid lied. "Dr. Coleman also suggested it."

"Great, I have a virtual appointment with Annette tomorrow." Claire was now in fix-it mode. "I'll get some names."

"That would be great." Astrid feigned enthusiasm. She had no intention of baring her soul to a professional but knew it would make Claire feel good to be given a task. "Let me know. Now go, break a leg."

"Okay."

Astrid turned off the phone and looked down the riverbank. Her well-meaning sister could wait one hundred tomorrows. Talking to a stranger about her mother's fixation on physical beauty sounded excruciating. What Astrid needed was to get away and think about her life for a while. There was only one place where this was possible. She needed to go to Bob's.

Thirty minutes later she pulled into the shaded parking lot attached to Lock 6 of the C&O Canal. A special National Parks Service sticker allowed her to leave the car here for as long she needed. Lock 6 was just down the slope from her parent's house but she didn't want Katrina to know she was so close. The park rangers knew her car and would leave it unmolested.

She opened the car door and stepped out into the wet September afternoon. Astrid had the parking lot almost entirely to herself. The earlier soaking rain had slowed to a drizzle but no one was braving the weather. She shook her head. Washingtonians were so silly. All year long they clamored for snow but hid in the house when it rained as if they might melt. It never made sense to Astrid. Rain was awesome but, like all weather, enjoying it was about having the correct gear. She zipped up her water-repellent Gowear shell and pulled on the hood.

Correct gear was the difference between a pleasant outdoor experience and a total nightmare. Snow enthusiasts knew this. They had appropriate boots for the few days a year it was necessary. But where were their rain pants and water shoes? Astrid didn't understand it. Some years it never snowed in DC at all, but it rained an average of one hundred and fourteen days a year. You could count on it. Nature was glorious in the rain. Today it was all gloriously hers.

The only other car in the parking lot was a vintage white Ford Bronco XL, Astrid's dream truck. Ford had stopped making the model in 1996 and was reissuing them for the first time this year. If Astrid had the option, and she didn't, as they were highly sought after and expensive, she'd choose the older model like the one parked a few spaces away. She'd written a blog on the subject earlier in the year called "Fantasy Ride" that had gotten more than a thousand comments. The Outsiders liked to use her subject as a starting point and then relay anecdotes of their own. It was funny. Some of them even seemed to know each other. They absolutely loved talking about their cars.

Whoever owned this one was a lucky individual. Astrid ogled the lines of the old 4 x 4. When the Volvo gasped its last breath, and she could put together enough cash, the Bronc would be her first choice. Ford had used the same V8 Windsor engines in their Mustang that year and it was a total beast. It would be a while before she could afford it and finding an affordable place near the river was her first concern. Hopefully some time away from the world would help her sort it all out.

She removed her inflatable kayak from the back of the station wagon and set to work inflating the boat. As much as she loved the streamlined agility of the bright blue, fiberglass Pelican that was still in Leigh's garage, the inflatable Firefly was convenient for unplanned outings, like today's. The sturdy little kayak was also more forgiving on the rocks, and, despite the more universal appeal of the Pelican, Astrid loved the stubby little inflatable she'd purchased on a whim at a boathouse close-out sale.

She locked the car door and slipped the key into an inside zippered pocket of her bright fuchsia snap-off rain pants. They weren't her favorite, but like most gear heads Astrid no longer saw color. It was a rule of the woods she'd learned as a teenager. Sure, it's nice to be matchy-matchy. Who hadn't salivated over pristine new gear in a catalogue? But performance was more important than color. The right fabric was the difference between having a comfortable outing and freezing your tits off.

She held the small, battery-powered hand pump steady as the boat filled out. The drizzle had now almost completely stopped and mist hung heavy over the river. Bob lived just beyond the kayaking course on an island in the middle of the river. A few miles upriver from the District line, the land was considered part of Maryland but controlled by the US National Park Service. As children, the neighborhood kids had been terrified of the hermit that lived on Snake Island. They'd swapped horrific made-up stories about severed heads and incest babies, the more outlandish the better. Astrid was embarrassed to have once abetted disseminating the local folklore.

She now considered Bob one of her best friends. At least once a month she came to Snake Island and helped him in his lonely pursuit to save the Potomac. Cruising the river bank in their boats they found all manner of garbage and hauled it to a designated spot to be collected by the National Park Service. Clearing the river helped clear Astrid's mind. It was therapeutic and Astrid considered it her public service. It was also great exercise and she almost always got an idea for *Outside Astrid* out of it.

As the boat inflated, her spirits began to follow suit. Katrina's obsession with cosmetic appeal bordered on the pathological. Claire had been right to classify their mother's childhood, spent competing in Atlantic City beauty pageants, as child abuse. Just because Katrina was emphatic did not mean she was correct. A big nose had never defined her, and neither would this newer, Claire-look-alike model. Astrid had never counted on a mirror to tell her who she was. Why would she start now? If required to choose a photo of herself that best depicted how she saw herself right now, Astrid would pick the x-ray.

Hoisting the kayak on her shoulder, she grabbed her paddle, PFD and water-proof stuff-sack. The well-known training course of the US Olympic Team was in a placid tributary, just a short portage away. On the other side of the inlet was Snake Island and Bob.

Astrid crossed the old mule towpath next to the romantic ruins of Lock 6. She wondered if anyone had slept in the lock keeper's house that night. The old waterway was nearly two hundred miles long and had once had seventy-five working locks transporting supplies down the Potomac from Cumberland, Maryland to Washington, DC. Several years ago, the National Park Service had refurbished seven of the original lock keeper homes and made them available for public use. *Outside Astrid* had featured the story and their bookings had doubled over night. The supervisor had been so thrilled, she'd offered to comp Astrid a free weekend. Leigh hadn't wanted to go, so it had never happened.

Leaving the canal behind, Astrid started down a wooded path to the river. Up the hill, in the opposite direction, was the house where Astrid grew up. Katrina and Jerry still lived in a gorgeous multilayered home overlooking the river. What they'd paid half a million dollars for in 1985 was now worth three point seven. This morning Astrid had planned on taking refuge in the basement, now she wasn't sure what she was doing. The lock house was looking better and better.

Careful of her footing, she stepped quickly toward water. The closer she got to the Potomac the lighter she felt. Bob would notice the cosmetic work done to her face but he'd be more interested in what Astrid had brought him to eat. If he was off on an adventure, Astrid wouldn't see him at all.

The launch site was a stretch of embankment where an oak tree leaned conveniently over the tributary, creating a kind of bench. A small island directly across the water buffered the practice course from the mighty Potomac on the other side. Astrid had paddled the area too many times to count. She'd first learned to kayak at age ten on a Girl Scout retreat in West Virginia and, according to her father, had not left the river since. Almost every day of her childhood, rain or shine, hell or high water, Astrid had explored the Potomac and its surrounding banks. When Claire went to ballet practice, Astrid went down the hill. It had a lot to do with personal passion but more to do with access. The Potomac was basically in her backyard.

The rain was done so she snapped off the all-weather pants and tugged the wind-breaker over her head. Stashing the gear in her stuff-sack in the stern, Astrid was now down to shorts and a tank top. She dipped her paddle in the water and pulled the boat forward.

The hanging PVC poles that served as training gates on the kayak course were barely visible in the mist. Astrid could only see one clearly and it beckoned her forward. She hadn't intended on working out but her body ached with the kind of tension that could only be alleviated by intense physical exercise or sex. Her hands itched on the paddle. She'd checked the water levels and knew the river was high, both from today's rainfall and yesterday's storm upriver in West Virginia. Astrid wouldn't advise a novice to come out but she was no beginner. She knew this course by heart, could carve the turns in her sleep. The inflatable wasn't the best vessel to work the gates, but it would have to do. Dipping her paddle in the water, she stroked forward.

For thirty solid minutes she pushed her body to the brink. Maneuvering the kayak through the gates upstream to the tip of the tributary, she then circled around and plowed back in the other direction. Again and again, until her back and shoulders burned. The cool air stirred up by the storm was long gone, leaving a blanket of humidity in its wake. Astrid's body was covered in sweat and she knew there was every chance she'd go swimming when she got to Bob's. One of the most inviting things about his compound was the beautiful private beach. She swiped a hand across her brow and flinched at the remaining tenderness across the bridge of her nose. Fuck. She'd just managed to push the surgery from her mind. It was never going away. She had to face it. *Ha ha.*

She paddled downstream until she reached the end of the barrier island protecting the kayaking course from the river and then turned into a wide creek. Snake Island was up river, closer to the Virginia side of the Potomac, and not yet visible through the fog.

Astrid had last visited Bob the month before the accident. She'd been doing a story on airplane noise along the river and wanted his opinion on how it affected the wildlife. She'd brought her own tent and camped near his compound, which had changed considerably since she'd first discovered it nearly fifteen years before. What was once a series of small tents was now an elaborate treehouse with a balcony and roof deck. Astrid never referenced Bob in her blog for fear of divulging the location of his compound or giving away his identity. She wouldn't dare. The only thing more thrilling than someone living off grid on an island in the middle of the Potomac was personal access to it.

She would likely stay the week. It would be enough time to make a plan and maybe get her head on straight about her new appearance. Blessedly, Bob would have no opinion.

She drew close to the island and movement caught her eye on the shore. Bob's compound was on the other side of the nearly five-acre island. A flash of red confirmed it was not him. Bob only wore muted colors that blended in with the environment. It must be the owner of the vintage Bronco in the parking lot. Astrid was intrigued. She wondered who'd braved the inclement forecast to spend time on the water. She didn't feel like making new friends right now, or ever really, but the journalist in her was curious to know. The kayak moved closer to the shore and she saw it was a woman.

CHAPTER FIVE

Loud and Queer

Astrid only had seconds to decide if she wanted to engage with the stranger. Bent over, messing with something in her kayak, the woman had yet to notice her. There was no law, of course, that said Astrid had to speak to other people she encountered in the outdoors. It was just etiquette she liked to observe. What she observed now on the shore did not make her want to change her protocol.

The woman was dressed almost identically to Astrid in a sports bra and boardshorts but the resemblance stopped there. Where Astrid's body was long and sinewy, a classic ballerina frame like her sister Claire's, this woman was a head shorter and all glorious curves. Light brown skin offset her yellow bra and shorts drawing Astrid further in. She leaned over to put something else in her boat and Astrid sucked in a breath. Squinting to see what it was, she slammed into the river bank.

"Fuck!" she said louder than intended, drawing the woman's attention away from her mysterious chore. They locked eyes for a brief second before Astrid was forced to drag hers back to the boat. The kayak's inflatable hull was trapped beneath the exposed roots of a large sycamore. Upended at the shoreline, the root-ball hung out over the water like a sculpture of Medusa's head. It was totally avoidable unless you were stupid enough to run right into it. *Double fuck.* Astrid pressed down on the rubber casing, trying to free the boat, but it didn't work. She shifted her weight, and a jagged tendril pushed harder into the kayak's side threatening to make her bad day even worse. *Fuck. Fuck. Fuck.*

The best way to get loose would be to get out of the boat. She dipped a hand in the water. At least it wasn't freezing. She'd planned on swimming, but not here. The current was too strong and if the boat capsized, she'd lose all her gear. Right now, losing her phone meant more than just a financial nuisance. It meant losing personal photos from the last year. Astrid couldn't remember the last time she'd backed up her personal photos. It was the easiest chore to perform, inexcusable not to do it as Astrid wasn't connected to the cloud. It would be so easy to set up automatic dumps, but somehow this step always escaped her. The last year of her real face was in the phone. Losing the photos meant losing a part of herself she could never recover.

"Let me help you." A warm hand landed on Astrid's shoulder and she almost fell out of the kayak.

"Watch out!" she shouted, desperately trying to regain her balance but the hand grabbed more firmly onto her arm.

"I've got you," the softly accented voice said, and Astrid's boat miraculously stabilized. "Give me your hand."

"Grab my bag first?" Astrid asked, and lifted the stuff sack from the bottom of the kayak.

"Sure." The woman leaned down giving Astrid a bird's eye view into her impressive cleavage.

"Thanks so much." Astrid choked.

"It's no problem. Let me help you, now." The warm hand was now on her arm. The sexy accent in her ear.

"Okay." Astrid looked up into her eyes and almost fell from the boat a second time.

"Simone?" She was a little older, but it was definitely her. The beautiful girl who'd awakened Astrid's sexuality twelve years before, had grown up into an even more beautiful woman.

"Claire?" Simone's pretty face clouded with confusion, while Astrid struggled to think of anything beyond the soft fingers gripping her flesh. "I thought you were on tour."

"I am on tour. I mean, she's on tour. Claire's on tour," Astrid rambled, while Simone looked more and more perplexed.

"Come out of the boat and explain," Simone insisted. Gripping Astrid's arm more tightly, she pulled her forward.

Astrid looked into the limpid brown eyes and did as she was told. Stepping shaky-legged onto to shore, she smiled, shyly. "Thanks for the assist. You probably don't remember me. I'm Claire's sister, Astrid. We only met a couple times."

Instantly, Simone's face lit with recognition and delight. "Astrid! Ciao! Of course, I know you! How wonderful." Leaning forward she clasped Astrid's shoulders and kissed both her cheeks, European style. Astrid knew the gesture was not meant to be intimate, but her nipples had never been to Europe and pebbled beneath her sports bra. If Simone noticed, she didn't let on.

Letting go of Astrid she stood back smiling, mischievously. The aura of fun that had once attracted Claire's friendship looked to be intact. Astrid remembered them always laughing.

"Claire's little sister is now a beautiful woman, brava."

Astrid's hand shot toward her face but she managed not to touch her nose. She'd never been called beautiful and now it had happened twice in the span of the afternoon. There was no doubt the plastic surgery had everything to do with it. For some reason it didn't lessen the effect of the compliment.

"Um, thanks. You too." She felt her face grow warm and fought from taking a second look down Simone's cleavage. She centered on Simone's face which only made her blush harder. Expressive brown eyes were offset by almost equally expressive eyebrows. Astrid wanted to dive head long into the warmth but forced herself to look away at Simone's hair instead. Mistake. Long dark curls corkscrewed through the back of a faded blue ball cap putting the whole visual over the top. Holy shit. Astrid recognized the logo of a boutique outfitter that had gone out of business years before and smiled. They'd made the best thermal hoodies. She still had one in her closet and wished she had four more.

"When did you get to town? Claire told me you were taking a place in her building." Astrid automatically kicked into interview mode. It was her default switch, a safe zone. Fortunately, what worked in her professional life also worked in the private sector. People liked to talk about themselves, allowing Astrid to disappear into the questions.

The beautiful brown eyes became even more playful. "I got here last week," she pushed softly at Astrid's shoulder. "Claire told me you would be there to give me the key. What happened?"

"Oh," Astrid hesitated. Telling the story to Simone meant discussing the accident and her transformative surgery. The bandage hadn't been off twenty-four hours. Astrid wasn't ready to go there yet. "I've been busy," she hedged, and Simone looked amused.

"You should see your face."

This time Astrid couldn't stop herself from touching her nose. "What's wrong with my face?"

"Nothing." Simone's hand closed over Astrid's and pulled it away. "You're beautiful. I told you this already. But you are guilty of something." She shrugged, drawing Astrid's eye back to her cleavage. Astrid wondered if she was doing it on purpose.

"Oh, um, sorry I couldn't be there to give you the key. I had some stuff going on," she said, then asked the question at the forefront of her mind. "What are you doing all the way out here in the rain?"

"What's wrong with the rain?" Simone challenged, and now it was Astrid's turn to laugh.

"Absolutely nothing," she said, smiling at the irony. "I happen to love being outside in the rain. But it's kind of *my* thing. Other people don't always like getting wet."

"Oh, I like to be wet," Simone replied and then seemed to hear herself. A slow blush crept across her cheeks. "You know what I mean."

"I do," Astrid said, utterly charmed. The afternoon was taking an unexpected turn. She nodded toward the red kayak on the bank. "I love your ride. I have the same one in green."

The brown eyes retained their sparkle. "Thanks. I bought it yesterday. It was cheaper to get a new one than ship from Torino. I cannot be without a boat."

"Because you like being wet so much?" Astrid couldn't help herself.

"Yes," Simone said simply.

"What are you collecting?" Astrid asked, more than a little curious. She'd almost punctured her kayak watching Simone putting the mysterious bags in the boat.

"Were you spying on me?" Simone said, and her voice rose in mock indignation.

"Yeah, I think I was." Astrid admitted. "I'm not used to seeing people out here. You made me run into a tree."

"I made you do that?" She laughed. "It was me?"

"Yep," Astrid matched her teasing tone. "But then you rescued me, so I forgive you."

Simone nodded, as if this all made perfect sense. "Want to see what I'm collecting?"

"I do."

"Free your boat and come see."

"Oh, right." Astrid looked down at the Firefly and felt a stab of guilt. Captivated by Simone she'd forgotten her old standby. Leaning over, she extracted the hull from the roots and pulled the undamaged boat to shore.

Simone smiled at her. "Come on."

Careful not to trip on exposed roots along the riverbank, Astrid allowed herself to be led across the beach. A sweet smell revealed the contents of the bags in the Simone's kayak before they came into view.

"Pawpaws?" Astrid asked and, for the first time, noticed scattered pieces of fruit on the shore. The size and shape of smallish mangoes, they were pale green on the outside and pale orange within.

"We don't have them in Italy," Simone looked excited. "We have papaya but these pawpaws are different."

Astrid couldn't help smiling at Simone's enthusiasm. "We have papaya in the USA, too. But they're different altogether. Tropical, so they mostly grow in Florida and California."

Simone picked a piece of fruit from the bag and held it up like a proud mother. "This one, I think, she is perfect."

"It's a girl?"

"Yes." Simone twinkled.

Astrid took the pawpaw from her hand. Careful not to bruise the flesh she pressed her thumb lightly into the side. Bob had first shown her how to test for ripeness years ago. Though if you found one on the ground, it was usually ready to eat.

"You were lucky to find so many good ones before the deer got to them." She handed the fruit back to Simone. "How do you know about them anyway? Pawpaws are pretty obscure. They only grow in the northeast US and Canada."

"I am a slow-food chef." Simone grew more animated. A dimple popped on her left cheek and Astrid was seized with the impulse to touch it.

"I didn't know that," Astrid replied, and busied her hands readjusting her ball cap. Claire had been sparse with details surrounding her old friend. The one glaring detail that stood out in her mind was Claire mentioning something about Simone maybe being gay. But that had happened just before Astrid had been hit in the head, so maybe she'd dreamed it. She struggled for something to say. "So, no more ballet?"

"No," Simone's smile faltered for a second before reigniting anew. "That dream didn't work out for this body." She ran her hands up and down her glorious curves. "Chef is a much better fit, don't you think?"

"I think you were a beautiful dancer," Astrid said, rushing to correct her faux pas. Asking an artist about why'd they stopped creating was a conversation you should never initiate. It was like asking a high school senior where they were going to college. Highly personal, possibly disappointing and none of your damn business. Claire had struggled for years with her injuries before finally making her dreams come true.

Simone's face softened. "You saw me dance?"

"Yes, I saw you do this butterfly thing one time. I thought you might actually fly off the stage."

"Sometimes, I wished I could have. Thank you." Simone executed a low, cleavage-displaying curtsy that made Astrid's throat go dry. "I still love to dance. Now, I just do it in my kitchen."

Astrid was happy to move on from the subject of dance. "You said you were a slow-food chef? What's that?"

"A slow-food chef cooks with only indigenous ingredients," Simone explained. "The rule is not to use anything produced more than one hundred miles away from where you are living."

"Is the mission environmental?" Astrid asked.

"Yes," Simone nodded. "But also, gastronomical. Fresh food just tastes better. When I move somewhere new, I always research the local food." She held up the pawpaw.

"You can't get more local than pawpaws," Astrid agreed, smelling both a story and Simone's faint floral perfume. *International chef sleuths out obscure local ingredients in sexy red kayak.* It would be catnip for her readers. "What other local ingredients are you using?"

"I only got here last week," Simone looked indignant. "Give me time, okay? I already found your mysterious pawpaw." She was clearly teasing. It almost felt like she was flirting.

Astrid couldn't help herself and leaned in. Standing half-naked on the misty riverbank chatting with this exotic creature was the most exciting thing that had happened to her in a long time, maybe ever. She wanted to see where it went. "You're right. I'm sorry," she said, and looked for something to keep the banter going. "But why come all the way up here? There are pawpaws all along the river. Even in Georgetown."

"Because this is Pawpaw Island," Simone replied, simply and spread her hands wide.

"No," Astrid dragged the word out to two syllables enjoying the look of confusion coming over Simone's face. She pointed to a smaller island down river where she'd once found a rusted-out service revolver. "That's Pawpaw Island. They call this one Snake Island."

"Snakes?" Simone looked around the beach like it might suddenly be teeming with serpents. "This is an island for snakes?"

"It's just the name." Astrid laughed. "As you can see, there are plenty of pawpaws here, too. Just like there are plenty of snakes over there." She pointed down river.

"Where?" Simone acted as if Astrid was pointing out a specific pit of vipers. She narrowed her eyes. "Where are the snakes?"

"Everywhere," Astrid spread her hands out to indicate the whole world and then laughed at the expression on Simone's face. "But you don't have to worry. The snakes don't want to see you either. Believe me."

Simone shook her head. "I must have read the map wrong. I thought this was Pawpaw Island." She pointed at the ground.

"Where did you find a Potomac island map?" Astrid asked. It wasn't as if they didn't exist, but they didn't give them away at gas stations either.

"We don't have pawpaws in Italy but we do have the Internet." Simone cracked and Astrid laughed out loud.

"I hadn't heard."

"It's true."

They stood smiling at each other for a few pleasant moments.

"What are you going to do with all this fruit?" Astrid nodded toward the bags in the boat.

"I'm going to make a cake," Simone said and the dimple appeared again. Astrid was beginning to understand this happened when Simone was excited about something. "Do you like pawpaw cake?"

"I don't like pawpaws much," Astrid admitted. "So, there's a good chance I won't like them in cake form either."

"You don't like pawpaws?" The dimple disappeared and Astrid felt an acute sense of loss.

"No, but Claire likes them a lot. When we were kids, she used to eat them right off the ground like a cow."

Simone laughed and the dimple was back. Score! "There is nothing about Claire that is like a cow."

"Except for the grazing," Astrid said, doggedly, and Simone rolled her beautiful brown eyes. They were back to flirting now.

"What do they taste like?" Simone asked. It was Astrid's turn to be dismayed.

"You haven't tried one yet?"

"Not yet," she admitted, and looked slightly abashed.

Astrid knew what was going to happen next as if she'd seen it in a movie. She took a pawpaw from the bag. Gripping it tightly between both hands, she split the fruit open straight down the middle exposing ripe, orange, flesh. The pungent smell, hanging all around them in the September air, suddenly intensified. Their eyes locked.

"No time like the present," she challenged.

Simone didn't hesitate. Bending down, she sank her teeth firmly into the flesh. Astrid felt the pressure of lips against her fingers but held steady as juice oozed onto her wrists. The moment was charged, erotic.

"Hmmm," Simone gave Astrid a look of wonder. "I taste mango and banana and orange. Hmmmm," she said again, and her speech trailed off as she dived in for another bite.

Astrid swallowed hard. Simone was making a great show of enjoying the pawpaw and treating Astrid to a front row seat. Where Claire had been vague about Simone's sexuality, Simone was not being vague at all. The signals she was sending Astrid were loud and queer. It felt like she was in a dream where anything might happen.

"You make it look really good," Astrid said, and flung the half-eaten pawpaw into the brush. "I might have to try that cake."

"Yes, of course." Simone nodded enthusiastically. She picked another pawpaw from the bag. Digging her fingers into the flesh she exposed the ripe fruit. "Hmmmmm," she hummed happily and devoured the second pawpaw. Smacking her lips, she smiled into Astrid's eye. "Your turn."

"I said I'd try the cake."

"When was the last time you ate one?" Simone challenged and split another piece of fruit in two, like she'd been doing it for years.

"I, um, don't remember," Astrid admitted, and Simone looked triumphant.

"Tastes change as we get older." She gave Astrid a knowing look.

"Fine, I'll try it." Astrid agreed. It was only fair. Dipping her head, she nibbled at the exposed flesh. Perfectly ripe, it had a creamy texture and tasted exactly as she remembered: like the frozen, orange, push-up pops from the pool canteen. No wonder Claire liked those nasty things so much. Astrid made a face and Simone put a hand on one hip.

"Eat some more." She insisted and Astrid complied. She had no illusion the taste would improve but wanted to prolong the intimate encounter. Placing her hands on Simone's, to position the pawpaw better, she fully committed to the second bite. *Okay, no.* Cloying sweetness flooded her senses and she struggled not to gag.

"Brava!" Simone laughed, and rubbed Astrid's back with her free hand. "Thank you for trying. Maybe you will like the cake better. When are you free?"

"Oh," Astrid said. "I'll be out here for a week. Can I come by next Saturday?"

Simone looked intrigued. "You are camping?"

"Yeah," Astrid fought off the impulse to invite her along. The hospitality of Bob's compound was not hers to offer to someone else. No matter how soft their brown eyes felt on her face.

"Okay, Saturday. Six o'clock, we will eat pawpaw cake and watch car races with Eartha Kitty."

"I told Claire no NASCAR!" Astrid said, and Simone smiled enigmatically.

"Let's see what happens."

"Okay," Astrid heard herself reply.

Watching Simone launch her boat, huge butterflies began a conga line in Astrid's stomach. Never before had she experienced such an immediate physical attraction to another person. It was probably tied to that fact that Simone had been the agent of Astrid's awakening, but who knew? The way Simone's eyes caressed her face made her feel special. Was that why Astrid had agreed to a date with her, this virtual stranger? Leigh had asked her out five times before Astrid had agreed to go.

It was curious. Astrid knew from researching human sexuality that animal attraction had the potential to make you act out of character. Though exhilarated, she would need to be careful. Simone was beautiful but way out of her league. They'd been reacquainted less than an hour and she already had Astrid eating out of her hands.

CHAPTER SIX

Off Grid

Bob's compound was located on the northeastern tip of Snake Island in the middle of the Potomac River. The land was not zoned for commercial or residential use. According to Maryland state law, fourteen days was the maximum time a private citizen could co-opt public land for a private encampment before being considered a squatter. Some national forests allowed thirty-day occupancy rates but Maryland capped their hospitality at a fortnight. Bob had been on the island for fifteen years. He'd definitely overstayed his welcome.

The National Park Service, responsible for policing the area, gave him a pass because Bob spent all his time picking up garbage. Trolling the river in a dented canoe called Sondro, he dragged away the flotsam and jetsam of the Potomac—parts of old docks, fuel barrels, and automotive debris fallen from the American Legion Bridge upstream—making the environment safer for wildlife and kayakers alike. Most of the items he collected were hauled to a spot designated by the Park Service for trash pick-up, others were incorporated into the infrastructure of his compound giving the place a steampunk Swiss Family Robinson aesthetic. It was unique. Each time Astrid visited he'd added something new. She had no idea what to expect next and neither did he. His projects were completely dependent on what floated down the river.

She didn't write about him. The kayaking community was already aware a garbage-collecting hermit lived on the point. They didn't know he was an MIT-educated engineer and they didn't need to. Astrid had written the article in her head a dozen times but never published it. She'd no doubt the public would be interested in Bob but Bob was not interested in the public. The special mindset that allowed him to lead a productive and fulfilling existence on the island wouldn't tolerate notoriety. Astrid was not an expert on the peculiarity of behavior, but she knew enough not to upset the balance of a happy life.

Depending on the year, Bob usually stayed on the island six months, then spent the winter in Georgetown with his parents who owned a rare-map store. His existence was fringe, but not entirely off grid and not the most extreme example of hermitage Astrid had ever witnessed, not by a long shot, not even on the Potomac. There was a notorious naked man living downstream closer to Georgetown, who made Bob look like a bon vivant.

Off-grid living was an increasing trend. Given her current state of homelessness, it was possibly something for Astrid to consider. She'd recently blogged about a couple she'd met at a music festival who were committed to the idea of existing in natural spaces. Jen and Chad were part of the "Boondocker" community. Moving from campsite to campsite, they kept no formal residence beyond a white van whose amenities included a stained futon and bucket. Astrid had lived with them for two weeks in a drafty teepee in the mountains near Asheville, North Carolina. She'd come away from the experience with a constellation of chigger-bites on her butt and a greater appreciation of what it meant to live that way. Choices had seemed much clearer when there was nothing to impose structure on her beyond the sun and tide. She hoped the trick worked again. She needed clarity more than ever.

Hoisting the Firefly on her shoulder, she walked north toward Bob's compound. The rain was now a distant memory and the September sun beat down on her back warming her skin. The encounter with Simone had been unexpected fun. The flirty Italian chef had lifted her flagging spirits if only for a moment. Bob did not flirt and rarely smiled but he was as constant as the current and always a safe harbor when she needed one.

Astrid knew he'd be grateful for the ciabatta sandwiches she'd remembered to pick up at the deli and happy to let her stay for as long as she wished. He wouldn't ask her any questions about her love life or her job, because it wouldn't occur to him. Bob never talked about subjects that didn't concern his immediate environment. This was Astrid's favorite thing about him.

She first passed through the forest of the lost-and-found. Here, Bob had covered trees with salvageable objects rescued from the river. Astrid's favorite had canoe and kayak paddles lashed to it with kudzu vines. It looked like a wild exotic bird. She eyed a graphite paddle, nicer than the one she'd brought with her, and considered trading up. Bob wouldn't mind. It made sense to him to take the stuff out of the river and sort it into categories, but he didn't care what happened to it after that. Each tree had a different theme as the debris tended to be either automotive, recreational, or marine. The fishing tree probably had five hundred dollars' worth of gear on it and the boating tree had a rudder Astrid knew cost more than a grand. Hikers were free to take what they liked, though people seldom did. Bob's reputation didn't invite curiosity seekers.

Also, there was Django.

"Hey Bob?" she called, smiling as the compound came into view. The first glimpse of the treehouse always captivated her. The central platform was a beautiful, nearly-intact deck made of solid teak. Three meters square, it was ten feet off the ground nestled in a natural cradle between the branches of a giant linden tree. It almost looked like an open palm holding the platform. Fastened to the trunk with heavy cables, the deck was protected from the wind by plastic barrels edging the exterior and creating a railing. The dwelling was windproof, waterproof and could probably sleep three people comfortably, though Astrid had never seen anyone there except Bob and Django. "You up there?"

"No."

The voice was so quiet Astrid almost didn't hear it. Whirling around she saw Bob coming up the path leading from the interior of the island. Dressed in cargo shorts and a clean Gowear T-shirt, his appearance did nothing to suggest he was an island-squatting hermit. Clean-shaven, with closely cropped grey hair, Bob might be any normal weekend warrior exploring the Potomac. Except today was Monday and Bob was anything but normal.

"Hi, Astrid," he said, walking purposefully toward her. His hands were full of pawpaws and a bulging bagful dangled from his wrist.

Astrid flashed to the memory of eating the ripe flesh from Simone's hands and smiled to herself. Had that really happened?

"Hey, Bob. You making some more of that shine? Last year's batch was a blaster." Astrid teased as he drew closer.

"I made the liquor last week," he said, his eyes glued to her face. "What happened to your nose? You look different."

Astrid was ready for the question. Bob was the most observant person she knew and had the least amount of filter. Over the years she'd discovered that guileless honesty was the best way to communicate with him, or anyone else for that matter.

"I got smashed in the face by a door. A plastic surgeon made me a new one."

He nodded thoughtfully. "You look pretty but you don't look like you. I like the old nose better."

Astrid smiled into his kind blue eyes. She knew she was getting his honest opinion. "Thanks. Me too."

"Can you get it back?"

"No, turns out I had a deviated septum. The doctor had to take out the bump." She pointed to her nose. "This is me now."

Bob shrugged his broad shoulders. "It looks good."

"Thanks." Astrid knew this was the last he would say on the subject. There'd be no discussion on the existential whammy of having her appearance altered. Bob wouldn't ask her how Leigh or her parents felt. He wouldn't ask Astrid about anything beyond what was in their immediate vicinity. This is precisely why she'd come.

He eyed her backpack. "You staying?"

"Yes, maybe a week." She still had two prewritten blogs in the can, and the bark muttsvah story was half written in her head. A week at Bob's was just what she needed to reset her compass. She hadn't spent any real time in the woods since before the accident. It felt glorious being outside. Let the inside world fuck off for a few days.

"Okay," he said, looking pleased. "I'll get your hammock set up on the lower deck."

"That sounds awesome. And I've got dinner." She slipped two wrapped ciabatta rolls from her bag and watched his eyes spark with interest.

"Italianos?"

"Yeah, I brought six. How do you think they'll taste with your pawpaw shine?"

"I think they'll taste good."

"Me too."

Two hours later, Astrid was blissed out in a linden tree, swinging high above the island in a hammock. Canopied by the hull of an old row boat Bob had wired in the branches with steel cables, Astrid was protected from wind and weather but could still see the stars. She reached up and touched the bark of the tree. It was probably just the effects of the pawpaw shine, which was cloyingly sweet and packed a big punch, but Astrid suddenly didn't feel quite so horrible. The breakup with Leigh was inevitable. Why be upset about it? They'd never been a true fit. Astrid had forced it to work like a pair of shoes that were too small. The real question was: why had it taken so long for her to walk away?

The immediate problem was finding a place to live. Astrid mulled over options. Her parents' house would be perfect if she were speaking to her mother. Steps from the river, the basement had a spacious room that opened to the backyard. But moving there now was not a possibility. River access and free rent were not amenity enough to cancel Katrina's hurtful stance about her nose.

Astrid took a swig of pawpaw shine from the corked bottle Bob had given her for a nightcap. Sleeping below her in a hammock tied above the lowest platform of the tree house, he mumbled in his sleep. Astrid wondered what he might be dreaming.

She took another sip of homemade liquor and grimaced. It was too sweet for her tastes but it helped fog over the scene in the doctor's office. Her mother could deny her joy all day long, but Astrid knew the truth. Katrina had always wanted Astrid to have her nose fixed. It was not a secret. She'd lobbied hard for it when Astrid was in high school and had only let up in recent years when it seemed like a lost cause. Now that it was fait accompli, she was taking no care to hide her glee. The look of approval in her eyes had been unmistakable. She much preferred the new version of Astrid to the old. The knowledge hurt Astrid more than the door.

Confiding her hurt feelings to Claire wasn't possible until after the tour. Astrid wouldn't burden her sister with information she could do nothing about. There was no changing Katrina, anyway. What was the point? Drifting off to sleep, she pushed it all from her mind and thought instead of Simone's soft brown eyes.

She awoke to a cat licking her neck.

"Django, hey, buddy." Astrid slid an arm out of the hammock and stroked the head of Bob's long-haired, Maine Coon cat. Perched on a branch of the tree, just to the side of the hammock, the eight-toed cat weighed twenty-five pounds and had a head the size of a cantaloupe. Backlit by the pink of the early morning sky, his long silky hair gave him the appearance of a mythical creature. "Who's the sweetest boy?"

Django trilled and leaned into the caress. He was the second in the breed since Astrid had started visiting the island twelve years ago and an inveterate snuggler.

"Well, good morning to you, too," She scratched the scruff under his neck and he trilled again. "You want to come in here with me?"

The cat placed a paw on Astrid's chest asking for permission and she happily obliged.

"Come on in. Okay, wow," she gulped as he landed his full weight on her body before settling beneath the crook of her arm. The cat heaved a deep sigh of contentment, as if there was no place on earth he'd rather be, and began to snore. Astrid smiled. There was something deeply validating when another animal, even a giant, long-haired cat that smelled faintly of the river, sought your company. It fostered a feeling of being desired, which in turn fostered feelings of security. It was primal, lovely.

Astrid stroked the top of Django's head and thought about creating a post for *Outside Astrid* around the idea. She'd written about pets before. Her readers were crazy about domestic animals and this would be a new spin. Astrid hadn't had a pet of her own since living with her parents. The one major drawback of the Mount Pleasant townhouse had been the no-pets rule. Randy, the owner and landlord, had lived next door, so there was no cheating with a secret backdoor dog. He'd made them Irish soda bread on St. Patrick's Day, which was excellent, but didn't make up for the unconditional love of an animal. Leigh, who'd been raised in a Chicago high-rise, thought animals belonged in a zoo.

Django chirped, and nestled more firmly into her side.

"Big night, boy? Did you stay out of trouble?"

Bob's first island cat, Clarence of the Jungle, had famously lost an eye to a barred owl. Life on the island was a tough existence, but Astrid was sometimes jealous of it. Rules didn't vary in Django's world. You might have to fight for your life every now and then, but at least you knew who your enemies were.

Perhaps she was being too hard on her mother. She needed to settle down. Employing a meditation trick she'd learned on a yoga retreat, she first assessed her physical comfort. Tightly cocooned in the large woven hammock, another heart beating against her own, she was supremely content, if a little hungover from the pawpaw shine. Things could be worse. Though her shoulders were sore from working out yesterday, it was the type of pain that inspired you to do more. She couldn't wait to attack the course again.

Floating in peaceful awareness of her body, Astrid next confronted her emotions. Her biggest concern was where to live. Money was tight. She didn't know anyone looking for a roommate and she'd never lived alone. These were the primary reasons she'd moved in with Leigh, though she'd pretended they were in love. What a mess. Right now, her best option was her parents' basement or breaking into a lock house on the canal. What was she going to do?

Drifting back to sleep, the plan came to her. It was just so obvious. Why not move into Claire's place to buy a little time? It would solve Eartha Kitty's loneliness issue and Astrid had two friends in the building. Tara's brother, Miles, had been Astrid's lab partner in high school. She hadn't seen him in a while but maybe they could reconnect. He was a stoner but low-key and hilarious.

And then there was Simone. Sexy, sexy Simone. Every time Astrid thought of their encounter on the beach, a small thrill ran up her spine. The woman was absolutely gorgeous. But maybe Simone looked at everyone like they were a hot-out-of-the-oven calzone. Astrid tried not to get too excited about the playful brown eyes. She knew she was fighting a losing battle.

"What do you think, Django? Am I crazy to think she liked me, too?"

Astrid spent the next week gloriously off grid. After securing an invite to the bark muttszvah and texting Claire her plans, she disconnected her phone and helped Bob collect the trash. His stretch of the Potomac had a storied history of which he was both curator and custodian. In addition to the important environmental work, Bob also delighted in finding and repurposing interesting things. A scavenger at heart, he had an impressive collection of artifacts displayed in a glass jeweler's case in his parents' Georgetown map store. Civil War bullet casings, beautiful quartz arrowheads—he'd amassed items of both historic and prehistoric value. Astrid liked tagging along because you never knew what you'd find. Last year, Bob found a metal, WWII era canteen wedged in between some rocks on a tidal island downstream. But mostly it was garbage.

Following today's scavenge, Astrid would pack her gear and return to civilization. She had to face Leigh, get the rest of her stuff and move out of the townhouse. She really wanted to get her good kayak. Just thinking about the future encounter was exhausting. Astrid put it out of her mind. Time at Bob's had rejuvenated her. She didn't want to go backward.

Claire knew Astrid's whereabouts and that's all that mattered. She never went off grid without informing her sister. It was irresponsible not to let someone know when you'd be out of communication. In Claire's case it would be unkind. She'd been out to Bob's once or twice and knew Astrid was in good, if somewhat eccentric, hands.

Right now, he was clambering atop a pile of driftwood the size of a mobile home, pulling out old tennis balls he used to create a soft patio around the treehouse.

"I'm going to grab this tent. Looks like it's in pretty good shape." Astrid steered her kayak toward a two-person, nylon tent hanging in the debris like a sheet drying on a clothesline. There was no way of knowing how it got here. It might have been left behind by campers or washed down river from Ohio.

"Great, I may need that," he answered and looked over her shoulder at something in the distance and then back at the pile of driftwood. Fishing out another tennis ball he tossed it in the boat.

"For what?" Bob was crafty but Astrid could not imagine what he'd do with a washed-out old tent.

"Your sister is here. If she's staying, I'll need to make another hammock."

CHAPTER SEVEN

Claire-ity

Astrid couldn't believe her eyes. It was, indeed, Claire. She knew the ballet company had time off following the first grueling leg of the tour, but Claire was supposed to be recharging her batteries at an eclectic spa in Arizona before for a big sweep through the heartland. The place was fabulous, offering both hot and goat yoga and every other spa amenity imaginable. Right now, Claire should be laid out on smoking-hot stones with her smoking-hot boyfriend. What was she doing standing in the high weeds of Snake Island?

"What are you doing here?" Astrid shouted. Steering the kayak toward her sister she tried to look angry but failed miserably. Claire was actually here. Her big sister, best friend, personal warrior—the girl who snuck home from New York to toilet paper the house of the high school basketball coach for not starting Astrid her senior year—was just ten feet of Potomac river away from a hug. A hug Astrid desperately needed. Her mouth twisted into a smile as tears stung the back of her eyes.

"I could ask you the same question," Claire shouted back. Astrid was now close enough to make out her sister's facial features. She looked worried. The bright blue eyes had small shadows beneath them and her normally radiant smile was forced.

Shit. This was not good. Claire needed to look her best right now, better than her best. The role was *The Sleeping Beauty*, not the *sleepy* beauty. The last thing Astrid wanted to do was cause Claire more stress. There would be plenty of time to discuss Astrid's issues after the show wrapped. Coty was scheduled to go fishing with his brother in Puerto Rico for a long weekend. Astrid had imagined she and Claire would have time to properly unpack her drama. She'd start by admitting the mistake she'd made moving in with Leigh and they'd take it from there. Astrid had it semi-planned out. They'd pop popcorn, maybe have a *Gilmore Girls* marathon. But Astrid had steeled herself to wait until the tour was over. What was Claire doing here now?

"I told you I was going off grid," Astrid managed before the waterworks began. Banking the kayak on the shallow beach, she scrambled out of the boat and, within seconds, Claire's arms were around her. Her sister wasn't dressed for a river rescue but she didn't seem to notice or care. Astrid felt the crisp white shirt crumple against her damp tank-top and started to pull away. Claire held on more tightly.

"Don't you dare." Easing Astrid's body down to the beach, she cradled her on the shore like a child. The sisters were nearly identical in size but Claire was a professional dancer and physically much stronger. Astrid worked out at least once a day and was no slouch, but Claire was a beast. Astrid always felt safest with the ropey ballerina arms wrapped around her body.

"Okay, Stinky, tell me where it hurts."

Astrid choked back a sob at the old nickname. From early childhood Claire had called Astrid "Stinky," for the smells she often brought back from the river and, in return, Astrid had called Claire "Slinky," for the moves she brought back from dance practice. A week bunking with Django in Bob's tree house and Astrid knew her nickname fit better than ever.

Claire stroked her hair. "It's okay, you're okay."

Astrid cried in her sister's arms. The days on the island had been restorative but her wounds were still fresh, and shockingly deep. She'd been so busy reacting to Leigh and Katrina's reactions that she'd just begun to check in with herself. Having her physical appearance altered was a seismic shift with lingering, existential ramifications. Astrid had yet to process it. Claire's look of concern gave her permission to begin.

"I can't believe you're actually here," Astrid said, and then started to sob again. Idly, she wondered if this much ugly crying could damage her new nose. Would it necessitate additional surgery? Could she get her old nose back? Did she want it back? When she finally pulled herself together enough to speak, she noticed Claire was smiling at her. "What?"

"I'm just so glad to see you." The sweet expression turned to one of joy when twenty-five pounds of Maine Coon cat joined their hug. "Oh, my goodness! Who is this handsome guy?" Claire asked, laughing, as Django forced his giant body between them.

"Django," Astrid replied, and stroked the ruff under his neck. "He belongs to Bob, or Bob belongs to him. That's probably more accurate. Django's been sharing my hammock."

Claire sniffed the top of the cat's head before giving it a tentative kiss. "That explains so much. Where is the infamous Bob?"

Astrid looked around the shoreline and up the bank. The nylon tent had been pulled from the debris pile but Bob was nowhere to be found. "I'm pretty sure he went to make up your bed."

Claire looked alarmed. She put a hand to her throat as if to make sure they were talking about the same person. "For me?"

Astrid nodded. Untangling herself from Claire's embrace, she rose to her feet. Django chirped twice and blinked happily back at her. Nestled atop her beautiful sister the cat was in no hurry to move. "Yeah, he's a great host. Last night we made roadkill fondue."

"Okay, no." Claire loved exercising outdoors and was usually game for glamping, but preferred not to know of Astrid's more gnarly adventures. She was particularly squeamish about food. "Don't tell me another detail, please."

Giving Django a last pat, she rose to her feet. Behind her Astrid saw a gorgeous Gowear kayak Claire must have rented from the boathouse along with the shiny new paddle and PFD.

"Do Mom and Dad know you're here?" Astrid asked bluntly and Claire nodded.

"Mom called me right after you did. She was just as upset about the scene in Dr. Coleman's office as you were."

"I sincerely doubt that." Astrid tried to keep the ice out of her voice. Katrina's shortcomings were not Claire's fault. She'd sacrificed sacred break days to come to Astrid's rescue and deserved nothing but kindness. Astrid hadn't known how much she needed her big sister until Bob had pointed her out on the river bank. She still hadn't said anything about Astrid's appearance which seemed weird. So, she asked her, "What do you think of my nose?"

Claire's smile widened. "Oh, are you ready to talk about it?"

"Isn't that why you came back?"

"Definitely, but only if you're ready. Are you?"

Astrid felt fresh tears. "I think so," she choked before Claire's arms were around her once more.

"You look amazing by the way," Claire whispered into her hair causing Astrid to hiccup.

"I look just like you."

"Like I said," Claire teased, "stunning." Gently letting go of Astrid's body, she took her face between her hands. "May I?"

"Okay." Astrid closed her eyes and allowed Claire to study her. Several moments passed. "What's the verdict?"

"I already told you, you're beautiful."

Astrid opened her eyes to find her sister smiling at her. "Yes, but do I look like me?" She was not even sure what she meant.

"Yes, definitely," Claire answered without hesitation. She then wrinkled her nose. "You certainly smell like yourself."

"Thanks a lot, Slinky."

"No problem, Stinky," Claire said, and then grew serious. "I'm so sorry this happened to you." She brushed her finger softly on the bridge of Astrid's nose and then gave it a light kiss.

Astrid frowned and stepped back a few feet. "I'm altered, right? Give it to me straight. A part of me is missing."

"Yeah," Claire said, now even more solemn. "It's true." She shook her head. "I never told you this, but last year, something similar happened to me."

"What are you talking about?" Astrid asked, suddenly feeling awful. Had Claire undergone a surgical procedure she didn't know about? They'd been distant the past six months but there'd been no falling out. Had something happened?

"I had a corn removed from my toe."

"A what?"

"Corny. He's gone," Claire said.

She wiped dramatically at her eye and Astrid knew that she was being teased. The sisters often used to improv to cheer each other up. Astrid might begin a discussion about how much she hated wearing an underwire bra and Claire would suggest she move to the moon where lack of gravity would make them irrelevant and they would laugh and laugh. The silly solution wouldn't make the underwire pinch any less but this wasn't the point. Some problems were unsolvable. It was nice to be with someone who understood that.

Right now, Claire had the deadpan look she often got before launching into a distracting story. Astrid wasn't sure if she was ready to joke about her face. "Claire, maybe don't," she said, but it was too late. Claire was off and running.

"You remember, *Corny*," she stroked the outside of her foot. "He was a part of me for so long."

Astrid sighed. "Are you seriously comparing a growth on your toe to my face? Are we really going there?"

"His name was Corny and don't disparage him," Claire said indignantly. "He operated under tremendous pressure." She glared at Astrid until she cracked a smile.

"Poor Corny."

"Thank you."

"Do you miss him?"

"I do not." Claire looked wistful. "We were toe-toe-ly in love but weren't growing at the same level, you know?"

Astrid couldn't stop a full smile. "How long have you been working on that one?"

"I thought of it on the plane," Claire admitted. "Speaking of which, we need to get back to the real world. People are worried about you. Mom's been stress shopping."

"You went by the house?" Astrid was confused. If Claire had stopped at their parents' house, why had she bothered to rent the Gowear kayak? At last count there were at least six boats in her parent's garage.

"Yes, I went by the house, and there are so many Zappos boxes on the front porch Dad has made them into a bench."

"Good," Astrid was defiant. If their mother wanted to work out her demons buying shoes, who was Astrid to stop her? "I hope she maxes out the credit cards."

"Do you, really?" Claire did her new eyebrow thing. "Okay, well, if Mom drives them into bankruptcy, they can move in with you. Our place is only a single. How do you think Leigh will feel about having Katrina and Jerry sleeping in the guest room? You ladies have two bathrooms, right?"

"I, uh, yeah, no." Astrid said, and looked quickly away. Now was the time to tell Claire that she was planning to move into her apartment, but she held back. Six months ago, Claire had voiced concerns about Astrid moving in with Leigh. Correctly guessing that Astrid was taking the path of least resistance on a road to nowhere, Claire had unwittingly put Astrid on the defensive. Consequently, Astrid had been too embarrassed to share any of the microaggressions that made Leigh impossible to live with. Claire seemed so blissful living with Coty. She reported candlelit dinners on the roof deck and spontaneous flowers once a week. Leigh marked her bananas with a Sharpie. It was all so mortifying. Astrid didn't know where to begin, so she addressed the issue with Katrina first.

"Mom really hurt my feelings. She was positively gloating in the doctor's office. It was just so obvious how thrilled she is about the change." Astrid touched the tip of her nose. "She's always wanted me to do it. Remember how much pressure she put on me my last year in high school?"

"I do." Claire frowned.

"She made all those comments about how beautiful the Long Island cousins were. I just ignored her. But it made me feel terrible."

Claire shook her head. She had an odd look.

"What?"

"I think you can expect Mom to tone it down. I was just with her, a little while ago, and she's a changed woman."

"What are you talking about?" Astrid was confused. As far as she knew, their mother was not capable of reining in her impulses.

"Dad said something to her."

"Whose dad?"

"Our Dad."

"You called Dad?" It was Astrid's turn to lift an eyebrow.

"What was I supposed to do?" Claire put a hand on her hip. "You were three thousand miles away and hysterical. I needed boots on the ground."

"But Dad never takes on Mom," Astrid said, slowly. "What would be the point of telling him?"

"Because I was desperate," Claire admitted, and then her eyes began to dance. "But it turns out I'm a genius because it worked."

"How, exactly?"

"Dad went Di-Bulldozer on her."

"No way."

Claire nodded.

"I don't believe you."

"Well, start."

"I can't."

"Try."

Astrid shook her head. Jerry Dibello was famous for his rarely glimpsed, though absolutely terrifying temper. Their uncles called it the Di-Bulldozer. Astrid had seen it only once when a Federal Express driver had gone through a stop light and almost run Claire over on her bicycle. Jerry hadn't laid a hand on the man, though somehow still rendered him unable to drive. Astrid wasn't sure if it was their father's physical size, righteous anger or thick Long Island accent but the man had crumpled like a wet napkin. While Claire had pedaled off to the park without a scratch, he'd been driven home by a FedEx supervisor who'd arrived by taxi from Rockville. Astrid couldn't imagine Jerry yelling at their mother.

Claire nodded. "I don't know exactly what he said, but she's different."

"Stress shopping seems like normal Katrina behavior to me," Astrid challenged. "Self-serving, appearance-oriented."

"See for yourself. When I drove up this morning, she was wearing a pair of your high school sweatpants and a Nationals ball cap."

"Okay, what?" It was a family joke that Katrina didn't come downstairs unless she was ready for a photographer from the *Washingtonian* magazine to show up and do a much longed-for profile.

"Yes, she looks like a skater-boi. And the Zappos boxes? They're all hiking boots."

Astrid smirked. "She's trying to buy me? We've seen this before, too. Remember when she bought you a horse?"

"She's not perfect."

"And not that smart, either. I rep an outdoor company, remember? Why would I need more hiking boots?" She kicked out her foot to show Claire the most recent footwear supplied by Gowear.

"The shoes aren't for you," Claire said, and lifted her eyebrow again.

"Stop it with the eyebrow. You look like Joan Crawford."

"Thank you." Claire looked genuinely pleased. "And the hiking boots are for her. Dad's speech went deep. It hit some maternal nerve no one know existed. She told me she wants to spend more time with you."

"You're lying," Astrid croaked while Claire burst out laughing.

"Nope. Didn't you see the new kayak?" Claire gestured over her shoulder to the beautiful boat on the beach.

"That's hers?" Astrid was aghast.

"I told you. She's different. Maybe you can introduce her to Bob."

"What a great idea." Astrid smiled at her sister. "Mom could start coming out on weekends. She could help Bob with the roadkill and the garbage."

"Mom would be so good at that."

Astrid pretended to consider the idea. "If she puts a hitch on the Mercedes, she could start doing the hauls to the dump. Save the National Park Service the trip."

"I love this plan. I'm sure her friends at the club will want to get involved."

"The only problem will be keeping it under the radar. If everyone starts collecting garbage there won't be any left."

"We should probably go talk to her." Claire stood up and linked her arm through Astrid's. They were no longer joking.

"Do we have to?" Leaving the island meant more than facing her mother. Astrid also needed to deal with Leigh, find a new place to live and buy a bark muttszvah gift.

What did you get for a thirteen-year-old chihuahua?

CHAPTER EIGHT

Home Cheapo

"Would anyone care for anything else? Can I get you another glass of wine?" The young waiter looked expectantly at Katrina Dibello. At Claire's insistence their mother was no longer wearing the Nationals ballcap and had exchanged Astrid's sweatpants for a pair of jeans. She now looked like their mother again, only less so. Without her fancy clothing, designer jewelry or heavy makeup, Katrina had succeeded in creating a minimalist version of herself. It was the opposite of caricature.

"Sancerre, please," she said, and grasped the arm of the server taking him visibly by surprise. Small and spare with a man-bun and a graphic T-shirt that substituted the word Kale for Yale, he had the energy of a high-strung but well-mannered dog. He was of obvious pedigree but perhaps a tad overbred.

"Yes, ma'am," he squeaked, and Astrid wondered if his voice might still be changing.

"Thank you for taking such good care of us, Todd," Katrina gushed. She was either oblivious to his discomfort or ignoring it. "This is a big day for our family."

"No problem, ma'am." Todd blushed to the roots of the man-bun and Claire did her eyebrow thing across the table at Astrid who tried not to laugh.

The faded version of their mother was more than a little drunk. Such was her relief at Astrid's return and acceptance of her heartfelt apology, that she'd invited them out to a celebratory lunch. It was touching, really. When Claire had suggested a funky U Street bistro Astrid had once profiled, Katrina had agreed without argument. Normally, she lobbied hard for the Chevy Chase Club where parking was easy and the cuisine familiar. At unUsual DC the only thing Katrina recognized on the menu was the wine list of which she'd availed herself liberally. Perhaps it was the two glasses of wine she'd had herself, but Astrid was inclined to be forgiving. Katrina was stepping outside her comfort zone. It was an act of contrition as obvious as the expensive new hiking shoes on her feet. That they were technically approach wear, not meant for use off-trail, and leaving huge black scuff marks on the polished wooden floor of the restaurant, were beside the point. The important thing was that Katrina was making an effort.

"I'll have a glass too," Jerry said, and smiled expansively.

It was no secret how much he loved having his family around the same table. Astrid could not remember the last time it had happened outside a holiday or milestone occasion. Claire's intense practice schedule was partly responsible, but most of the blame lately was on her. Leigh had never meshed well with the family. Coty had been on a first name basis with her parents five minutes into their introductory meeting. Leigh had never progressed beyond Mr. and Mrs. Dibello. Both gluten-and dairy-free, it had been nearly impossible for her to share a meal with them. It was no longer a problem, as they were no longer a couple—a fact Astrid still hadn't managed to tell her family.

They'd been at the table nearly an hour. Claire had to leave for the airport soon. If Astrid wanted sanctioned use of her apartment, she needed to tell them now.

"Should we just get another bottle?" Jerry asked.

Astrid could feel his happiness. Unlike his wife, Jerry was an adventurous eater and satisfaction at the duck confit he'd just devoured lingered in his eyes.

"No," Astrid and Claire said, in unison, while Katrina answered, "Absolutely."

Jerry just laughed. He might be a hothead but he didn't bear grudges. Holding Katrina's hand across the table, lovingly stroking the tops of her knuckles with his thumb, it was as if their quarrel had never happened. If Claire hadn't told her about the Di-Bulldozing, Astrid might be convinced Katrina had been given some sort of magic potion. It wouldn't have occurred to her that Jerry, though he'd been her champion in every other realm of life, had finally stood up to his wife. The knowledge warmed Astrid more than the wine.

The waiter coughed nervously and Astrid felt sorry for him. Her family could be a lot to take and today was no exception. In addition to Katrina's colossal buzz and the large black streaks she was leaving on the floor there was the fact of Claire's beauty. Poor little man-bun. Every time he looked at their side of the booth his overly large Adam's apple betrayed his discomfort. Bobbing relentlessly about in his neck, Astrid was afraid it might shoot into his skull and give him a stroke.

"Two glasses please," Jerry said.

"Coming right up. Anything else?" He kept his eyes trained firmly on the ground.

"A slice of pie?"

"Sure. Would you like to see our dessert menu? We have a few different options."

Jerry shook his head. "Do me a favor? Pick one that looks good and us bring four forks. We trust you, right, girls?"

"Of course," Claire said and the Adam's apple quivered at the sound of her voice.

Astrid had seen this reaction to her sister's beauty too many times to doubt its power. She likened the response to being hypnotized by a cobra. Claire was not remotely vicious, but her beauty generated the type of reaction that allowed her to talk her way into restaurants and out of speeding tickets. Right now, she was using it to avoid a mystery dessert.

"One fork, please," she told Todd who blinked at her as if he were staring into the sun. She smiled at him. "Daddy's going to eat the whole thing, anyway. Right, Stinky?"

"Right, Slinky," Astrid responded, and Todd turned to her.

To Astrid's surprise, the nervous manner didn't abate. If anything, he grew more discombobulated. Putting his hands on his head, he inadvertently freed the bun and hair fell into his face. "Oh shit, my bad," he said, struggling to contain it.

"No, you're good," Astrid said, and shot a look at Claire who was giggling into her hand.

"Just bring us the wine and a slice of pie, son." Jerry dismissed him with a wave of his paw. "We'll figure out the rest."

"Yes, sir." Todd tripped off into the kitchen and Jerry chuckled.

"Poor guy," Jerry said, fondly. At six-four, two-hundred and twenty pounds, another glass of Sancerre, or three, wouldn't affect his ability to drive. Astrid suspected he only drank it to be companiable with Katrina, whose tolerance was much lower. Claire didn't imbibe during ballet season but lubricating the conciliatory lunch had seemed like a no-brainer to Astrid. She was also experiencing the endorphin boost of using soap for the first time in a week. Reentry sometimes felt akin to being reborn. Coupled with the carb-rush from the fried chicken special, Astrid's happiness, though undoubtably chemical, was also undeniable. She lifted her glass.

"Here's to *The Sleeping Beauty*." She locked eyes with Claire, grateful to her big sister for putting the family on a healing path. Katrina might be full of Sancerre, but her apology had been sincere. It was all Claire's doing. Wielding a human bulldozer, the artful ballerina had moved their mother to a place of understanding. Astrid had every hope they were at the cusp of a new direction in their relationship. By the look of the boxes in the garage, Katrina had more than enough gear for anywhere they chose to go.

"Here's to Claire, who's so pretty!" Katrina sang happily and then clamped a hand over her mouth. "I mean her job. I meant the dancing," she said, through the vent of her fingers.

Astrid noticed that her nails, though buffed and clean, had been scrubbed of polish. She reached across the table. "It's okay, Mom. We know what you meant. And it's fine to say Claire is pretty. It's not a crime—it's a fact."

"Hear, hear!" Jerry chimed his agreement and Claire picked up her glass of iced tea and tapped it against Astrid's wine stem.

"Aw, thank you, Stinky."

"No problem, Slinky."

Tears welled in Katrina's eyes. She raised her glass again. "And here's to Astrid who is nicer than I deserve and uses words so beautifully."

"Here's to beautiful words!" Claire echoed. "And here's to Daddy, who's paying for lunch and my Lyft to Dulles."

Jerry laughed his big booming laugh. Starting deep in his chest, it washed over the table pulling them all in. "Indeed, and here's to the chef, whose duck makes me miss my Nona Pacelli." He kissed his fingers and Claire startled to attention.

"Oh, my gosh. We know her."

"Nona Pacelli died before you were born, honey." Katrina said. She put a hand on her chest and seemed surprised to find no necklace there.

"Not Nona Pacelli. The chef. I know the chef, or the future chef, rather." Claire turned to Astrid. "I forgot to tell you, but Simone got a job here."

"No way." Astrid thought of the encounter on the beach and experienced the same pleasant tingle she'd felt in the treehouse.

"It's true," Claire sparkled happily. "I was just texting with her this morning. She doesn't start until next month but it's totally on." The eyebrow went up. "She also told me she ran into you kayaking a few days ago."

Astrid tried to appear nonchalant. Remembering eating a pawpaw out of Simone's hand, sticky juice running down her fingers, made this difficult. She squirmed in her chair. "That's right, she did."

"Are you talking about Simone, from ballet?" Jerry asked. Ballet hadn't permitted Claire to have more than a handful of close friends but, self-appointed chief of carpooling, Jerry had known every one of them. It was his observation that you got more information out of teenage girls by plying them with Starbucks and listening to their conversations—*wind 'em up and watch 'em go!*—than by questioning them directly. "Simone was good fun, a really nice kid."

"I remember Simone," Katrina said. "She was the ambassador's daughter. She had the most beautiful eyes, and what a figure. But she was too curvy for ballet and, of course, she couldn't compete with Claire." She seemed to hear herself and shook her head. "What is wrong with me?"

"Baby steps, Mom. You're doing great." Claire rubbed Katrina's shoulder while Jerry frowned into his plate.

Astrid sensed the precious moment of family unity slipping away and made a tactical decision. It was time to come clean about her breakup with Leigh. She had to do it sometime. Why not now, when it would provide cover for her struggling mother?

Leaning in over the table, she lowered her voice. "I think Simone is gorgeous too. I kind of have a date with her tonight."

"Excuse me?" Claire squeaked, sounding not unlike the waiter.

"A date?" Jerry echoed but Katrina asked the most salient question.

Perking up considerably, she gave Astrid a shrewd look. "What happened to Leigh?"

"Yeah, that," Astrid swallowed hard. There was no way around the facts. "It didn't work out," she said, and shrugged her shoulders as if the Dibellos were the type of family that might accept such a simple explanation.

"Since when?" Claire said, her voice rising. The normally warm blue eyes felt like lasers pinning Astrid to the back of the booth. "Why didn't you tell me this sooner?"

"Because it just happened a few days ago, and I'm still processing it," Astrid replied carefully. She might make her living as a journalist, but at a personal level Claire posed much tougher questions.

"When did it happen, exactly? Tell me. What day?" There was no fear in her. Astrid suspected that it was because she was pure of heart. She wasn't afraid to ask the hard questions because she wasn't afraid to hear the answers. It was inspiring but daunting if you found yourself on the other side of the interview. Claire didn't beat around the bush. If she smelled a rat, she came into the darkness with a flashlight and a machete.

"It was the day after the bandage came off. Leigh was pretty mean about it," Astrid began and saw Jerry's nostrils flare. There was no going back, now. Pride wasn't the only reason she'd kept her problems with Leigh under wraps. Once her family got a whiff of trouble it would be like making dinner with hungry children in the house—endless hounding until she coughed up the goods. They would now demand the full buffet.

"The bandage came off more than a week ago," Claire reminded Astrid. "What happened? What did Leigh say to you?"

Astrid blew out a small breath. This was the most painful part of the story. She hated thinking about it. Saying the words aloud would be even less fun. "She accused me of taking advantage of the accident to have my nose fixed. She said I'd always wanted to look like my Barbie doll family and now I'd finally belong in the Dreamhouse, too."

"No," Jerry said simply while Claire expressed herself more colorfully.

"Fucking bitch."

"And, she's fucking wrong!" Katrina said, dropping the first f-bomb ever in Astrid's earshot. "I know that you didn't want to have your nose changed. I'm happy to tell her that. Or I can have Dr. Coleman do it."

"Thank you, no." Astrid imagined what things Leigh might say to her mother or the nation's sexiest doctor and shuddered. It was all a big mess and Leigh was not solely to blame. Astrid had ignored warning signs that now seemed preposterous. She wasn't proud of it but it was the truth. It was time to tell her family everything. "Moving in with Leigh was a mistake from the beginning. I never said anything before, because everyone warned me against it."

"So, you just decided to suffer instead? How did that work out for you?" Claire now looked truly angry. If Astrid's perfect sister had a flaw it was that she was too protective of the people she loved. She also had no patience for self-destruction. Astrid supposed it was because she'd worked so hard at the incremental gains in her own life. Watching others take willful steps backward didn't make sense to her and she was rarely quiet about it.

"It totally sucked." Astrid admitted. "There are so many stories I've been dying to tell you." Shamelessly she tried to pull Claire off the warpath with the lure of gossip. Her sister wasn't taking the bait.

"I'm sure you could write a book," she said coldly. Her phone beeped and she took the opportunity to turn away.

"What did Leigh do?" Katrina was game for the tale.

"Yes, tell us, honey," Jerry encouraged, gently.

"Okay."

Astrid glanced at Claire. So many times, Astrid had wanted to tell her sister the details of the sitcom absurdity she was living with Leigh. Some of the stories were downright hilarious. The chance had finally come and Claire was scrolling through Instagram. But she was still at the table, so Astrid started the narrative.

"First off, she wrote her name on the fruit, so I wouldn't eat hers by mistake."

"That's bananas," Jerry deadpanned while Katrina looked appalled.

"And so petty," she narrowed her eyes. A stereotypical Italian mother, Katrina took great joy providing food to the people she loved. She was better at catering than cooking, but there was always food on the table. "What else did she do?"

"She charged me for hot water," Astrid said, and looked to Claire for a reaction. Finding none, she pressed on with the story. "She put this weird timer thing on the shower. I started taking sponge baths because it was cheaper."

"No!" Katrina shouted. She sounded aghast but looked a little thrilled. "Where would you even buy something like that?"

"Home Cheapo?" Jerry cracked, but the disgust in his voice was as clear as the blob of duck confit on his tie. "You can shower at our house any time you want, honey."

"Thanks, Daddy. But I don't want you to get the wrong idea. It wasn't entirely Leigh's fault."

"How do you mean?"

"I always knew she had a weird relationship with money. Our first date she took me to the public library."

"That's because you're a writer. I thought it was romantic," Claire interjected and Astrid fought to contain a smile. Attacking herself, she'd managed to flush out her protector.

"That's true. But then we went Dutch to a taco-truck."

Jerry looked disgusted. "She asked you out and then made you pay? She's a dentist!"

"Yes, but I can't really fault her because she was totally upfront about it. We had this big conversation about the importance of keeping things separate. But then she asked me to Venmo her for a sip of beer."

"Oh, come on!" challenged Claire.

"Okay, maybe not for a sip, but if I ever wanted one out of a six-pack, then she most definitely charged me for it," Astrid replied.

"Is that a thing people do?" Katrina looked at Claire who shrugged.

"It's something Leigh did. I knew it going in. I thought she might change. I'm sorry I didn't tell you all sooner."

Confession done, the Dibellos said all the right things.

Katrina was quick to shift the blame. "It's not your fault. Love makes us do crazy things."

Jerry offered absolution. "Don't blame yourself, honey. We live and we learn."

But it was Claire said who provided the most comfort, saying the words Astrid most longed to hear.

"Move into our apartment until you figure this out."

CHAPTER NINE

The Diplo-cat

"No, ma'am. I said *get back*, Eartha." Using the tip of her boot, Astrid gently nudged the cat back inside Coty and Claire's apartment. "I'm sorry, sweet girl. You weren't invited for cake."

Eartha didn't make a noise but Astrid imagined she saw sadness flicker in the yellow eyes.

"I promise we'll watch some more NASCAR when I get back," she said, and reluctantly closed the door.

Eartha Kitty was a total lover. Astrid had only spent a fraction of an afternoon with Claire and Coty's new calico and was ready to sign on as the president of her fan club. She reminded Astrid of a cat they'd had as children, named Zsa Zsa. Sister-cat to the much-maligned Eva, who lived with their cousins on Long Island, Zsa Zsa was the type of cat who'd made it her mission to seek out cat-haters and win them over. Jerry had called her the diplo-cat. No one's familiar, she could be counted on to make everyone feel special. When she died, Jerry had buried her in the back yard, marking her grave with a piece of snow-white quartz Astrid had dragged up from the river.

She completely understood why Coty and Claire were obsessed with Eartha Kitty. Like Zsa Zsa, this cat was a giver. Hilariously chatty, she was also playful, affectionate and absolutely gorgeous. Spending a week with Django had reminded Astrid how much she missed having a pet in her world. The hospitable Eartha Kitty only strengthened the feeling. Astrid made a promise to herself then and there. As soon as she found a new apartment, she was getting a cat of her own.

She walked the short distance down the hallway to the staircase. Living alone was going to be a change. Leigh had once accused her of being too needy and there were too many jokes about navel-gazing writers to disavow the notion that her profession attracted validation seekers. Shit. Is that why she liked animals so much, because she was needy? It was entirely possible. She'd welcomed a half-wild Maine Coon cat into her hammock without batting an eyelash and Eartha Kitty had stolen her heart with a single swish of her feathery tail.

Unfortunately, the charismatic calico couldn't be included in tonight's party. Astrid had once written a blog about people who brought uninvited pets to social engagements. Everyone she interviewed, animal loving or not, thought the habit to be rude. Showing up with a cat tucked under her arm would be rude and strange. Simone might be allergic. Though she was supposed to be helping to feed Eartha in Claire's absence, so maybe not. Perhaps, when Astrid knew Simone better, she could bring Eartha upstairs to visit. The thought made her blush and she cautioned herself that Simone was an old friend of Claire's and possibly just being polite. Tonight might be a one-time thing. Astrid needed to calm down.

The attic apartment was located directly above Coty and Claire's on the third floor. Until recently, it had been full of items from the old Turkman estate. According to Coty, who'd helped Miles drag the stuff down to his apartment in the basement, some things looked to be of local historical value. Astrid was particularly interested in seeing the gilded Tiffany weathervane that had once topped the old Turkman department store. She was mulling over a story about ornamental nods to nature in

DC architecture. There were two stone llamas in front of an apartment building on Connecticut Avenue she was dying to spotlight. The weathervane might be a good side bar. She made a mental note to visit her old lab partner tomorrow.

A polished-wood handrail made the ascent easy and she half pulled herself to the top floor. Simone had texted earlier. Astrid was expected at eight. She'd tried not to put romantic aspirations on the evening, but found it impossible, so had stopped. The way Simone had looked at Astrid on the beach had sparked a small flame. She was mostly convinced the beautiful Italian woman only wanted to see her because she looked like her sister but Astrid was still eager to see where the evening might go.

Before leaving for the airport, Claire had spun a fanciful narrative where Astrid and Simone fell in love, got married and took turns having babies who became ballet prodigies and danced a pas de deux at Madison Square Garden. There was also something about retiring to a beach house in the Outer Banks to raise corgis but Astrid had stuck on the first part of the story.

The idea of being married to Simone, having a family with her... It was completely preposterous but she couldn't stop the images from looping in her head. Women this beautiful had never noticed her. Astrid wasn't even sure how to respond if Simone did make a pass at her tonight, though the thought made her pleasantly warm.

Was it even appropriate to entertain thoughts of other women yet? She and Leigh had only been broken up for a week. Astrid's belongings were still in their assigned spots in the Georgetown house. She was pretty sure there was still a lime in the refrigerator with her name on it and a few onions of shared custody. Should Astrid even be here?

"Are you going to knock?"

A muffled voice, coming from inside the apartment brought Astrid back to reality. How long had she been staring at the door? Something flickered in the peephole. She was being watched. Dumbly, she reached out to knock but the door opened before she could make contact. Standing in the entrance wearing a red tank dress, and not much else, was Simone.

"Hi."

"Hey," Astrid said, looking up into the twinkling brown eyes. *God, she was pretty.* "Sorry, I think I may have spaced out there for a second."

"Are you back?" Simone asked sweetly, and the dimple formed on her cheek. Her dark hair was loose. Curling madly around her face, it swept down onto her shoulders dragging Astrid's gaze along with it.

She swallowed hard. "Definitely."

"Good, come eat some of my cake."

"Okay," Astrid agreed, and wondered if the word meant something different in Italian. The sexy energy from the encounter on the beach had returned twofold. Astrid could not be the only one feeling it. Entering the apartment, she brushed Simone's bare arm and experienced a flutter low in her stomach. Was it an overreaction? Standing face-to-face with the woman who'd prompted her sexual awakening, it was impossible to tell.

"Come, sit in the Papasan chair. Do you like the Papasan?"

"The what?" Behind her, Simone was saying something about a chair. Astrid tried to focus. "What type of chair?" She turned and nearly ran into Simone. "Oh, I'm sorry!"

They were so close. Astrid could smell vague hints of honey behind the much bolder lavender of Simone's body lotion. Her lips were not painted but glistened where she'd licked them with her tongue. Did she want to be kissed? Astrid hadn't properly kissed anyone in a long time and wondered if she remembered how.

"It's a Papasan chair," Simone said, and hit Astrid playfully on the arm as she walked past her into the open space. "Come meet Papa."

More contact, more butterflies. Astrid ignored them. She looked into the nearly empty living room and saw a yoga mat stretched in front of a large wicker chair shaped like a pasta bowl. Resting on a matching pedestal, the chair had a faded orange cushion and sat in the very middle of the room. Next to it, acting as coffee table, was a single folding TV tray. She approached the chair cautiously.

"Hi, Papa."

Astrid was not unfamiliar with the low circular design. She hadn't recognized the name but her Aunt Carol had one in her Hicksville living room and Astrid had never figured out how to sit on it without feeling as if she might pitch over. "Is he friendly?"

"Sit and see," Simone ordered and then skipped off into the kitchen, touching Astrid again as she left the room.

What was going on? She'd never been on a hookup site but imagined it must feel something like this: the possibility of sex with a stranger. It was as if Simone was the male cardinal, preening in her red dress, and Astrid, the drab female in an earth-tone Gowear T-shirt. She couldn't look away and she didn't want to. The feelings were exciting, incredibly erotic. They were also incredibly premature. Perching carefully on the edge of the chair, Astrid vowed not to give in.

"No," Simone called loudly from the other room as if reading her mind.

"What?" Astrid said, but couldn't help smiling as Simone bounced back into the den with two pieces of a spongy looking yellow cake. Artfully plated, with a dusting of powdered sugar on top and a sprig of mint on the side, it looked delicious. Simone put their plates on the TV tray and then went back into the kitchen returning with two glasses of wine, and an open bottle of Pinot Noir. She set these down next to the cake and turned to address Astrid.

"Don't sit like that." She shook her head and her curls shimmered in the low light of the room. Astrid wanted to touch them. "You must fully commit to Papa."

"Okay," Astrid said. Obediently, she pulled her long legs into the chair and tucked them beneath her. It wasn't the least bit comfortable but Simone could ask her to crab walk to the Washington Monument right now and, as long as she was wearing that dress, Astrid would comply. "Like this?"

"Yes, much better," Simone said, with so much authority Astrid laughed. Her feet were beginning to tingle but she ignored it.

"I didn't know there were rules to sitting in chairs."

"There are no rules, just technique."

"Where are you going to sit?" Astrid asked, and for a delicious moment imagined Simone might settle in her lap.

"On the floor," Simone said. Picking a wine glass off the table, she handed it to Astrid, and took the other for herself. Taking a sip, she then lowered herself gracefully onto the yoga mat. Her dancer's pedigree was on full display, as was her cleavage. "Are you ready?"

Astrid knew she was referencing the pawpaw cake but teased herself there was another question on the table besides the dessert.

The answer to both was the same. "Yes."

"I think you'll love it," Simone said, with the perfect amount of confidence. Rising to her knees, she took a plate from the table and handed it to Astrid. She took the other for herself and lifted her fork to her mouth. "Hmmm," she hummed happily as her lips closed over the cake.

Just watching her eat was a sensual pleasure. Astrid felt a ridiculous stab of disappointment when she put down the fork.

"Now, you try it. See what you think you think. Be honest."

"Always," Astrid promised her, and took a tentative bite. Her eyes fluttered shut as the pleasant texture of the sponge landed on her tongue. "Okay, yum. This is really good," she said, chewing slowly. "I taste the pawpaw but there's something else, too. Something that works really well with the flavor. What is it?"

"Guess," Simone encouraged her.

Astrid took another bite. "It's a spice," she thought hard. "And it's brown. I know that. I can see it. Gosh, it's literally on the tip of my tongue. Give me a hint?"

"Okay," Simone thought for a moment while chewing her own piece. "Oh, I know," she smiled mischievously. "It is what Italian soccer players do to American soccer players."

"Nutmeg!" Astrid laughed but then pretended to grow serious. "But only the men's team. I won't hear a word against the US women's national team. It's something you need to know if you expect us to be friends."

Simone's face clouded over. Quick as a switch, the light disappeared from her eyes and her smile became a distant memory. "Aren't we already friends?" Her beautiful bottom lip trembled.

Astrid didn't know how to respond. "Yes, of course, Simone. I was just kidding. I promise I…"

But Simone was now doubled over laughing in child's pose. The line of her vertebrae looked like a strand of pearls.

"Oh, so you're teasing me?" Astrid said, and shook her head. This was precisely something Claire might do. It shouldn't surprise her that Simone had a similar sense of humor.

Simone sat up and reached for her wine. "Sorry. I couldn't help it. The joke was too easy."

"Low hanging fruit?" Astrid asked.

Simone nodded. "Like the pawpaws."

"Your cake is fantastic."

"Thank you."

They smiled at each other. Astrid wondered what it was about this person that she found so compelling. It had to be more than the childhood crush. Astrid had famously crushed on Tara, too. Hell, she'd crushed on most of Claire's friends and some of Katrina's, but she'd never felt reciprocity to this degree. Simone's gaze was electric. No one had ever looked at Astrid this way. Could that be it? Was the feeling of being desired, in itself, an aphrodisiac?

She lowered the heat a notch. "Claire told me you landed a job at unUsual DC. Congratulations."

"Thank you," Simone sat up a little straighter. "I'm excited to get started."

Astrid tried not to peek down her dress and failed miserably. "Will you create a whole new menu?"

Simone smiled and her dimple popped adorably. "I'm going to create a whole new everything." She went on to detail her plan for a complete kitchen overhaul and dining room décor upgrade.

"That's fantastic. Is the owner giving you carte blanche?"

She shrugged her shoulders. "It's an evolving situation, but I'm optimistic that I'll win."

"I wish you the best," Astrid said and hoped whoever the owner was had deep pockets. It would take super human strength to say no to these dancing brown eyes.

"Thank you."

"I'm excited for you. Have you discovered any other local flavors you want to sample?"

"Yes," Simone said, slowly and then winked slyly at Astrid. "There's one local flavor I'd really love to try."

Astrid almost dropped her fork. "Um, what's that?"

"Crab cakes," she laughed. "But so many others, too." She winked again.

"Oh," Astrid said, and reminded herself they were just flirting. Simone was discussing her job. Astrid needed to get her mind out of the bedroom and back into the kitchen.

"The embassy cook used to make them for me. They were my favorite."

"Don't you have crabs in Italy?" Astrid asked.

"Yes, *granseola* live in the Adriatic, but they're too small to make cakes."

"So, you put them in cookies?" Astrid joked, and was rewarded with the dimple.

"Spaghetti," Simone said, drawing out every syllable as only a native speaker could do.

"I know how to make crab cakes," Astrid volunteered, shyly. It wasn't normal for her to share unsolicited information, but nothing felt normal about her rapport with Simone. Also, it was true. Authentic Maryland crab cakes was one of the few recipes Astrid knew how to make well enough to prepare for others.

Simone sat back on her heels. "Is that an invitation?"

"Um, sure," Astrid said. "Absolutely. You were nice enough to cook for me tonight. It's only fair." She lifted her fork where to her surprise only a bite remained of the pawpaw cake. "I'm actually staying downstairs for a little while."

"In Claire's apartment?" Simone asked. Her unmistakable enthusiasm felt like an overture and Astrid couldn't help matching her smile.

"Yes, but I hear Miles is now renting out the sleeping porch," she joked.

Simone looked confused so Astrid explained. "Every now and then, he reshuffles the layout of the townhouse to add another apartment. More rent money means more income."

"Does he have another job?"

Astrid shook her head. "Not that I'm aware of. Their grandfather made a lot of money. I think Miles lives off his inheritance. Lucky guy."

"I don't think that's so lucky," Simone said, enigmatically. It was the first note of discord in the conversation all evening and Astrid wondered if she'd hit a nerve. According to Tara, Simone's family was fabulously wealthy. Yet, here she was living in a rented attic with borrowed furniture. Had something happened to cause estrangement from her family? The question felt too personal, so Astrid stayed with Miles.

"Your apartment is the fifth residence he's carved out of this townhouse."

"Really? He carves the house?" Simone made a cutting motion with her hand.

"Yes," Astrid, gestured to their surroundings. "This space used to be the attic over Claire and Coty's apartment."

"That explains the door in the floor." Simone nodded thoughtfully.

"There's a door?"

"Yes, I discovered it yesterday." Rising from the yoga mat, she walked across the living room and dragged a small rug a way to reveal a section of plywood with a recessed metal latch. "Here."

"It must be the old trap door." Astrid carefully extracted herself from the palm of the Papasan chair and joined Simone on the floor. "I can't believe Miles didn't take this out. What a lazy fucker. Have you tried lifting it?"

"Maybe." The brown eyes danced.

"Where does it go?" Astrid asked.

"Open it and see."

Astrid lifted the door and then peered down into the room dark below. Her throat went dry. The trap door was located directly over Claire and Coty's bed, the place where Astrid would sleep until she found a place of her own. Sitting on the mattress, looking up at them quizzically, was Eartha Kitty.

CHAPTER TEN

Floored

Astrid looked through the trap door and then back at Simone who seemed completely delighted that an extraneous hatch had been left in the floor.

"Ciao, Eartha." She waved down at the cat, who sat unblinking on the floral duvet cover in the apartment beneath them. "Hi, baby." The cat made a purring noise and rolled over onto to her back. Astrid laughed despite the swarm of butterflies taking flight inside her. Simone shifted positions and the dress slid up her leg. "Is that where you'll be sleeping?"

"Yes, it's Claire's bed," she replied. The mahogany spindle four-poster had been a birthday gift to Claire from their maternal grandmother.

"And Coty's bed, too," Simone reminded her and Astrid nodded slowly.

"Yeah, him too."

"Don't you like Coty?" Simone's expression shifted from playful to concerned. It occurred to Astrid that she could be worried about Claire's wellbeing.

"Oh no! Coty's super nice. Everyone loves him." She rushed to clarify. Coty was the agent of Claire's happiness and therefore her own.

"But not you." Simone was now watching her closely. Astrid felt put on the spot but not unpleasantly so. Commanding Simone's focus gave her a heady sensation. It was as if the gawky fourteen-year-old was being plucked off the back porch and brought along to the party. Astrid was happy to answer any of her questions. And she had more than a few of her own.

"I do like Coty."

"No, you don't. Why not?" The brown eyes were brimming with curiosity. Astrid wanted to fall in, share the secrets of her soul. A voice in the back of her head told her to be careful. Astrid told the voice to fuck off. She might tell Simone her social security number and all her passcodes. Fortunately, Simone only wanted to know about Claire's boyfriend. "Tell me what's wrong with Coty?"

Astrid thought of where to start. The two had met last year, dancing roles in the *Nutcracker* at the Kennedy Center. Coty had literally swept Claire off her feet. It was to be expected that he'd fall in love with her. Everyone fell in love with Claire. But Claire had fallen in love, too, and that was a first. Their relationship had precipitated Astrid's disastrous decision to move in with Leigh. It wasn't fair, but someone had to be held accountable and Coty had drawn the short straw. But Astrid didn't want Simone to get the impression he was a creep. It wasn't fair and it wasn't true.

"Claire and I had this great townhouse in Mount Pleasant," she began, and Simone gave her a funny look.

"It's about a house?"

"It was a townhouse," Astrid explained, "and my bedroom was in the turret." Simone only seemed more perplexed so Astrid elaborated. "A turret is a little tower that comes to a point?" She steepled her fingers together. "It's usually associated with castles."

"Toretta? You were like a princess?"

"Yes, Dad found us the apartment through a friend of his. Claire's room was even better than mine. It took up the whole second floor, looked right over Seventeenth Street. We had the wildest parties during Pride." She shook her head, reminiscing.

Simone smiled sweetly. "It sounds amazing."

"It really was. We had biggest private balcony on the parade route. The dancers from the Washington Ballet always have a float. After the parade, they'd come back to our house and party like maniacs."

"Why didn't you just get another roommate?"

"The landlord was selling."

"That's bad luck," Simone said.

"I won't argue with that," Astrid replied. Needing something to do with her hands, she put her glass on the floor and began toying with the lace of her boot. "I don't blame Mr. Felton for taking back the townhouse. The area is really commercial. A restaurant group had been after him for years. Our house is now an upscale fish taco place."

"I love fish tacos," Simone enthused.

"I loved that apartment," Astrid countered. "When Coty heard that we had to move he asked Claire to move in with him."

Simone made a tsking noise. "How does that make him responsible for you losing the princess house?"

Astrid scrunched her eyes closed. "It doesn't. I know. It's not fair. Coty's great and he's been great for Claire. She's so happy. I've been a huge asshole." This was the first time Astrid had admitted this to another person. Luckily, Simone seemed to understand.

The brown eyes, though brimming with questions, held no judgement. "What did you do to him?"

"Do?"

"You said you were an asshole."

"I haven't done anything. I just haven't been very warm."

"Is that it?" Simone seemed disappointed there wasn't something more scandalous to report.

"Yes, but it's hurt Claire's feelings. I know it has, and I feel bad about that."

"So, stop," Simone said, gesturing dramatically with her hands. "You don't want to be a bitch? Stop being a bitch." Rising from the floor, she went to retrieve the bottle of wine from the TV table. Astrid had drained her own glass minutes before and accepted a refill gratefully. She'd been drinking off and on since the family lunch and was floating in a rarified plane of lucidity that sometimes came with consuming too much alcohol. Or maybe it was just Simone.

"Just stop being a bitch. It's that simple?"

"Why not? The next time you see Coty, give him a hug," Simone suggested.

"You make it sound easy."

"Because it could be." She shrugged, and sank gracefully back to the floor.

Neither of them suggested they move back into the living room. It was not remotely comfortable on the floor, but Astrid didn't want to break the magical spell of the evening. She couldn't remember the last time she'd had such an intense conversation with anyone, including Claire. What at first had felt like a seduction had blossomed into a heart to heart. Simone was warm and witty. She'd called Astrid on her bullshit without dressing her down...and that dress. It felt like the beginnings of a new friendship with the possibility of something more to come.

"Where did you go when they moved here?" Simone was looking down at the bed.

Astrid took a large swallow of wine. She'd known the question was coming, but dreaded answering it. Introducing Leigh into the conversation felt like opening a can of rancid sardines in a room full of roses. But it was unavoidable. If they were going to be friends, and it felt like they were, Astrid had to be honest. "I moved in with my girlfriend, Leigh."

"O-la-la," Simone trilled, deflating Astrid a little with her enthusiasm.

"Yeah, but it didn't work out."

Simone watched her carefully. "Did you love each other?"

"You get right to the point, don't you?"

"Do you prefer dull?"

"No, I don't," Astrid answered laughing. "And ultimately that's what broke us up."

"Leigh is dull?"

"She's just different. It was fun for a little while but we weren't compatible. The breakup was for the best, trust me." Astrid didn't want to go into a litany of Leigh's imperfections. Maybe, when they got to know each other better, she'd tell Simone more about Leigh's hurtful behavior. Right now, she wished Simone looked less sympathetic about her newfound status as a single woman.

"I'm going to stay here and take care of Eartha Kitty until I figure it out." She pointed to the bed beneath them.

Simone seemed to sense her reluctance to further discuss the topic and tactfully changed the subject. She looked down into the hole. "Why do you think Miles left the door here?"

Astrid felt a rush of gratitude and happily made the pivot. "Because he's lazy."

"Ah-hah." Simone nodded. "There are lots of lazy people in Italy."

"There are lazy people everywhere," Astrid smiled. "I'm lazy on occasion myself but Miles takes the cake."

"There is a lazy cake?" Simone looked truly excited and Astrid laughed.

"No, but there should be. Taking the cake means he wins the prize for being the laziest. Miles was in my high school class. We were lab partners in chemistry and he never did any of the reading. He would come in and start throwing chemicals around, drove the teacher crazy, caught things on fire a lot. It doesn't surprise me at all that he wouldn't take the time to seal the trap door properly." She looked down into the apartment below. Eartha Kitty had lost interest in them and was no longer on the bed. "Does it bother you?"

Simone shook her head and curls danced in the candlelight. "Are you kidding? I love this hole. In Turin I lived in an ugly new building. There were no secret places."

"Secret places are the best," Astrid agreed and thought suddenly of Bob's compound. How much fun would it be to show

Simone the treehouse? Have a sleepover in the hammock? She shook her head. Where had that come from? Claire had never even been to Bob's, and now Simone was already spending the night? She needed to get a hold of herself. She looked around the bare walls of the converted attic. "There could be more hidden doors, you never know."

"I hope so," Simone's eyes danced. "I hope lazy-cake Miles left hidden doors everywhere for me to find."

"Here's to hidden doors." Astrid tapped her glass against Simone's. How was it almost empty again? "And Miles is a good guy, really. He's lazy but he's also really nice. You've got a great landlord."

"We've got a great landlord," Simone corrected her. "You live here now, too." She stood abruptly and began walking toward what Astrid assumed was her bedroom. "I'm going to put on something warmer. Can I get you anything?"

"A one-bedroom apartment, in my price range, preferably near the river." She called after her, vaguely disappointed Simone had gone in search of additional clothing. The evening had begun with such potential. A hot, red dress and candlelight were universal signs of interest. Had the conversation been too real? "Oh, and it would be great if there was a place I could keep my boat."

Simone emerged from the bedroom wearing a soft looking pair of navy-blue sweatpants and a long-sleeved Gowear T-shirt. "I'm happy to help you look. I don't start my job for two weeks, so I've got lots of time." She shrugged her shoulders, Astrid thought it impossible, seemed unsure of her reception. "I mean, if you want me to."

"Yes, I want you," Astrid started, and then corrected herself. "I mean…that would be great." She rose to her knees. "Would you like me to close this door?"

"Sure, unless you want to leave it open." Simone picked up the wine glasses from the floor. "We could talk to each other during the night."

Astrid smiled thinking of the things they might say to each other. Lifting the trap door, she held it on its hinge suspended over the open hatch. "Yeah, but what if you got up in the middle of the night for a glass of water and fell in?"

"Are you imagining what I do in the middle of the night?" Simone winked at her.

"What time is it?" Astrid asked, still holding the door. She truly had no idea. "These new jeans were too tight to bring my phone." She said, and then realized she'd given away the care she'd taken to prepare herself for the evening.

Simone laughed. "I like those jeans." She winked again. "There was no room in my dress for a phone either."

"I noticed that." Astrid smiled, and the brown eyes twinkled.

"I checked my computer in the bedroom and it's after ten."

"Really?"

Astrid was shocked. Aside from a small cramp in her back from sitting on the floor, she'd no idea how long they'd been chatting. "I should go. I had no idea it was that late. Let me close the door."

Simone held her gaze. "If I fell in the hole, I'd land in bed with you."

Astrid dropped the door in the frame and it landed with a loud bang.

Simone laughed. "Or on top of you," she said, and walked toward the kitchen.

Astrid rose to her feet. Standing dumbly by the Papasan chair, she wondered how to respond. Her teenage fantasy was unfolding in front of her. The timing was uncomfortably close to her breakup with Leigh but the chemistry was undeniably real. She let the wine tip the balance.

"I don't think I'd mind that so much."

Simone walked back into the living room. "Really? What else wouldn't you mind?"

Astrid took a deep breath. "Truthfully? I'd really like to kiss you right now. I've actually wanted to kiss you all night."

"Okay." Without missing a beat, Simone moved forward and kissed Astrid tenderly on the lips.

"Oh," Astrid let out a small sigh. "Thank you." The pressure of Simone's mouth against her own felt shockingly intimate.

Her sex life with Leigh had sometimes involved orgasms but there was never any kissing on the lips.

"My pleasure." Simone twinkled, and kissed Astrid again, this time slipping her tongue inside her mouth. Wet heat flooded Astrid's core threatening to knock her off balance. Clinging to Simone, she was able to keep her feet.

The kiss, best described as delicious, continued for another moment before Simone pulled away. Rubbing her lips with her fingertips, she picked up the dessert plates and walked calmly back into the kitchen.

Astrid struggled to think of something to say. Shaken by the kiss, her thoughts were fractured and bounced around the room like light through a prism. Did Simone kiss other people this way? Was she kissing Astrid because she looked like Claire? Right now, she was acting if it had been no big deal. Astrid would follow her lead.

"Thanks for offering to help me find an apartment. I may take you up on that."

"I hope you do," Simone called from the kitchen. Astrid heard the faucet running. "I just went through it. Some of the leads may still be hot." She walked back into the living room wiping her hands on a towel. "How much time do you have?"

"As much as I need really," Astrid replied, marveling at Simone's composure. Other than her slightly swollen lips, there was no hint that two minutes ago they'd been pressed together intimately. She continued to play along. "Claire's tour only lasts another two weeks. But if I can't find something else, I can always move in with my parents."

"Would that be bad?"

"No, not at all." Astrid thought of the new and improved Katrina Dibello and smiled. Before dropping her off at Claire's apartment, her mother had promised to meet her that weekend for a cocktail paddle under the Key Bridge.

"Do they still live in the beautiful house on the river?"

"Yes."

Astrid wondered if Simone remembered their first encounter on the back deck. She didn't look much different from the seventeen-year-old girl who'd first rocked Astrid's world, but Astrid had changed dramatically. At some point she'd have to tell Simone about the accident and the nose job. Right now, they were talking about apartment hunting together, and acting as if they hadn't just shared a magnificent kiss. First things first.

"The house isn't the problem and neither are my parents. It's me. I think I need to live alone for a while."

"Why alone?" Simone asked.

"Because I never have," Astrid swirled the remaining wine around in her stem. "I hate being so needy. I moved in with Leigh because I didn't want to be alone."

"That is such an American thing," Simone said, surprising Astrid with her dismissive tone. "Italians do not live alone. We are smarter."

"How is that smarter?"

"It's better for the environment and better for the soul," she said. Waving her hands around, she began to get excited. "Humans are animals. We're supposed to live together in packs. Physical contact is necessary." She grabbed Astrid's wrist, taking her by surprise.

Astrid looked down at her hand. They were in danger of kissing again. She licked her lips. "I guess I do like it better when I have a roommate."

"Then find one," Simone said. "If you don't know anyone then ask around."

Astrid met her eyes. "I don't remember you being this bossy."

"But you do remember me." Simone said. It wasn't a question.

"I do," Astrid replied, and closed her eyes as Simone moved in for another kiss.

CHAPTER ELEVEN

The Bark Muttsvah

"Mazel-tail!"

"Mazel-tail!"

Congratulatory cries arose from the bark muttsvah audience. Seated in folding chairs with herring-and-dog-bone-patterned cushions in the large-occasion room of the Castle Resort in Bethesda, the crowd applauded Arfunkel's call to the Tal-mutt. Blasphemy aside, Astrid found everything about the event to be hilarious. Her readers were going to love learning about the cottage industry that celebrated a dog's thirteenth year with lavish parties, flowing freely with first-rate Champagne and lower-tier puns.

Most of the canine guests were cavorting on a lush-looking AstroTurf carpet spanning the back of the room. They were not focused on the celebrant. Sniffing each other or engaging with one of the teenagers Astrid supposed had been hired to keep them in check, not one of them had paid attention to the dog-park video testimonials or puppy-grows-up photo montage that had comprised the nearly forty-minute ceremony. Arfunkel, to his credit, had remained compliant through most of it, but the Chihuahua was so ancient that it was likely sleeping.

"Stop your humping, Kevin!" a woman hissed at a wild-eyed Pomeranian attempting to mount a boxer four times his size on the AstroTurf. "He only does this when he's around other dogs who haven't been neutered," she assured Astrid.

A tiny girl with a pointy chin offered conflicting evidence. "Sometimes he does it to my stuffed monkey."

The woman glared at her and resumed her hissing. "Kevin! I said stop it!"

"What's Arfunkel eating?" Simone asked, quietly. She and Astrid had exchanged several incredulous looks during the ceremony but hadn't had a chance to compare notes. Astrid looked forward to hearing Simone's take. Following her direction now, she looked center stage, and found the guest of honor gnawing on something that looked like a doormat.

"It's his rawhide Torah portion," a man said to their left. "They make them at a place in Brooklyn." He didn't appear to be kidding.

"Really?" Astrid replied, quickly sizing him up. His commemorative purple yarmulke matched one pinned to the head of a standard poodle sitting upright in a chair on his other side. If she was lucky enough to get him talking, he might write half her story. The dog gave them a sleepy look. Astrid wondered why it wasn't in the play area.

"Latte was bark muttsvah'ed five years ago," the man began, with an unmistakable air of superiority. The poodle closed its eyes. "But we do things differently on the west coast and, of course, we're Ortho-dog."

"Ortho-dog?"

Simone snorted and Astrid grabbed her hand. Part of being a professional journalist was not making fun of the people you interviewed. The bark muttsvah was a serious test of this resolve but Astrid had no hope of succeeding if her beautiful plus-one succumbed to a giggle fit.

"We go by dog years," the man explained and Simone begin to titter. Astrid could feel her shoulders shaking and a smile threatened to overcome her own carefully arranged features. *Shit.*

They'd spent the last week in nearly constant company. Parting only to shower and sleep, they'd managed to keep their magical first night conversation afloat like some kind of enchanted balloon. Simone's offer to help Astrid find a place to live had been real. As the daughter of the former Italian ambassador, she had access to an international community who didn't advertise on Craigslist. So far they'd looked at a penthouse in Kalorama and a funky little basement in Cleveland Park. After the event Simone was taking her to see a houseboat for rent on the wharf. Astrid had no interest in living on a boat. Making out with Simone on the boat was another proposition.

She squeezed her hand, glad for any excuse to be touching her. They'd continued to engage in lovely little kissing interludes that they hadn't discussed, but were increasing in frequency and passion. It was both maddening and blissful, a moment in time that couldn't possibly continue because it was dynamic. It felt like they were moving toward something. Astrid wanted to press pause and fast forward at the same time.

"We had Latte's ceremony when he was eighteen months old." The man was now explaining. "It makes more sense when you think about it." He thumped a finger on his skull and the dog startled awake.

"Why does it make more sense to do it earlier?" Astrid asked him to elaborate. The best parts of a story often came from off-the-cuff remarks. You never knew what someone might say, especially after a few of glasses of Zinfan-tail.

The man dropped his voice as if to avoid being overheard. "This feels more like a celebration-of-life party to me."

"Like sitting shiva?" Astrid asked

"Yes," he agreed enthusiastically. "That's precisely it."

"Dogs must be great at shiva. You just say sit, right?" Simone cracked and Astrid stepped hard on her foot. Fortunately, the man hadn't heard.

"A true bark muttsvah is supposed to be a coming-of-age celebration." He explained and Latte yawned audibly, exposing pink and black spotted gums. "Excuse his manners. He's still tired from the Ativan he had on the plane. Aren't you, boy?"

"You flew in from the west coast?" Astrid tried to keep the surprise from her voice.

"Yes, we live in Sacramento. Arfy and Latte are cousins."

Simone squeezed her hand and Astrid squeezed back harder. "Can you please explain again why Latte had his ceremony at eighteen months?"

The man thumped his skull again. "Think about it. Eighteen months translates to thirteen in reverse dog years. It just makes sense."

"Reverse dog years?" Astrid repeated dumbly while Simone made a choking noise. Squeezing Astrid's hand one final time, she rose abruptly from her seat.

"I need to find the ladies' room," she said. Wiping tears from her eyes, she walked away.

For an awkward moment Astrid feared the man knew Simone had been laughing at him. She started to apologize and then saw he was watching her fondly make her way across the room. He gave Astrid an indulgent look. "These things can be very moving."

"Yeah, I think she may be a little cur-klempt," Astrid tried.

He nodded. "Indeed."

She took the opportunity to introduce the subject of her article. "Can I ask you about the reverse dog years idea again? I'm writing a story about today's celebration for my blog. I'd love to hear more about Latte's bark muttsvah." She handed him her business card.

Hearing his name, the poodle seemed to wake up a little more. Astrid wondered how much Ativan the dog had taken and if he had his own prescription. There were so many questions she wanted to ask and hoped the man would agree to the interview. Most people were tickled to talk to her but you never knew.

"Can I see some identification, please?" the man requested.

"Absolutely," Astrid replied. The absurdity of the subject matter didn't negate his right to protocol.

She slid her driver's license from the sleeve attached to the back of her phone and handed it to him. The story was a perfect fit for *Outside Astrid*. Her readers loved anything animal-related. Astrid had reported on the bald eagles nesting at the National Arboretum, a deer walking into the Polo store in Georgetown, and a live frog found in someone's Lebanese take-out food. If it had a natural outdoorsy bent, she put it into the blog.

The man studied the driver's license for a long moment and then gave it back to her. "This doesn't look anything like you."

Astrid's hand flew to her face. Spending all her time with Simone, someone who had little memory of her pre-nose job, she'd all but forgotten it had happened. "Oh, my nose." She laughed ruefully. "That's a long story. Well, not anymore. Haha."

He didn't get the joke.

"Does Miriam know you're here? Who invited you?" His voice rose in pitch causing Latte to jump from the chair and put his head in his lap. A few people turned to see what was happening and Astrid rushed to stop a potential scene from escalating.

"I met Miriam at Dr. Coleman's office." She played the celebrity card firmly and heaved a sigh of relief when the man looked dutifully impressed.

"Oh." He paused adjusting the dog's yarmulke. "*People Magazine* voted him sexiest doctor."

"That's right. I feel so lucky."

"Miriam invited him, of course. He has a French bulldog, you know." The man was beginning to thaw. Astrid was only too happy to help him along.

"Yes, Maurice," Astrid replied, thankful Katrina had made her read the fluff piece on the doctor that mentioned both his pets and pastimes.

"It's too bad they weren't able to make it." The man looked over his shoulder as if the famous doctor might materialize after all.

"It really is," Astrid replied, though she was secretly thrilled the doctor wouldn't be at the event. She still hadn't told Simone about the surgery. It was the one thing they hadn't discussed.

Simone knew all about the Leigh disaster. Heck, after last night's Ben and Jerry's run, she knew Astrid's favorite ice cream flavor. But for some reason, Astrid hadn't told her about the accident.

"What did I miss?" A warm hand on her shoulder alerted Astrid to Simone's return.

"I'm trying to lock down an interview." She gave the man a winning smile, and willed him not to reference Dr. Coleman again.

A commotion on the AstroTurf saved her from the worry. Kevin, the randy Pomeranian, was fighting with another small dog over a commemorative yar-mutt-ke. Growling and snarling, they began a vicious game of tug-of-war. The teenaged minder was clearly in over his head. Activating a loud rap song on his phone, he tried to get them to separate. It only added to the melee. The other dogs went crazy. Storming the barricade that divided the AstroTurf from the seating area, they either went for their owners or the buffet.

"Please, Kevin!" the woman wailed.

Latte took an interest and made a beeline for the turf with Kevin's owner in close pursuit.

"Latte!" The man next to Astrid sprang from his chair.

Thirty seconds later, the entire gathering exploded into total chaos. Dogs of all shapes and sizes ran freely around the room doing exactly as they pleased. The waiters abandoned the lunch without a fight. Astrid could hear the catering manager fleeing the event room and screaming into his cell phone as the dogs helped themselves to platters heaping with deli meats and shrimp cocktail.

Clutching Arfunkel to her chest, Miriam stood stunned and alone in the front of the room.

"The poor mother!" Simone voiced the thought in Astrid's head. "She looks so sad. All the work she put into this crazy puppy-party, and now it's ruined."

"We should rescue her," Astrid suggested. She was half joking but Simone sprang to action. She took Astrid's hand.

"Let's do it."

Threading their way quickly through the pandemonium, they slowed down only to sweep Miriam and Arfunkel into their wake, and left the room. The older woman kept the dog tucked beneath her arm like a football and they reached a bank of elevators unmolested. Astrid made a quick decision. She'd been to the Castle Resort a million times. It had been the venue for her high school senior prom and next year would host their ten-year reunion. There was an intimate back bar off the first floor that opened onto a small patio. Once, on a dare, she and Claire and climbed over the fence and gone skinny dipping in the adjacent pool. Calm and quiet, it was the perfect place to escape a pack of wild dogs.

Astrid sat them down in a booth and called for the waiter. "We need some drinks over here, please. Oh, and a bowl of water."

"I was hoping to try the Zinfin-tail after the ceremony." Miriam sniffed, and sunk her face into the back of Arfunkel's neck.

"Oh, here you go!" Simone surprised Astrid by producing two small bottles of the boutique beverage from her purse.

"Where did those come from?" Astrid asked, in surprise.

Miriam was elated. "Thank you." Accepting a bottle, she twisted off the cap and sipped delicately from the neck.

"They were in the gift bags, by the door," Simone replied.

"I totally missed that." Astrid shook her head. "Maybe you should be the reporter?"

"Or maybe we just make a great team?" Simone countered.

"I won't argue with that." Astrid smiled.

Miriam perked up. "They are doggie bags and you were supposed to take one. I made them myself. All of Arf's favorite treats are in there, and some of mine."

"Will you show us?" Simone asked, and Astrid wanted to kiss her. Well, she pretty much always wanted to kiss her, but even more so now. The bark muttsvah story was mentally half written, and now Simone was doing additional correspondent work. Astrid took her hand under the table as a waiter approached the booth with a bowl of water and a reproving tone.

"Someone order water, in a bowl?" he asked, as if it couldn't possibly be true.

"It's for Arfunkel," Simone pointed to the chihuahua. "Today we celebrate his bark muttsvah." She beamed.

The waiter scowled. "That dumb dog party is supposed to be upstairs." He jerked his thumb toward the ceiling.

"The dog party is called a bark muttsvah," Simone informed him. Though still pleasant, her voice now rang with a faint challenge.

Astrid suppressed a smile. The ambassador's daughter had arrived.

Beside her, Miriam inflated. "Arfy's thirteen," she volunteered and kissed the dog on his head.

The waiter dug in. "The party is contracted for upstairs."

"Upstairs or downstairs, inside or outside. As clients of this hotel, they should be afforded every amenity. Don't you agree?" Simone's voice took on more authority. "Or should I call my friend, Alex?"

The waiter stared at her dumbly. "Who is Alex? My boss is named Carla."

"Alexandra Castle is the co-owner and CEO of this hotel." Simone pulled out her phone and began to scroll. "We went to boarding school together. I don't know Carla, but maybe we should put her on the phone call, too? What's her number?"

The waiter paled. "I'll get you the wine list," he said and tried to back away from the table.

"Actually," Simone thought for a moment. "Can you please go up to the Roosevelt Room and get Miriam some more Zinfin-tail. Grab a bottle of the Char-dog-nay, too. I'm dying to try it."

"Yes, ma'am," he said, and scurried away.

Astrid burst out laughing. "That was awesome. Do you really know Alexandra Castle?"

"I do." Simone looked surprised at the question. She put down her phone. "She will pee in her pants when I tell her this story." She turned to Miriam. "How are you feeling?"

"I'm much better." Miriam patted Simone's hand as if she were now a beloved niece and not someone she'd just met during an elevator getaway. "I need to get back to the party soon. I can't imagine where they think I've gone."

"Would you like us to take you?" Simone asked.

Miriam wouldn't allow them to further inconvenience themselves but was visibly pleased when Simone bullied the waiter into the job a few minutes later.

"Thank you, dear," she kissed Simone's cheeks and then came for Astrid. "I'm so glad to have met you in Dr. Coleman's office. Isn't he wonderful?"

"Yeah, yeah, he's great," Astrid said, so quickly that Simone gave her funny look.

Miriam smiled. "Call me next week, and Mazel Tail!"

"Mazel Tail!" repeated Astrid and Simone.

As Miriam disappeared around the corner, they lifted their glasses of Char-dog-nay. Simone smiled at Astrid and then, squeezing her hand, addressed the elephant in the room.

"Tell me, who is Dr. Coleman?"

CHAPTER TWELVE

About Face

Astrid took a sip of wine. The Char-dog-nay was too dry for her liking, but it was better than the Zinfin-tail and it bought her a few precious moments to collect her thoughts. Telling Simone about the surgery was unavoidable. Each day that had passed in the miraculous week they'd spent together, the omission had weighed more heavily. Astrid worried she'd already let it go too long. Simone knew Astrid's favorite brand of organic toothpaste and her mother's inappropriate obsession with Timothée Chalamet. They'd talked about so many obscure things. How had Astrid not told her about the nose job that had completely transformed her face?

"Dr. Coleman was my surgeon."

The brown eyes filled with concern. "Were you sick?"

"No, not sick. I was in an accident." Astrid shifted in her seat, searching for a way in to the narrative. "It's a long, weird story."

"Then we'll need food," Simone said, and looked around for the waiter.

"Poor George is probably still busy with Miriam." Astrid raised her eyes to the ceiling. There were no longer sounds of dogs barking or running feet. "We may have missed our chance at the buffet."

Simone shuddered. "I am happy to let the dogs have that food. A buffet is how you feed horses."

"Tell me how you really feel." Astrid laughed.

"I hate them," Simone said, emphatically, her hands helping to explain as she grew more excited. "The Swedes started this thing with their smorgasbord," she said, like a mother pointing to the bad influence on the playground. "They brought it to the USA and you Americans went crazy." She jabbed a finger at Astrid who grabbed it, and held on.

"Tell me what did we did?"

"You invented the all-you-can-eat."

"Oh, my God. That's sounds just like us." Astrid pulled Simone's finger to her lips and gave it light kiss. She needed to get the conversation back on track, but flirting was so much more fun.

"Even horses do not eat all day," Simone said, but her voice was faint and Astrid wondered if she was reacting to the physical contact.

"They might, if given the chance," Astrid pointed out and Simone didn't disagree. Astrid began to play with her fingers. They needed to talk about the surgery. There was no reason they couldn't hold hands during the conversation.

Suddenly, the waiter reappeared holding a cheese board, charcuterie plate and what looked to be a caprese salad. Behind him, a tiny woman with an asymmetrical hair cut was standing at attention. Astrid looked askance at Simone who didn't seem surprised. Who had ordered all this food? What was going on?

"Compliments of Ms. Castle," the waiter said. He set the heaping platters down on the table as well as two small plates, napkins and silverware. His manner had miraculously transformed from sullen to sycophant. Simone didn't seem surprised by this either. Nor was she holding a grudge.

"George! Thank you." She gave him a winning smile and then looked over his shoulder at the tiny woman standing behind him. "And you must be Carla?"

The woman stepped forward and gave a tight bow. "Please ma'am, accept Ms. Castle's apologies for any inconvenience you may have experienced." She shot a look at George. "It is our hope at Castle Resorts that all our customers feel valued."

"Tell Alex thank you." Simone indicated the platters of food spread before them on the table. "Everything is perfect."

Carla looked relieved. "If you need anything else, anything at all, please let us know."

"Do you have olive oil?"

"Of course." She snapped her fingers and George shot forward.

"And maybe choose a Chianti? I can no longer drink this dog wine," Simone called after him.

Carla collected the empty glasses and, making sure everything else was to their liking, left them alone.

"What just happened here?" Astrid surveyed the food with wonder. She hadn't realized how hungry she was until the platters had appeared in front of them.

Simone looked smug. "This is the hospitality industry working as it should." She picked up one of the small plates and began loading it with food.

"I don't understand," Astrid said. "And how did you know that the woman was Carla?"

"How?" Simone crossed her arms, and mimicked Carla's pinched expression. "She was obviously his boss. You saw her mad face."

Astrid laughed. "She did look pissed."

Simone shrugged. "I've worked in restaurants a long time. George must have told Carla we had a problem so she fixed it. I would have done the same thing. Nothing corrects a negative impression more quickly than free food."

"Do they teach you that in culinary school?" Astrid asked her.

"On the first day," Simone deadpanned.

"But why so much food?" Astrid eyed the heaps of mozzarella.

"That's the Castle effect," Simone conceded looking slightly abashed. "Regular people maybe just get a bruschetta."

"Aren't we regular people?"

"No, we are not."

Before Astrid had a chance to question her about this cryptic remark, George returned with a decanter of olive oil and a bottle of Chianti. He showed Simone the label and poured a small amount into a glass for her inspection. Gaining approval, he poured Astrid a glass and scurried quickly away.

"I think George may be scared of you." Astrid teased.

Simone smiled. "I think he's growing as a person."

The back and forth was so much fun. Also, not a chore, was looking at Simone. Astrid watched fascinated as her hands fluttered around the platters.

"Now we can talk, properly," Simone said. "Empty stomachs affect our emotions. You've heard the term gut reaction?"

"Sure."

"Your brain doesn't work properly on an empty stomach." She handed Astrid a heaping plate.

"This is for me?"

"Eat," Simone commanded and popped a cherry tomato in her mouth. "You should never do anything important unless you're properly nourished."

Astrid liked the idea that Simone thought of the conversation they were about to have as important. She thought of all the meals she'd skipped at Leigh's and frowned. "I never put that together." She picked a plate and helped herself to salad. "But it makes sense."

"Think about it." Simone thumped her head in an uncanny impression of the man at the bark muttsvah making Astrid crack up.

"You're so funny," she said, through a mouthful of prosciutto.

"And you're beautiful," Simone replied.

Astrid suddenly had trouble swallowing. Every time someone commented on her appearance it threw her off guard.

What did it mean to be called beautiful? Is this why Simone kept stealing kisses, because of some cultural definition of what was pretty? In the beginning she'd thought Astrid was Claire, which was even more disturbing. Coughing, Astrid reached for her glass of wine.

"Are you okay?" Simone looked concerned. "Do you want me to ask George to get you some water?" She started to rise from the booth but Astrid waved her back in her seat.

"Leave that poor man alone," she choked and took a liberal sip of Chianti. "I'm fine." This was the time to tell Simone the truth. But how to frame the words? Thinking again of the bark-muttsvah man, an idea occurred to her. She slipped her driver's license from her wallet and lay it on the table in front of Simone.

"What's this?" Simone picked up the card.

"It's my driver's license."

Simone stared at it for a long moment and then raised her eyes and looked thoughtfully at Astrid. "You used to look more like your Dad. I remember that, now. What happened to your nose?"

"I got hit by a door."

"Oh, no."

"Yeah, it only happened a few weeks ago. The reason I haven't told you about it is because I'm still processing it."

"Oh, baby." Simone slipped from the booth and joined Astrid on the other side. "I'm so sorry." Reaching up, she laid her hands onto Astrid's face. Her warm leg pressed against Astrid's under the table. "Tell me what happened. Tell me everything," she commanded.

"Okay."

Astrid brushed their lips together wondering for the hundredth time what was going on between them. On so many levels it felt as if they were already a couple. Last week Simone had been a memory, now she was the first thing Astrid thought of in the morning. And the last thing at night. It was time she knew the whole truth.

Starting with the robbery attempt at Closet Diva, Astrid laid out the details of the story. She told Simone about Tara's problem with sticky-fingered prep-schoolers, her own attempted heroics and the resulting rhinoplasty with the sexist doctor alive. Simone stopped her there.

"Wait a minute," she said, munching a piece of cheese. "Why does it matter if the doctor is sexy?"

Astrid shook her head. "I really don't know. But my mother was very impressed."

Simone chewed thoughtfully. "Ah ha, Katrina, the beauty queen. How is your mother?"

"Still a piece of work," Astrid said, but without malice. The one time she'd managed to drag herself away from Simone that week was when she'd met her mom for a hike in Rock Creek Park. Katrina had been wearing makeup again, though not as much, and the groovy, Gowear hiking pants with little turtles on them that Astrid had coveted in the catalogue.

"Your mother is from another generation," Simone said. She picked up another piece of cheese and stacked it on a toasted piece of bread.

"Can we send her back there? I'll drive, if you make the snacks," Astrid quipped, and then saw the heaping cracker coming toward her. "Is that for me, too?"

Simone hand fed Astrid the snack. "I'd love to take a drive with you." The innuendo was clear. "We can even take my truck."

"I'm so jealous of that Bronco," Astrid said, and struggled to ignore the lingering feeling of Simone's fingers on her mouth. "You know that's my dream truck?"

"So you said." Simone smiled, enigmatically.

"You still haven't told me where you got it or how much you paid."

"That's a story for another time," Simone said, frustrating Astrid further. Simone had been weirdly reticent on details involving the purchase of the Bronco or the kayak. Astrid knew rich people could be funny about money so left it alone.

Simone pushed the conversation back on track. "We are talking about your accident, now."

"Okay, right, the story," Astrid sighed. "My mother was very impressed with sexy Dr. Coleman and even more impressed with his work." She tapped the end of her nose.

Simone leaned in to kiss it. "Your mother likes this nose better? Why? I thought you were Claire when I saw you on the beach."

"I do look like Claire, it's so weird. Even I think so. I don't recognize myself."

"That must be hard," Simone squeezed her hand.

"It really is," Astrid confessed and felt a weight lift. "I've been lying low, avoiding mirrors. It's easier hanging out with you, because you didn't know me that well before."

Simone's face fell. The dimple, which had been popping all day, disappeared like the sun behind a cloud. "Is that why you've been spending so much time with me? Because I don't make you feel strange?"

"Oh, no," Astrid nearly shouted. "Are you kidding?" She struggled for the right words. "You do make me feel strange, Simone. But it's a good kind of strange. The best kind of strange," she clarified.

Simone didn't look convinced, so Astrid kissed her. Pressing their lips firmly together, she tried to communicate everything she was feeling. When she was finished, Simone fell, dazed, against the back of the booth. After a moment, she seemed to recover herself, but to Astrid's frustration didn't address the kiss but went back to the original conversation.

"Mothers can be crazy. We must always try to forgive them."

"It sounds like you have some stories of your own."

Simone nodded. "There are too many stories. My mother is the queen of crazy. She would love your sexy doctor. If she sees your nose, she will want his number. But we are not talking about Queen Claudia." She made a face. "You were telling me about your surgery. We keep getting off track."

"We seem to have a lot to say to each other." Astrid smiled into her eyes.

"Tell me what happened."

"Okay."

Astrid went on to describe Leigh's reaction to her new face and Simone looked aghast.

"You were in an accident." She stabbed an artichoke heart with her fork.

"Leigh didn't see it that way. She implied I'd done it on purpose and then suggested I was turning into my mother."

Simone slammed down the fork. "She criticized your mother, too?"

Astrid laughed. "You look like you want to beat her up."

"No, I feel bad for her."

"Why?" Astrid was confused.

"There is obviously something wrong with her brain if she let you go," she said softly and pecked Astrid on the nose.

"Thank you for saying that."

"It's how I feel." She kissed her nose again. "And your new nose is beautiful. But your Leigh sounds like burnt toast."

"Burnt toast?"

"Something that once held promise that's turned to ruin."

"Leigh is definitely burnt toast, and on gluten-free bread." Astrid nodded. "But she isn't mine anymore. I've still got some stuff at her house but the relationship is finished."

"Good, because the new woman in your life would be very jealous."

Under the table, Astrid felt a warm hand land on her thigh. She turned to meet Simone's eye. "We wouldn't want to upset her."

"She is very sensitive."

They stared at each other for a long moment and then resumed eating. Simone's comment was the first verbal acknowledgement something was happening between them. She'd just stepped out on a limb. Astrid wanted to join her. She looked for the right words to express her feelings.

"I really like you," she said, quietly.

"I like you, too," Simone replied without hesitation.

The last week had been amazing. After almost a year with Leigh, spending time with Simone had been a revelation. It had quickly risen near the top of Astrid's favorite things to do, slotted directly between kissing Simone and looking at pictures of Simone on her phone. It was all moving so quickly. Astrid felt like she was swimming in a beautiful, glorious river with no idea of the topography. There were quite possibly falls ahead but she was helpless against the current. Simone seemed to read her mind.

"I'm happy to take things slow. I know you just got out of a relationship."

Astrid frowned. Simone didn't need to know the grim reality of her sexless life with Leigh, she did need to know Astrid was available. "Leigh already feels like a long time ago."

Simone picked up her wine glass and swirled around the contents. "Making love is not just about sex."

"That's true." Astrid took her hand. "And I can wait as long as you need too."

"Me?" Simone nearly spit out her wine. "I'm not the one who needs to wait. I haven't had a girlfriend in…" She made a funny face. "I can't remember."

"Do you want one?" Astrid laid her cards on the table.

"I thought we were talking about sex," Simone said.

"That would be a big part of it, at least at first, it would," Astrid said. "Am I being crazy here? What do you think?" she asked.

Simone looked around for the waiter. "I think we should get the check."

CHAPTER THIRTEEN

Room Serviced

"I can't believe we're doing this." With a growing sense of anticipation, Astrid surveyed the elegant penthouse room. The Castle Resorts suite was much nicer than the room Paige Turner had procured for them on prom night. The thought that this room would be used for the same carnal purposes with Simone made Astrid feel a little wobbly. She sat down on the bed. "I mean, I want to do this. Don't get me wrong." She licked her lips and looked around the expansive suite. "It's just seems so extravagant."

"No more talking." Simone walked toward her with purpose. Stopping in front of the bed, she rested her hands on Astrid's shoulders, and gave her a light push onto the mattress. Astrid fell onto the crisp, white duvet that smelled of rosewater and money and reminded her of no other hotel room she'd ever been in.

"Okay, but I need this on the record. I appreciate you going to all this trouble. It's not necessary, but it's really nice." Astrid stared up at Simone. As usual her eyes were smiling but there was something else there, too. Something that was eroding Astrid's ability to form a thought that didn't include this moment, this woman.

"Where is this record? Who keeps it?" Simone asked. Positioning a knee between Astrid's legs, she hovered deliciously over her.

"I guess, we do? We're in charge," Astrid whispered, and Simone nodded.

"Yes." She dipped her head, pecking Astrid's lips. "And I'm good at being in charge."

"That's why you make such a great chef."

"Stop talking," Simone ordered, and slid her knee higher on the bed. It was now perilously close to Astrid's center and the focus of her entire universe. Simone snaked her tongue into Astrid's mouth and then back out again.

"So good," Astrid moaned.

"Shhhhh," Simone commanded, and lowered herself completely on top of Astrid. Kissing her more deeply, she moved her body in slow, rhythmic undulations creating fantastic friction.

"Oh my God." Astrid recognized the signs of an early orgasm and tried to hold back from grinding into Simone's thigh. It had been months since Leigh had touched her like this. Frankly, it had never been anything like this with Leigh. Simone on top of her was like being led by an expert partner in ecstatic dance. A few more seconds of contact and Astrid would almost certainly flame out. The same thing had happened on prom night, actually, but Astrid was now a grown woman and Simone had paid five hundred dollars for the penthouse. She'd tried to hide the receipt but Astrid had seen. It was embarrassing. She needed to slow things down.

Breaking the kiss, she put a hand on Simone's chest and gently pushed her back. "If you don't stop doing that, right this second, I'm going to explode." She warned her, and then screamed when a hand slid into her panties.

"What about this?" Simone asked. Firmly cupping Astrid's sex, she laid a finger just outside her opening.

"Oh my God." Astrid desperately wanted to bear down but held back.

Simone moved her finger a fraction of an inch forward and bit Astrid's neck. "It's okay, lover. Let go."

Astrid didn't need to be told twice. Her loose linen pants gave Simone plenty of room to position her hand and she entered Astrid with the skill of a long-time partner. There was no hesitation, only certainty and then bliss. Radiant pleasure ripped through Astrid's body like splinters of lightning. She was soaring, transcendent with feeling.

"God, yes!" She bucked into Simone's hand, shamelessly taking what was offered.

"Will you please stop talking?" Simone laughed into her neck. Fucking her gently through the first orgasm, she latched onto to the sweet spot behind Astrid's earlobe, discovered in one of their earlier make-out sessions, and began to suck.

The pressure in Astrid's center built again, shocking her with its intensity. Rarely was she able to come so soon after a first orgasm but when Simone's thumb found her clit, she was halfway there.

"I can't. This is too much. Don't stop," she cried as Simone slid a second finger inside her and began to thrust.

"Let go," she whispered.

But the command wasn't necessary. Astrid's brain had given over control to Simone's fingers. So complete was the allegiance, that free-falling through ecstasy, Astrid began to chant her name. "*Simone. Simone. Simone.*"

"I've got you."

Pops of white light exploded behind her eyes. The waves of pleasure Simone was coaxing from within her seemed endless and eternal. Pumping her hips up into Simone's hand she gave herself savagely. Even the gradual descent to earth felt like bliss. When Astrid came back to herself, Simone was sucking her nipples through the fabric of her shirt. She'd slipped her fingers from Astrid's depths but kept her hand inside her pants. Somehow, they were both still fully dressed. How was that even possible?

Astrid pushed against Simone's fingers, and enjoyed an aftershock and then another one. "That was incredible."

Simone lifted her head. "We can rest if you want."

"What? Oh, no." In a single motion, Astrid flipped Simone on her back, topping her like a professional wrestler. She stared into surprised brown eyes. "You're in the USA, now. So, we must be democratic. It's the law." She sighed, as if resigned to doing a chore.

Simone looked serious. "The law is important."

"I wouldn't want you to get deported," Astrid said. Reaching a hand between them, she began to unbutton Simone's dress.

"Do what you must." Simone let her arms fall to the side.

Astrid could feel the heat from her pussy through the fabric of the dress. She wanted to push it over her head and throw it across the room but undid the buttons one by one because it seemed sexier. Simone was her adolescent fantasy. A version of what had just happened had run in Astrid's head a million times. Now she was being given a chance to return the favor. She wanted it to be perfect.

"Hurry up," Simone pleaded, and Astrid leaned down and licked a stripe from her cleavage to her neck. She knew all too well the tortuous tension Simone was experiencing. But she had a front row seat to the action, and would not leave it under a shroud.

"Give me a minute," she said, and then gasped.

Astrid wasn't surprised that Simone was braless beneath the dress. She'd been watching her breasts all week and knew they'd come unchaperoned to the bark muttsvah. Still, she gasped when they came into view. Round and full, they were deserving of statuary tribute. Astrid ached to test their weight in her hands. The only thing Simone was wearing now, besides a please-fuck-me expression, was a black lace thong.

She took a moment to savor the visual before dipping her head and kissing a pink tipped nipple. Encouraged by a plaintive noise, she licked the other one and Simone bucked her hips. "You like that?" Astrid pushed her knee between her hips, spreading her wide.

Needing to feel flesh against her skin, she tugged off her own pants and bikini briefs drawing a whimper from Simone. The smell of her own arousal filled her nostrils, imbuing her with renewed ardor. Emboldened, she slipped off her shirt and bralette and let her hand wander down Simone's curves into her thong. "You're so wet," she gasped and quickly withdrew her hand.

"Don't stop," Simone started but then ceased protesting when Astrid's mouth closed over the thong.

"I want to taste you," she murmured and snaked her tongue around the fabric for one delicious deep swipe before nudging the material back in place and licking her again through the lace.

"Astrid, please," Simone cried and threw an arm across her brow like a silent film star.

"What do you want?" Astrid asked. Grabbing the thong from behind she used the scratchy edge of the lace to her advantage. Pulling it tight against Simone's pussy she tugged it back and forth creating friction. Simone's body began to shake and Astrid knew she didn't have long. Yanking off the thong, she dove between her legs just in time to catch the first tremor against her tongue. Holding her down, she spread her wider.

"*Merda, merda,*" Simone was crying above her.

Marveling at the taste of her, the texture, Astrid held her firmly in place. Later, she might describe it to Simone in sommelier terms and make her laugh. Faint hint of salt with undertones of orange. Later. The idea of it drove her to work more intricately. Tonguing Simone deeply, she sensed another vein of arousal and tapped it hard. Simone began to pedal her feet on the bed. Astrid felt a hand close on the back of her head and smiled. She certainly wasn't going anywhere. Happiness completely flooded her consciousness. Their week together was culminating in an unmatched display of physical passion. Whatever was happening between them seemed momentous and did not invite questions. This was fortunate, because Astrid didn't have any answers, beyond that there was no other place she wanted to be.

Simone climaxed in a fantastic, shimmering display of ecstasy. Watching from the supreme vantage point at the cleft of her thighs, Astrid nearly came undone a third time. After a moment, she crawled up Simone's body and snuggled into her side. Simone grabbed her hand and trapped it in the warm spot between her breasts then, murmuring softly, slipped it down to her pussy.

"You're incredible," Astrid whispered, and gently stroked her slick, hot folds. She kissed the side of her face and neck before finding her lips.

Each kiss they'd shared that week had been special in its own way. Astrid had listed several in her journal, citing duration and location. A quick make-out session in the kitchen, ten glorious minutes in the Papasan chair, they paled in comparison to the intimacy of what they shared now. Their bodies were gloriously fluid, lubricated, hot and wet. Astrid kissed Simone languidly, reveling in the taste of her. Gone was the urgency of the first frantic coupling. They were now making love on the most intimate terms. Astrid had never felt so connected to another person. She had no idea where this was going, she only knew she didn't want it to stop.

Hours later, she awoke to a breakfast picnic. Somehow, without waking Astrid, Simone had managed to summon room service and set it up on the bed like offerings in a Bedouin tent.

"What's all this?" Lifting her head from the pillow, Astrid surveyed the spread. Simone was still blessedly naked and stirring what appeared to be a cappuccino with a tiny spoon. Her smile was radiant.

"Sustenance," she said, and set the spoon down on a tray next to a teapot and pitcher of milk. "Are you ready for tea? I got Lemon Zinger."

"Hey, thanks." Astrid sat up all the way in the bed. Maybe it was the lingering emotion from their night together, but she was incredibly touched Simone had remembered her preferred breakfast beverage. It shouldn't be a surprise, Simone worked in hospitality after all, but tears threatened all the same.

Simone set down her cappuccino. "Are you okay?" Leaning forward she laid a hand on Astrid's cheek. "Was last night too much? Did we move too quickly?"

Shocked to hear uncertainty in her voice, Astrid rushed to disabuse her of any regret. "I don't think so," she said, "that's not what I think at all. Last night was incredible." Taking Simone's hand, she kissed her palm. "I'm just touched you remembered my tea."

Simone threw her head back and laughed. The rich sound brought back the conversations of the past week and their easy blossoming friendship. That she had just given Astrid three incredible orgasms seemed unbelievable. "They're lucky they had it. I would have made them find it for you." She leaned forward. "May I pour you a cup?"

"Yes, please." Astrid rubbed at her eyes. Simone's breasts were on fabulous display and she tried not to be too obvious with her ogling. Last night she'd had complete access. Touching and tasting them had been pure heaven but the visual was doing things to her that threatened to upstage breakfast. "This looks amazing," she said, tearing her eyes away to focus on the food. It looked as if Simone had ordered a sample of everything on the menu. She felt like Julia Roberts in the classic movie *Pretty Woman* and told her so.

"I love that movie," Simone enthused, and picked up the teapot. "Claire actually introduced me to it." She carefully poured a cup and handed it to Astrid.

"That's not a surprise." Astrid smiled. "It's our mom's favorite film. We watch it every year on her birthday with chocolate covered strawberries and Champagne."

Simone smiled. "I love that."

"Me too."

"Take care a you!" Simone shouted in perfect imitation of the wise cracking sidekick, making Astrid laugh.

She shook her head. "There's something about a rags-to-riches story I find really compelling. It took me years to understand Julia Roberts was a prostitute."

"The Pretty Woman was a prostitute?" Simone clapped a hand to her chest in feigned shock and Astrid nearly spit out her tea. "I thought she was a race car driver."

"That must have been lost in translation." Astrid laughed. She was enjoying herself too much to tell Simone that Leigh and Julia Robert's character shared the same rule about kissing on the mouth. Astrid didn't want to talk about Leigh at all. After a year being with the spartan dentist, time with Simone was like a full-spa immersion. Astrid was completely caught in her spell. Smart and beautiful, Simone was also really funny, surprising Astrid at every turn with her wit.

"I like it when she goes shopping on Rodeo Drive," Simone said. She wrapped a piece of prosciutto around a ripe wedge of cantaloupe and handed it Astrid who took it without comment. "Big mistake. Big. Huge," she quoted the movie again.

Astrid sobered. "Just as long as you're sure this wasn't," she wagged a finger between the two of them.

Simone frowned. "It's the second time you've brought that up. What are you worried about?"

Astrid put the tea down on the bedside table and visored a hand over her eyes. It would be much easier to say the things in her heart without risking the wrong look on Simone's face. "I'm worried that I'm falling for you too fast. I never told you this, but my feelings have a bit of a head start on yours."

"I don't understand," Simone said, softly. Astrid felt her come closer on the bed.

"You were my very first crush," Astrid told her, and relayed the story of her sexual awakening.

"You liked me in high school?" Simone's body was now even closer and Astrid could feel her breath on her face.

"I'm not sure that word is strong enough."

"What word would you choose?"

"I can't say it was love because I barely knew you. Maybe it was an identity crush? It wasn't just that I wanted you." Astrid struggled to assemble the right words. "I was too young to really know what that was. I think I wanted to be you. Does that make sense?" She peeked through fingers and was met with a searing kiss.

Releasing her lips, Simone held her face in her hands. "That's the most flattering thing anyone has ever said to me."

"Flattering?" Astrid pulled her face away. "It's the truth and I don't know what to do with it."

Simone stroked her arm. "We can take a step back if you like."

"No," Astrid said, quickly. "That's not what I want, not at all." She couldn't stand it anymore. Leaning over she took one nipple in her mouth and the other between her fingertips. Of all the breakfast offerings there was a clear winner.

Simone didn't push Astrid away. Cradling her head against her chest she stroked her hair. "Why don't we just keep doing what makes us feel good?"

Astrid lifted her head just enough to speak. "This feels really good to me," she said, and went back to work.

CHAPTER FOURTEEN

Clich-Gay

"We don't need a U-Haul."

"Please."

"It isn't necessary. I barely have enough stuff to fill the Volvo." Astrid leaned back against the old, red station wagon and pulled Simone to her chest. Nuzzling her neck, she enjoyed the smell and feel of her freshly shampooed hair. They'd just had their first shower together. Simone had fucked her hard and fast under the spray. Astrid felt vital, alive, awake. She did not feel like she needed a U-Haul.

"But it's an American lesbian cliché, it's clich-gay," Simone laughed, and kissed Astrid's ear. "I want to participate. I'm a joiner."

Astrid snuggled in closer. "How about we rent an RV and go camping instead?"

"Yes, I like that idea, too," Simone was enthusiastic. "Let's do both."

"We're not getting a U-Haul." Astrid laughed. The idea was preposterous. Aside from her kayak, which was safer on the cartop rack, the largest thing she had at Leigh's townhouse was her pillow. Never was she so thankful of her ex-girlfriend's parsimonious hospitality. Astrid was confident the two plastic storage bins she had in the back of the car would be sufficient to pack her clothing and any possessions that had collected in her six months' residence. All her other stuff was still boxed up in her parents' basement. Add that to the items at Leigh's, and it still wouldn't be enough to warrant a U-Haul.

"Hiya, ladies."

Astrid was pulled from her thoughts by a voice coming from the other side of the car. The Volvo was parked in one of five smallish spots delineated by painted white lines along the elegant circular driveway of the townhouse. Suspicious blotches made Astrid certain there had previously been four. Claire and Coty paid an extra three hundred dollars a month for the amenity and had kindly relocated their Prius to Jerry and Katrina's garage during Astrid's stay. Also parked in the circle was Simone's Bronco and a beige minivan that belonged to Miles.

"Ciao, Miles," Simone said and stepped back discreetly from Astrid. They were no longer touching, but still close enough to touch.

Astrid turned her head. "Hey, bud."

She didn't know if her former lab partner had seen the PDA and she didn't care. Miles was certainly aware she was gay. Astrid had been out since junior year of high school when she'd openly dated a transfer student from southern Maryland. Paige Turner, the girl with a punny name and a serious jump shot. They'd been together nearly two years so Astrid's sexuality was hardly a secret. How to classify her relationship with Simone was another question. They'd taken a big step confiding their fledgling feelings to each other. They hadn't discussed what they might tell the public.

"How are you ladies doing?"

"We're great," they said in unison and then grinned stupidly at her other.

Miles cleared his throat. If he hadn't suspected anything was going on between them before, he certainly did now. Thankfully, he didn't go there.

"I still can't get over the new schnoz, dude." He tapped his nose. "I mean, I keep forgetting it's you."

"It's me," Astrid assured him, annoyed he'd broached the subject in front of Simone. She understood it was a big change, something that would take time for other people to get used to, but Astrid had seen Miles several times since moving into Claire's and he couldn't seem to let it go.

"You look so different," he continued, his manner mildly flirty. This was something else that bothered Astrid. There'd been a change in Miles' energy that she could only attribute to the change in her appearance. He let his eyes linger on her face for longer periods and with seemingly more approval. It was the oddest sensation. Most alarming was that it wasn't wholly unpleasant. In the past Astrid been made to feel this way when she'd lucked into a great new haircut or was wearing a hilarious Halloween costume. But this change wasn't temporary and it wasn't a joke. She hated how much she liked it.

"I promise, it's me." Astrid did not encourage further discourse.

The whole experience was giving her insight into her mother's warped value system. Katrina had been five when she'd started the pageant circuit. Judges had bestowed literal crowns on the girls deemed most beautiful. Miles was one person delivering an opinion in a driveway and Astrid could feel herself responding to his approval. It was beyond fucked up.

"You look so much like your sister," he went on. Walking around to their side of the car, he gaped openly at Astrid's face. "I mean, you could be Claire's twin. It's wild. I mean, it's cool. Um, you look great," he said, and then stood back looking pleased with his speech.

"Thank you for letting me borrow the Papasan chair." Simone took a tiny, protective step in front of Astrid.

Astrid's heart swelled. They'd talked a great deal about the existential issues of having her appearance altered and Astrid had made it clear she was still processing.

"Uh, no problem," Miles said, and turned his focus to her. The flirtatious energy did not abate. Shoving his hands in his pockets, he leaned back on the heel of his work boots. "That chair is pretty wild, huh?"

"Yes," Simone replied, and Astrid hid a smile. The day before, Simone had flipped the Papasan upside down, and taken Astrid across the back of the arch like she was a picnic on a sand dune.

"I don't have a coffee table yet but maybe I'll get one soon. I need to go furniture shopping." Her eyes slid hopefully to Astrid.

"What?" Astrid didn't remember having a conversation about furniture shopping though it was entirely possible one had transpired. She and Simone talked about everything under the sun, but they were usually naked and Astrid was inclined to get distracted.

"We could take our U-Haul shopping."

"We're not renting a U-Haul." Astrid laughed. Forgetting herself, she grabbed Simone by the waist and tickled her.

Simone squealed with glee while Miles looked on, slightly dazed. "Um, I've got a U-Haul."

"You have one?" Simone squealed.

"We don't need it."

But Simone was doing her happy dance. "Miles has a U-Haul. Did you hear that? Can we have it? Can we rent it?" She reached for a tiny Gucci wallet tucked into the back pocket of her faded Levi's.

"We don't need a U-Haul," Astrid said, but Simone was already negotiating. Astrid frowned. She appreciated Simone's generosity but the experience with Leigh left her wary of being financially incongruent with her lover. It was clear Simone enjoyed a much higher socio-economic status than she did. Just because she was free with her credit cards did not mean Astrid should take advantage. Also, they didn't need a fucking U-Haul.

"One hundred dollars. But you have to get it back by three this afternoon."

"Why? Will it turn into a pumpkin?" Simone narrowed her eyes and Miles scratched at the back of his head.

"The truck doesn't actually belong to me?" He looked at Astrid as if she might help him explain the origins of the mysterious U-Haul.

She gave him no quarter. "Where did you get it?"

He shrugged his shoulders calling attention to a small hole in the armpit of his graphic T-shirt advertising a defunct 90s grunge band. "I rented it this morning. I had to haul some books to a consignment shop in Wheaten. They buy them by the pound up there. My Grandad had a shit-ton."

"How much is a shit-ton in kilos?" Simone joked.

"A hundred and thirty-four dollars," Miles said, looking pleased with himself. "I could have gotten more if I'd sold them piecemeal on eBay, but that's a real job," he said, and Astrid was reminded of the boy who'd failed to keep a log of their final experiment and cost her a letter grade.

"If it's not your U-Haul, then we pay you half," Astrid asserted.

"Cash?"

"Your choice," she said, and reached for the Gucci wallet. Astrid repeated what now sounded like a mantra.

"We don't need a U-Haul."

Forty minutes later they were pulling up in front of Leigh's Georgetown townhouse in a fifteen-foot truck. A lucky fire hydrant sat directly in front of the tidy colonial, permitting ample space for Astrid to position the U-Haul. Thank God Leigh's dental practice was open Saturdays and she wouldn't be there to see it. She knew Astrid was coming today but if she saw the truck, she might think Astrid was there to rob her.

"This was your house?" Simone asked. She looked thoughtfully out the window and then back at Astrid. "It's very English. I love the roses."

"Those are Leigh's roses. She has a bigger garden out back with vegetables." Astrid surveyed the precision of the beautiful thorny flowers, unbuckling her seat belt. "And this was never my house." She shook her head. "I barely have any stuff here, you'll see."

Activating the hazard lights to avoid a parking ticket, Astrid got out of the truck and joined Simone on the sidewalk.

"Thanks for coming with me," she said.

"Coming with you, is one of my new favorite things," Simone said. As always, the warm brown eyes were brimming with humor. Astrid marveled at her luck. She was about to perform the painful chore of dismantling the physical effects of a failed romance and she was giggling on the sidewalk like she was on her way out of a John Waters movie. Simone made everything fun.

"Me too." She leaned in to kiss her and then stopped herself and squinted at the front door. Leigh's Nest Cam caught everything from the front door to the sidewalk. She wasn't sure if they were in range but it was too close for comfort.

Simone noticed the hesitation. "You okay?"

Astrid explained the police-sponsored, motion-activated video camera attached to Leigh's front door. Simone shook her head. "Most public spaces in Italy are monitored by government-controlled cameras. They do not ask for permission. You have to be careful."

"It's scary," Astrid admitted, eyeing the front door. "I don't know if she can see us from here. But I don't want to chance it."

"Chance what?" Simone wanted to know. "Does she watch the tapes?"

Astrid hated to answer the question. "Maybe?"

"She spies on the mailman?" Simone giggled and put a hand over her mouth.

Astrid allowed herself to smile. "I think she gets an alert on her phone every time something activates the camera. She usually watches the videos when she gets home from work."

"Every day?" Simone laughed harder.

"Pretty much," Astrid replied. She hadn't argued when Leigh had signed up for the surveillance program two months prior. It wasn't Astrid's mortgage payment, so it wasn't her call. The house had a back door, after all.

Simone stepped purposefully closer into the range of the camera. "Does she ever see anything interesting?" she asked, a mischievous look forming in her eye.

"Not unless you find squirrels interesting," Astrid told her, shaking her head. "What are you doing?"

"I'm going to give her a show," Simone explained, and walked closer toward the front door. Definitely in view of the camera now, she put her hands above her head and did a serious of quick pliés and then, legs extended like the professional ballerina she'd almost been, jetéd toward the front door.

"You're crazy," Astrid called after her, softly. She could only imagine what Leigh would say when she opened the file and found Simone leaping toward the house.

She jetéd all the way to the doorway and stopped at the last step. Rising on the tips of her toes, she executed four tight pirouettes before flinging herself dramatically out of the frame and into Astrid's arms.

"That was incredible," Astrid said, pulling her into the side yard.

Simone melted dramatically against her. "I live for the dance."

Astrid knew the statement had once been true and didn't allow it to pass as a joke. "I mean that. You move beautifully."

"Thank you." Simone accepted the compliment.

They were out of view from both the camera and the street, so Astrid took the opportunity to kiss her. Pulling back, she looked into the warm brown eyes. "And you make me laugh."

Simone wrinkled her nose. "My psychiatrist says that is a defense mechanism."

"Well, I'm defenseless against you." Astrid pecked her nose.

They embraced for a long moment and then Astrid let her go. "Let's get my stuff and get out of here."

"Okay."

Holding hands, they walked around the side of the house. Astrid had a key to the back door. Once inside she'd have to run the length of the house to tap in the alarm code on the box in the foyer. There was a plant she had to avoid knocking over but it was otherwise a straight shot and it beat being caught on camera. Simone had given Leigh enough of a show.

"What's that?"

"What?"

Mapping out her sprint to the alarm box, Astrid didn't hear the music until they were on the back patio. She stopped to listen. It was a Tom Petty song, one she knew, but she couldn't think of the name.

"It's music."

"It's 'Runnin' Down a Dream'!" Astrid snapped her fingers. She looked triumphantly at Simone who was not looking back at her. Astrid followed her gaze through the back window and saw a party going on inside the house.

Instinctively, she dropped Simone's hand. "Oh, shit."

"Maybe it's a going away party for you?" Simone suggested and Astrid shook her head.

"No way," she said. Reaching back, she tightened her ponytail, nervously.

What the hell was going on? Leigh almost never had parties. Her dental practice thrived on regular Saturday hours. It was always the busiest day of her work week. The only Saturdays Leigh didn't miss work were days before a big race when she carbo-loaded with the other members of the Gowear running team. Could that be it? The Marine Corps Marathon was coming up. Astrid searched her mind for the date.

"We should probably go." She kept her gaze fixed on the people in the room. No one had noticed them yet but it was only a matter of time.

"Of course," Simone said, sympathetically. "We'll come back."

But it was too late. A lanky redhead opened the back door and blew their cover.

"Astrid? Is that you?"

Despite the awkward circumstances, Astrid felt her mouth twist into a natural smile. Hannah Richards was the daughter of the Gowear founder, and co-owner of the company. A near-celebrity in the local lesbian community, the athletic redhead modeled for the catalog and championed the company's LGBTQ outreach. She also ran on their marathon team, which had to be why she was standing in Leigh's back yard holding an empty gallon-sized jug of coconut water.

"Hi, Hannah." Astrid tapped her nose. "Come meet the new me."

Hannah walked closer. Astrid saw she was wearing a custom made, team-Gowear jersey, and knew she'd been correct. The marathon team was indeed there. Astrid couldn't imagine how Leigh had come to host the all-important, pre-competition meal. What the hell was she feeding them? Last year, Hannah and her wife Camille had hosted a New Orleans themed party at their Dupont Circle townhouse. Astrid had gorged herself silly on crispy fingerling potatoes with aioli dressing. They'd served waffles, French toast, Cajun-seasoned steamed shrimp and made-to-order omelets. The women were carefully building energy stores they would need to compete the next day. Leigh kept a garden, but she didn't cook very well and mostly ate vegetables raw. Astrid hoped she'd had the event catered.

"Leigh said you got hit by a door? Ouch." Hannah was looking intently into Astrid's face.

"Yeah." Astrid nodded. "Knocked me out, cold."

"No, shit?" Hannah looked empathetic. Wealth and local fame aside, she was also really nice. Astrid had once spent an afternoon playing flag football with her to benefit a local theater. When the event hadn't raised enough money, Hannah had donated a hot pink motorcycle whose auction price more than made up the difference.

"Glad you're okay," she smiled. "And don't take this the wrong way, but you look good. Like, really pretty."

"No offense taken," Astrid said, and felt heat hit her face as the endorphin rush of approval washed over her. She needed to get used to these compliments. Hannah Richards, lesbian-extraordinaire, was not hitting on her. She was just being friendly, and Astrid needed to get a grip.

"I understand what you mean. It's been fucking weird." She looked over her shoulder at Simone and wondered how to explain her presence. It was beyond rude to show up at Leigh's with her new lover. The fact that Leigh had given her no indication there would be a party didn't make it any less so. It was asking for drama and as clich-gay as the U-Haul blinking in front of the fire hydrant. "This is my, um, friend…"

"Simone?" Hannah said in surprise as Simone blew past Astrid.

She stood transfixed as Simone double-kissed the Gowear heiress and then pulled her into a warm embrace.

"You gals know each other?"

"Hannah was my climbing instructor in the Dolomites," Simone said. Letting Hannah go, Simone turned back to Astrid, beaming. "I got to watch them shoot her on a catalogue cover."

"You were on *that* shoot?" Astrid was stunned. The iconic photo of Hannah hanging from one hand off an Italian mountainside was taken roughly five years ago. Astrid had written about the event, before and after, in her blog. The picture was still used in Gowear promotional material and for years it had filled in two stories of windows of the Georgetown store. To think Simone had been present on the shoot was a reminder of all the things Astrid didn't know about her.

"Yes, it was great." There was nothing in Simone's manner to suggest anything was amiss but Hannah Richards was another story. Her previously relaxed vibe had shifted a notch off center. It wasn't anything Astrid could put her finger on, but something seemed different. It was almost as if Simone made Hannah nervous.

"That was a long time ago." Hannah pulled at the end of her jersey. "Was it five years ago, six?" Squinting into the sun, she rounded up. "You know I got married, right?"

"No, that's wonderful. Mazel-tail!" Simone grinned back at Astrid who faked a smile as the realization hit. It may have happened long ago, in a country far away, but there was no doubt in her mind.

Hannah Richards had definitely fucked her girlfriend.

CHAPTER FIFTEEN

The Skin of Your Nose

The back door of the townhouse swung open once more, saving Astrid from the moment.

"Hi, ladies."

A pretty blond woman came smiling toward them. Astrid recognized Hannah's wife Camille from the flag-football event. She had great hands and had been on the receiving end of more than one pass thrown by her wife, including the game-ending touchdown. The two clearly had a special connection. Astrid needed to relax. Hannah may have had a fling with Simone years ago on a climbing adventure, but she was presently devoted to her wife and looking more than a little relieved to see her.

"Hey, baby." Hannah grabbed onto Camille like she was a life raft in the current. "Missed you."

Camille kissed Hannah's cheek. "Missed you, too baby. Is that you Astrid?"

"Yeah," Astrid admitted, and wondered how many times the scenario was going to play out today. Maybe it would be better to call everyone outside right now, and stage a formal unveiling.

"Can you believe it?" Her voice cracked a little and Camille frowned.

"You look really pretty," she said. "Leigh said you stopped a shoplifter?"

"Yeah, but just by the skin of my nose," Astrid tried the joke her Dad had used on her earlier and scored a laugh. She shook her head. "I was just telling Hannah. The experience has been pretty weird."

"I bet. I'm so sorry this happened to you."

"Thanks," Astrid said, and wondered if she'd ever get used to people's reactions. Right now, every reveal felt like pulling off a Band-Aid. "It'll take time to sink in."

"I get that." Camille nodded sympathetically.

Simone put a supportive hand on Astrid's shoulder. Without thinking, Astrid reached back and laced their fingers together pulling a knowing look from Camille and Hannah. Astrid didn't care. As tacky as it was bringing Simone to Leigh's with a fifteen-foot U-Haul, part of her was still happy to have her there. Spending time with Simone was the only silver lining in this strange new reality. She may well be attracted to Astrid's symmetrical new face too, but she hadn't seen her since she was a kid, which somehow made a difference. Astrid was more relaxed in her presence because Simone's opinion of her hadn't changed. It just was.

She took a deep breath. Another positive thing was that Hannah and Camille didn't know Claire, so wouldn't comment on Astrid's astonishing resemblance to her sister. It was a whole other layer to the onion she'd rather not add to the pre-race buffet.

"She looks just like her sister."

Suddenly, Leigh was standing at Camille's elbow. Wearing the same cool running jersey as Hannah, her face did not hold the same relaxed smile. Astrid started. How long had Leigh been standing there?

"Hi, Leigh. Sorry, I'm so early," Astrid said, truly apologetic. There were few places on earth she wouldn't rather be right now.

Leigh's eyes flashed to the hand on Astrid's shoulder. "Who's this?"

Astrid pulled Simone into the circle. While shooting rapids if there was no other way around the rocks, you went straight through the bullseye. But Simone was an old family friend and might be passed off as such. Astrid gave it a shot. "This is Simone," she told Leigh. "I've known her since I was a kid. She and Claire did ballet together in high school."

Only when Leigh's jaw dropped open did Astrid remember telling her the story of her sexual awakening. *Shit.* Leigh had heard all about Astrid's unrequited adolescent lust for the sexy, older, European girl. The sexy girl who'd grown into the sexier woman now standing in front of them. *Shit.* This wasn't fair. The story was dear to Astrid, sacred in a way that only childhood things can be. She'd only told Leigh in a last-ditch bonding effort. Never in a million years had Astrid imagined a world where something so precious would come back and bite her in the ass. Leigh was never one to turn the other cheek.

She gave Astrid a scathing look. "Simone? The Italian ambassador's daughter," she asked incredulous.

"You know my father?" Simone said, the slightest edge in her voice.

Shit. Astrid wanted to crawl under the deck. Her relationship with Leigh had never really worked but, up until two weeks ago, they'd been an acknowledged couple. Leigh deserved better treatment than this. Just because they no longer had sex and had never really mixed their fruit did not mean it was cool to flaunt a new girlfriend.

"We'll come back later," she said, and started to back away when Camille spoke up.

"Simone Galliano?" she asked.

Oh shit. Astrid watched transfixed as understanding dawned in Camille's intelligent green eyes.

"Yes?" Simone smiled at her.

Hannah was quick to get out ahead of any misunderstanding. "Simone was on the Gowear cover-climb with me in the Dolomites. I told you all about her, honey. You remember? We were just catching up."

Leigh's eyes nearly popped from her skull but Camille merely looked bemused. Before settling down, Hannah Richards had been a notorious player. Astrid remembered seeing her in pictures with actresses and world-class athletes. She could only imagine the number of times Camille had been placed in the situation of meeting an old flame. Apart from the age difference—Astrid was guessing ten years—Simone fit her profile. They were both rich and beautiful. Counting herself in their number is what felt weird.

If Astrid was weirded out, Leigh looked stricken. Making an excuse about checking something on the stove, she ran toward the house. Camille stuck out her hand.

"Yes, I do remember hearing about Simone." She smiled, graciously. "It's so nice to meet you."

Simone took Camille's fingers. "Thank you." She smiled warmly and then held on to her hand to examine the giant diamond solitaire and sapphire studded wedding band. "And congratulations. I am so happy to meet Hannah's wife. Did you have a big wedding?"

"It wasn't small," Camille hedged, and Hannah exploded with laughter easing the tension.

"I'm surprised you didn't get an invitation." She raked a hand though her glorious, red hair. "We let my stepmother plan it, and she invited the entire world."

"Really? The only person I noticed there was you." Camille kissed Hannah's cheek and Simone clapped her hands.

"You guys are sweet. Who made the food?"

"I literally have no idea." Hannah looked at Camille. "Do you know who did it?"

"Of course, I do!"

Astrid laughed. "Simone's a chef," she explained, happy at the turn in the conversation. "She just got a gig working at unUsual DC."

Hannah looked interested. "I heard Pedro sold that place. Are you working for the new owner?"

"I am the new owner."

"Wow!"

"Congratulations." Camille and Hannah were enthusiastic while Astrid struggled to control her facial expression. Simone owned unUsual DC? Not once had she mentioned buying the boutique restaurant. They'd talked about the menu, Simone's commute, even the shoes she planned to wear the first day on the job. They'd not discussed she would be wearing a second hat.

"Isn't that cool?" Astrid said, tightly. Her eyes slid to Simone who gave her a nervous smile.

"Pedro actually sold it to my uncle Giovanni who lives with his family in New York. Giovanni is an American citizen so it was easier to set up the finances."

"That makes sense," Hannah agreed as Astrid digested another new piece of information. Simone had family in New York? She wondered what else might be revealed if they stood there another five minutes. Was there a secret wife, a secret life?

"Hannah owns a gym in Georgetown," Camille was saying. "There's a lot of municipal crap you have to deal with. She might have some tips for you."

"That would be great." Simone took down Hannah's contact information.

The conversation was interrupted when the back door flew open and Leigh ran out carrying a giant, steaming pot. Holding it away from her body like it was toxic waste she shot into the backyard and disappeared behind the shed. Something had clearly run amok with brunch.

"Oh, no," Camille said.

"I think she burned the pasta," Simone was empathetic.

"No, that doesn't look good," Hannah agreed.

Astrid excused herself. Thankfully, no one made a move to follow her. Leigh was sure to be furious, and rightly so. Astrid had just rolled up in a U-Haul with a hot new girlfriend, ruining her party and her pasta. Whatever she had to say, Astrid had it coming.

She found her digging out the bottom of the stockpot with a garden spade.

"How ya doing?" Astrid approached her, gently. Leigh was not confident in her cooking and was likely to be mortified at such a public disaster. She was also likely to blame Astrid. Had she not been distracted by the commotion in the back yard, the Gowear marathon team would likely be preparing to eat whatever Leigh was now attacking with the trowel. "What's going on back here?"

"I'm just relaxing with some gardening," Leigh said, acid in her tone. "I find it helps my tomatoes if I burn up a four-hundred-dollar Le Crueset pot and then scrape the leavings into the soil around the roots."

"I'm so sorry about this, Leigh."

"It works especially well if you have twenty elite runners in your house waiting for brunch."

"I said, I'm sorry." Astrid lay a hand on her arm and Leigh flinched.

"Please do not touch me."

"Okay." Astrid drew back her hand. "Listen, I'm sorry I showed up early. I truly had no idea you'd be here."

"Is that why you brought your new girlfriend?"

"That was a mistake. I shouldn't have brought Simone."

Leigh grew more animated and began chopping harder at the bottom of the pot. "It proves my point, you know?"

"What point?"

"That you've changed." Leigh stabbed the shovel at Astrid.

Astrid was indignant. "I told you I was sorry for bringing her to your house. That was rude. I admit it, but I'm still the same person."

"Really?" Leigh began digging at the bottom of the pot again. "Are you sure? You never would have dated someone like Simone before the surgery."

"What does that mean? Will you please put that down and look at me?" Like their relationship, Astrid feared the pot was beyond saving.

Leigh threw the pot into a bush but kept the spade in her hand. She glared at Astrid.

"Part of my job is making people look good. Before I do anything radical, I show the client the change they can expect.

It helps them prepare emotionally. Reconstructive surgery is a big deal."

"I'm aware of that. But I didn't have a choice. The door hit me, remember?"

Leigh shrugged. "And now the culture places more value on your face."

"That's your opinion."

"If someone told you last year that you'd be dating Hannah Richards' old girlfriend, how would you react?"

"I'm not sure Hannah and Simone were actually girlfriends."

"You know what I'm saying."

"I do. Okay, I might be surprised but only because you and I were dating this time last year."

Leigh's face softened. "I'm sorry it didn't work out for us. And I'm glad you've found someone new. Just make sure she's not just with you for that pretty face."

"You broke up with me because of this pretty face," Astrid countered and Leigh pursed her lips.

"You know it wasn't working between us."

"I do."

"And now is probably not the best time to talk about it." She looked pensively back toward the house.

Astrid agreed. "How did you end up hosting this thing?"

"It was supposed to be at Shoshana's." Leigh sighed, and leaned back against the shed,

"Shoshana the lawyer?" Astrid perked up at the name Leigh said a little too often. She'd always suspected a crush and wondered now if something more was going on.

"Yeah, but her fancy new oven broke." Leigh looked over her shoulder toward the house and then back at the burned pot.

"Fancy new oven? That sounds hot," Astrid made an attempt at levity but Leigh just looked sad.

"I tried to fix it but only made things worse."

"Oh, no."

"Yeah."

"You're so good at electrical stuff." Astrid was sympathetic.

Leigh was a self-defined handy-woman who unironically wore a tool belt and a Rosie-the-Riveter sweatshirt. Though untrained, she'd done most of the work on the townhouse to great success. Botching the job on Shoshana's new oven would be a blow to her ego.

"I messed this one up."

"What happened?"

"I really don't know. Shoshie's going to have call a technician tomorrow. When she asked if I could host the brunch, I had to say yes."

"Shoshie?" Astrid said, and knew the hunch had been correct. Her mood lifted a notch. Maybe she wasn't entirely to blame for Leigh's agitation.

Leigh's blush confirmed her suspicions. "Yeah, I was going to tell you about Shoshana this afternoon. I was hoping we might get a chance to talk. Seems like you may have some things to tell me, too?"

"I do, actually," Astrid agreed, her mind now spinning. How long had Leigh been involved with Shoshana? Is that why they'd stopped having sex? Astrid yearned to get out her reporter's notebook and begin the interview but Leigh was impatient to get back to the house.

"I promise we can talk about everything, later. Shoshie's starting a new batch of pasta and I need to help." Leigh gave Astrid a nervous look. "We had to use your stockpot. It was the only one big enough. I'm really sorry."

"That's fine."

"And your pasta, too."

"It's fine, Leigh."

"And olive oil, I'll replace everything, I promise."

"Don't worry about it," Astrid assured her. "You were the only one who ever cared about mixing up our stuff."

"Thank you." Leigh kept her eye on the house. "Let's try and find some time to talk later this week, okay?"

"Of course."

Astrid gave Leigh a moment before following the path back around to the house. She was surprised to see that Simone was no longer standing on the deck. Another couple was now talking with Hannah and Camille. Hannah waved her over.

"Simone wanted me to tell you that she went in to help with the brunch."

Astrid felt the air leave her body. "No fucking way."

Hannah laughed. "Don't shoot the messenger. Come meet our friends."

Faced with the decision of cooking with Simone and Leigh—a new horror-based reality show apparently already in progress—or meeting the attractive couple standing with Hannah and Camille, Astrid chose the latter. Stepping onto the deck, she approached the group.

"Hi, I'm Astrid," she said, with more confidence than she felt. Playing host on Leigh's deck had never felt natural and today was certainly no exception. Hannah explained Astrid's presence at the party as if it had nothing to do with the burned pasta or the U-Haul blinking in front of the fire hydrant.

"Guys, this is *Outside Astrid*," she said. "I'm proud to say that Gowear was one of her earliest sponsors."

Astrid appreciated the gesture but was willing to bet her lesbian membership card that this nameless couple knew every detail of the drama playing out in the back yard. They'd probably known all about Leigh and Shoshana too.

"I'm an Outsider," the shorter woman said shyly. Curvy and blond, Astrid thought she might be Camille's little sister.

"Really?" Astrid was shocked. Writing about the DC nature scene since high school, her local following was vast and various. It was not uncommon for people to recognize her name, but she'd never met an actual Outsider before.

"Yes, and I loved that piece on the apartment building near the zoo. I can't believe those people wake up every morning to lions roaring."

"The landlord lists it as an amenity and charges extra for that side of the building." Astrid laughed, repeating her favorite detail of the story.

"I remember that." The Outsider smiled, and Hannah took the opportunity to introduce her.

"Astrid, this is Lillian. She's a lawyer at Camille's firm."

"I thought she was Camille's sister," Astrid admitted and the group erupted into mysterious laughter. "Did I say something wrong?"

Lillian shook her head. "Camille and I *are* sisters, in a way, but that's another story."

"It's more like a novel," Camille corrected her.

"It's more like two novels," Hannah said, and introduced the tall brunette next to her. "This is Lillian's girlfriend, Charlotte."

Astrid couldn't remember meeting Charlotte though she looked familiar. Beautiful with broad shoulders tapering down to a narrow waist, Charlotte had a figure you didn't forget. She was wearing the same cool Gowear T-shirt as the other people at the party. Maybe she was on the running team, too. Was this where Astrid had seen her?

"Have we met?" Astrid asked.

Charlotte shook her head. "I don't think so."

Astrid searched her memory and flashed to an image of a woman singing the national anthem. "You're Nurse Nightingale! You sing babies to sleep at the hospital!"

"Bingo!" Hannah smiled.

"There was a story about you in the *Washington Post*. I saw a clip of you singing at a Washington Nationals game. You were fantastic," Astrid said, remembering clicking on the video link in the article. Astrid had been fascinated with the primal aspect of babies responding to the sound of a human voice and considered blogging about it.

"She's also a badass athlete," Hannah asserted, and high-fived Charlotte above Camille's head. "The Gowear marathon team is lucky to have her."

"Are all of you running?" Astrid asked the group.

"Not me," said Lillian.

"Lily illustrated the jersey, so she'll be with us every step of the way," Charlotte said, drawing an appreciative "Awwwww" from Camille, and a blush from Lillian.

"I've been eyeing those," Astrid told her. "Any way I could score one?"

"It would be my honor." Lillian beamed causing Astrid to question her protocol of not engaging with her readers. This woman seemed really nice. Was it possible Astrid was missing out on meeting more people like Lillian?

Hannah laughed. "Simone just asked us the same thing."

"Really?" Astrid inflated at the small proof of their connection. Leigh's assertion that Simone's attraction was merely appearance-based had affected Astrid's confidence more than she cared to admit.

"Yes, she wants to do something for the restaurant. It's so exciting she bought unUsual DC. It's the coolest place. You must be freaking out."

Astrid looked toward the house. "You've no idea."

CHAPTER SIXTEEN

Holy Tara

A wonky grocery-cart wheel impeded Astrid's progress down the narrow aisle of Dupont Circle's notorious Soviet Safeway, known among locals as the Siberian Safeway for the long lines and sketchy produce. Already at a disadvantage in the unfamiliar terrain, Astrid tried not to let frustration take over. Yesterday, Leigh had stuffed a wad of twenties in her pocket to replace the items Simone had used to cook spaghetti carbonara for the Gowear marathon team. The women had devoured the impromptu offering of pasta, bacon and eggs and were hopefully showing well in today's competition. If not for the race, Astrid would be doing her shopping at an organic market in Woodley Park. But traffic in the city would be paralyzed until the last runner crossed the finish line at the Iwo Jima statue in Arlington sometime around midday. Astrid wanted to complete the chore early so had braved the foreign market.

She was also buying the dry ingredients needed to prepare crab cakes. The promise to demonstrate the recipe for Simone was still out there. They'd yet to set a date, and maybe it would never happen, but Astrid wanted to have things on hand just in case.

Yesterday had been strange, to say the least. Astrid was still processing how the scene in Leigh's backyard had played out. She'd started to text Claire about it but found she didn't have the words. It had become even weirder once Astrid had gone back inside and found Simone had become the life of the party. Completely at home in Leigh's kitchen, she whipped up an exceptional meal and had everyone laughing at stories from culinary school.

Shoshana had eaten two helpings and afterward organized a bucket brigade to ferry Astrid's few possessions to the U-Haul. The only thing that made the bizarre experience livable was the fact that everyone acted as if Astrid and Leigh had merely been roommates. It wasn't every day your ex-girlfriend's new lover helped your new girlfriend and her old lover put your pillow into the U-Haul.

Astrid stopped in the baking section to look for breadcrumbs. She never knew whether to look for them here or in the bread section. Each grocery store chain seemed to have its own notion of where they belonged. Given agency, she wondered how the breadcrumbs might self-identify and then worried she'd gone crazy. Sane people did not empathize with breadcrumbs. She was looking forward to showing Simone how to make crab cakes. The secret was not to overpower the meat with too much filler. An authentic Maryland crab cake was ninety-nine percent crab. She scanned the shelf.

"Hey, gorgeous."

"Oh, hey."

Astrid was surprised to see Tara standing in the cramped poorly lit aisle. Claire's sophisticated friend did not have a reputation for personally performing menial chores. In high school she'd famously paid a boy to do her community service hours. When confronted by a school administrator, she'd hired a lawyer who'd successfully argued that the language in the student handbook was too nebulous. *Wasn't paying someone to make peanut butter and jelly sandwiches for the homeless shelter the same as performing the task if, in the end, the work was accomplished?* By the time Astrid was a senior, they'd changed the wording in the handbook and Tara was two years into a business degree at Princeton. Jerry referred to her, lovingly, as Holy Tara.

"How's that sweet pussy?"

"*Excuse me?*" Astrid sputtered in surprise. She knocked Tara's cart with her own. The flirty component of their relationship always came from Astrid's end. *Always.* She played the besotted sophomore and Tara, though bisexual, never said anything remotely reciprocal, not even when she was drunk. This was their game and it never varied.

"Get your mind out of the gutter," Tara commanded, but her smile looked like it was already there. "I was asking about Eartha Kitty." She swatted Astrid's arm, putting her on alert.

What the hell was going on?

"Are you buying her treats right now? I'm here to get chicken broth for the Noodle. She won't drink broth made from a bouillon cube anymore."

"Noodles is on to you." Astrid took a small step back. Whatever Tara was playing at, she wanted no part of it. She was already walking an emotional high wire with Simone. Add Tara to the balance, and she'd lose her footing entirely. She forced a smile. "And cat treats are not necessary. Claire and Coty have enough supplies to last a year. I found a pantry full of crap. They could open a store. Eartha has more closet space than I did at Leigh's."

Tara's predatory expression changed to one of sympathy. "So, you two broke up? Miles told me you'd been sleeping at Claire and Coty's. I saw the little red wagon outside the house."

"Yeah, we weren't meant to be." Astrid tried out the new narrative.

"Are you sorry you moved in with her?" Tara asked.

Astrid was a little surprised by the intrusive nature of the question but Tara was an old friend and it looked as if she truly wanted to know. Maybe she was going through stuff of her own. Who knew? Maybe that's why she was acting so weird. Astrid hated to jump to conclusions. Tara had been a good friend to Claire and she deserved an honest answer.

"A little. I think I did it because I was lazy." She shrugged, and Tara laughed.

"Tell me something I don't know."

Astrid smiled. For a moment she'd forgotten Tara had known her since she was a ten-year-old girl who'd had to be bribed to make her bed or brush her teeth.

"It was too soon for Leigh and me to move in together, we weren't ready for that level of commitment."

"But you did it anyway?"

Why was Tara so curious? Astrid frowned. She picked out a small jar of mayonnaise and added it to the cart, followed by Dijon mustard. She was sure Claire had these condiments in the house but she'd decided to buy anything that might have possibly expired. Contaminating the crab with compromised ingredients would not impress a professional chef. She pulled her mind away from Simone to answer the question.

"At the time, I hoped the relationship was going to work out."

"How long had you two been dating?"

Astrid ran a hand through her hair, thinking of how to best articulate her motivation without sounding like a complete asshole. "Six months. I told you it was too soon, but I had to make a decision quickly. Claire and Coty were moving in together and I needed a place to live. Leigh asked me to move in and I jumped at it." She made a face. "And Leigh's house is really close to the river."

Tara threw back her head and laughed. "I knew you had an ulterior motive. You and that sporty dentist were never a match."

"I should have listened to you." Astrid shuddered. "Looking back, I think I wanted what Claire and Coty have."

Tara groaned. "And what *is that*, exactly?"

"Magic," Astrid said unhesitatingly. Was that what she and Simone had too? Were they magic? Up until yesterday, Astrid's level of certainty had been very high. Now she didn't know what to think. Simone's lie of omission about the restaurant had allowed doubt to creep in. Perhaps the sparks flying between them were nothing more than smoke and mirrors. Maybe it was too soon to tell.

"Magic?" Tara spat the word like it was the name of a secondhand shoe store in northern Virginia.

"Yes, I think so," Astrid said. She knew Tara was talking about Claire and Coty but her mind remained firmly fixed on Simone. Would she see her today? Later tonight? Would they text? Simone had meetings all day with the restaurant's staff to determine who would stay under the new management. She'd explained the process to Astrid the day before when Astrid had pretended not to be upset that she hadn't known Simone was the owner. She didn't know how long the interviews might last, and Simone hadn't said.

Tara narrowed her eyes. "I thought you blamed Coty for making you homeless."

"That was stupid." Astrid shook her head. She hated that her grudge against Coty was public knowledge and hoped to correct it when he returned. "He could have timed the whole sweeping-Claire-off-her-feet thing a little better for my personal timeline, but how can I blame him for falling in love with my sister? It is Claire we're talking about."

"That's very mature of you." Tara lay a hand on Astrid's arm causing the hair to stand-up on the back of her neck. "Sounds like you're growing up."

"I'm trying to."

They started down the aisle together. The wonky wheel of Astrid's cart made it impossible to walk in a straight line and twice she bumped Tara, who acted like she was doing it on purpose.

"Keep it in your pants," she joked, and Astrid laughed because it was easier to pretend everything was normal. Tara had never shown the slightest romantic interest in her. Why was she being so flirty now?

"It's not me, it's the cart," Astrid said, and pushed it further away from Tara. They were now in the produce section and she picked up a bunch of scallions. Despite the distraction of Tara, Simone and crab cakes were still at the forefront of her mind. She added a red pepper to the cart and Tara grew curious.

"What's for dinner?"

"Oh."

Astrid looked down at her groceries. She knew the question was an invitation for her to offer one of her own. It was curious. Tara didn't seem to know anything about Astrid's developing relationship with Simone. Miles might have told his sister Astrid was staying at Claire's, but true to form, he'd only given her half the story. Astrid said a silent thank you to her old lab partner. Once upon a time Tara had been very jealous of Simone's friendship with Claire. There was no point stirring up the old rivalry, especially if nothing was being contested. Astrid wasn't sure what was happening. A day ago, she'd been ready to make a public declaration, today they'd barely texted at all.

"Nothing in particular," she lied. "Just getting some roughage."

"You like it rough, Astrid?" Tara asked, softly. Astrid had no idea how to respond.

"I guess I do. Um, sometimes?" she said, and struggled to think of how to change the subject. Tara's behavior was now making her uncomfortable. Astrid suspected it was about the nose job which made it even worse. Why was everyone so hung up on her new face? "You don't know of any apartments for rent, do you? Claire and Coty get back next week. If I don't find a place, I'll have to move in with my parents."

Tara stopped short in the aisle, a happy smile blooming in her eyes. "Yes, actually, I do."

"What? Really? Where?"

Astrid was intrigued. Later that day she was supposed to see a place in Cleveland Park but didn't have much confidence it would work out. It was too far away from the river and had the stigma of being the first apartment tour without Simone, who made everything infinitely more fun. Last week, she'd pretended to be Astrid's pregnant wife and ranted at a potential landlord for putting their unborn baby in danger when mold was discovered growing on a radiator. She'd done it for no other purpose than to make Astrid laugh and somehow managed to score them a twenty-dollar Starbucks gift card.

Going without her today felt wrong. Astrid had almost lulled herself into the belief they were looking for a place together which was stupid. Yes, they'd been fucking like college kids on spring break but, like those kids, they barely knew each other. Now, Astrid was worried the vacation might be over.

"The apartment is in my building, actually," Tara said.

"The Cairo?"

"Yes, the woman across the hall works at the World Bank. They're sending her to Turkey or Tasmania or Tanzania or something." Tara shrugged as if the places were as exchangeable as nail polish color. "She's having a cocktail party tonight. Come with me and ask her yourself?"

"I can't do that," Astrid said.

"Why not?"

"It would only be a tease," Astrid replied, and immediately regretted her choice of words. But what was Tara playing at? Astrid could never afford anything at the Cairo and she knew it. The landmark building had the distinction of being the tallest residential building in the city and was listed in The National Registry of Historic Places.

"You could check out the view from my apartment?" Tara offered, hopefully. "I won't make dinner but I'm great at ordering things. Come on, have dinner with Noodle and me?"

"How is Ms. Noodle?" Astrid asked. "I saw photos of her pedicure on Instagram last week. Are you using a new groomer?" Astrid was happy to talk about Tara's sweet-as-pie Yorkie-poo who had big soulful eyes and perfectly done nails.

"Come see for yourself. Tonight, at dinner."

"I'm pretty busy," Astrid wavered. Tara looked genuinely lonely. Astrid had been so focused on how much she'd personally been missing Claire she hadn't considered how much her absence might be affecting Tara. She hated thinking of her ordering dinner with her dog. There was also something undeniably flattering about having an old crush suddenly pay attention to her.

"Come on, stop by." Tara smiled.

Astrid found herself nodding. *What was she doing?* This was a horrible idea. She'd no interest in furthering a flirtation with Tara. Astrid didn't need a crystal ball to know that they weren't a good match because Astrid knew Tara. Her store might be named Closet Diva, but Tara was a fully out-and-proud diva. Astrid couldn't imagine Tara kayaking or camping or doing anything outside, really. Why lead her on?

Six hours later, she found herself revisiting the question. Perched hesitantly on Tara's immaculate white couch, the Noodle pliant at her feet, Astrid knew she'd made a terrible mistake. The lovely penthouse had been stage set for seduction. Candlelight, wine, Sara Vaughn album playing on a vintage record player; there was no misreading Tara's intentions for the evening. There was also no sign of dinner. Idly, Astrid wondered if Tara was planning on offering herself as the main course. It was way too much and not what Astrid wanted at all. She addressed her concerns head on.

"Is this supposed to be a date?" she asked and wantonly stuck her hand perilously close to the flame of the candle to remind Tara exactly who was sitting next to her. Astrid might look like a different person but she was still the same all-weather tomboy who'd once carried bait crickets around in her backpack.

"Why not?" Tara frowned at Astrid's fingers but still looked hopeful. She handed Astrid a glass of wine, and sat down next to her. "We've known each other a long time."

Astrid sipped her wine and tried to pretend she wasn't mentally mapping the apartment exits. There had to be a way out of the situation that did not involve the fire escape. She needed to think of one and soon, because Tara was moving closer. Thinking quickly, she reached down and scooped the Noodle against her chest. "I've also known the Noodle a long time."

The snow-white Yorkie-poo was as soft as a stuffed animal and smelled of coconut cake.

"Don't make jokes," Tara said, and put her glass on the table. "We're both single, consenting adults. You've made it clear that you find me attractive." She blushed, and looked away. "I mean, I think you find me attractive."

"I do," Astrid said, too quickly. "I mean, come on, you're gorgeous." She forced a smile. The dry Cabernet had leached all the moisture from her mouth but she held onto the glass for protection. Tara's body language indicated she was about two seconds away from making a move.

"So, why not see where this goes?" she said and inched even closer to Astrid on the couch.

Astrid played the most obvious card. "Because I just got out of a relationship with Leigh. My head is all over the place."

Tara wasn't buying it. She put a hand on Astrid's knee. "You told me two hours ago that your relationship with Leigh was a mistake. Were you ever even in love with her?"

"No," Astrid choked, as warm fingers slid up her thigh. "I never was but this is still too soon. Please, listen to me."

"How will we know unless we try?" Tara slid her hand a fraction further and Astrid went Di-Bulldozer.

Standing abruptly, she splashed her nearly-full glass of Cabernet all over Tara, the couch and the dog. "Because I know!" she screamed. "Dammit Tara, will you please listen to what I'm saying?"

Noodle made a run for it as Tara scrambled to her feet. Covered in the deep-red wine, she looked like an actress from a low-budget horror film. When she shook her head, wine dripped off her chin and onto the floor. "Jesus fuck, Astrid. Look what you've done," she said, and stalked off to the kitchen.

Astrid felt bad, but not overly so. She called after her. "Is there anything I can do?"

"Just don't make it any worse. God, you're such a klutz," came the snappish reply.

Astrid smiled. The formally immaculate sofa now looked like a crime scene, but Holy Tara had blessedly returned to normal.

CHAPTER SEVENTEEN

Cirque du Ceiling

Astrid lay staring at the rectangular indentation in the ceiling above Claire and Coty's bed. Made visible by light coming through a leaded transom above the bedroom window, it was like a lit stage in an otherwise darkened theater. The trapdoor to Simone's apartment had been closed since the night of the pawpaw cake. As cool as it was, it was far too dangerous to leave such a wide opening exposed in the middle of the floor. Astrid wondered if she'd made the same mistake with her heart.

It was three a.m. and she couldn't sleep. Scenes from the last two days played though her mind like a silly, over-the-top movie she would only watch if trapped on an airplane. Had all that really happened in Leigh's backyard? Had she really spilled wine on Tara's dog? It seemed impossible to believe. Rolling over, she draped an arm across Eartha Kitty and pulled the cat in close.

"Come here, baby."

Eartha made a noise of pleasure low in her throat and twisted onto her back to give Astrid better access.

"You like that?" Astrid dug her fingers into scruff beneath Eartha's neck and the rumbling increased tenfold. Astrid giggled. "Oh, I think you do."

The massage continued until Eartha seemed to reach some sort of internal limit and flung herself from the bed. Landing with a thud she disappeared into the semidarkness.

"Hey!" Astrid called after her. "I'm sorry. Did I go in too hard? Come back. I promise I'll be gentle."

She received no response from Eartha but a creaking board overhead alerted her that someone else might be paying attention. Was Simone eavesdropping on her? It seemed unlikely that she'd be lying on the floor in the middle of the night, though Astrid didn't find the visual unpleasant.

She straightened her pillow. It felt wrong not to have Simone snuggled against her right now. They'd only been together two weeks and Astrid already missed the curve of Simone's naked body pressed into the recesses of her own. She missed her soft hair, her exotic perfume. She missed the laughter. This was the first time they hadn't shared a bed since the wild night together in the penthouse of the Castle Resort. The night Simone's fancy name and credit card had given Astrid a peek into her world of extreme wealth. A night when Astrid should have been paying more attention.

Could Leigh be right? Was Simone too good for her? She'd never thought in those terms before and she didn't like thinking in them now. Leigh acted as if categories of people could be categorized like they were Consumer Report listings. She'd insinuated that Astrid's surgery had bumped her up to a luxury item. Was this the only reason Simone was interested? It was entirely possible. The woman had slept with Hannah Richards for fuck's sake.

Earlier, Astrid had tortured herself by Googling the iconic Gowear catalogue cover. A younger Hannah was hanging by her fingertips on a precipice in the Dolomites. Though it hadn't been part of their story, Astrid imagined Simone to be the person on the other side of her golden gaze. Maybe Hannah had fucked her afterward and they'd shared a bottle Chianti and a plate of puttanesca Simone had cooked for them, naked.

The image had put Astrid in such a foul mood she'd declined Simone's text earlier in the evening offering to sleepover. Making up a bullshit story about being on deadline, she'd slunk off to nurse her wounded ego and wound up cuddling a cat. She hadn't seen Simone since that morning when she'd left her for the meetings at the restaurant. Avoiding her hadn't been intentional but Astrid hadn't sought her out either. Every time she pictured her face, she remembered the lie.

"Come over here, lover," Astrid called after Eartha, ramping the volume just in case Simone was listening. She hated that things felt weird between them but didn't know what to do about it. Why hadn't Simone told her about buying the restaurant? The question led to the unsettling but logical conclusion that other things might have been withheld as well. What else wasn't she telling Astrid? Simone could have a condo in Paris, a bastard child by an Armenian prince. Given her wealth and Astrid's imagination, the possibilities were endless. Making matters worse was that Simone had been so quick to share the restaurant ownership with Hannah. Perhaps that's what hurt Astrid the most. Why hadn't she told her?

"Hey!" she shouted, in surprise when Eartha Kitty suddenly reappeared in her lap. The cat pushed a foot into Astrid's stomach and then another. "Knead something?" Astrid joked, and another creak over head confirmed her suspicions. Simone was indeed up and listening. Astrid smiled to herself suddenly feeling very happy. Who was this wild woman? It was time she found out.

Nudging Eartha from her lap, she stood on the bed and pressed her hands lightly against the trapdoor. She imagined she could feel Simone's cheek on the other side. The situation was ridiculous. Had the experience with Leigh taught her nothing about communicating? She tapped on the board.

"Who is it?" a nonchalant voice asked from the other side and Astrid smiled as relief flooded her body. She was up.

"Um, pizza delivery?" she replied and was rewarded when the door cracked open a tiny bit. Astrid felt warm air on her face though nothing was visible. She had no idea of Simone's emotional state, so she stayed with the joke. "You ordered double cheese?"

"I was worried you were delivering to someone else," Simone said, softly, and Astrid was surprised to detect a note of vulnerability. The idea that Simone could be jealous seemed preposterous until she measured it against her reaction to finding Simone had slept with Hannah. The affair had been five years ago and a small part of Astrid had been ready to challenge Hannah to a duel.

"No, I'm only delivering for you," she said, and pressed her fingers more firmly against the wood. The door hinged back further and she saw Simone's silhouette against the ceiling. Waves of hair spilled over the elegant lines of her shoulders and back. She was either naked or very close to it. Astrid's breath caught. "You okay?"

"I miss you," came the reply, and the door gave way completely.

"I miss you, too," Astrid said. "I may be going through withdrawal."

"I've been looking at pictures of you on my phone," Simone confessed. Reaching a hand through the door she touched the tip of Astrid's finger with her own.

"Really?" Astrid asked and clasped her hand.

Neither spoke for a moment. Astrid still couldn't see Simone's face though her exotic fragrance had entered the room the moment the trapdoor opened. Astrid could feel her proximity and longed to have her nearer. Gently, she tugged her hand toward her. Simone didn't fight it. Holding onto Astrid's wrist, she lay on her stomach and leaned down through the opening until she was hanging halfway through the trapdoor with her hands resting on Astrid's shoulders.

"Hi," she said.

"Hey." Reaching up through the darkness Astrid found Simone's face and cradled it with her hands. "Thanks for dropping in."

"No problem."

Their lips met in a tender kiss and then another. It was a marvelous reunion. Kissing Simone now felt like sustenance to Astrid. She sank her fingers into her hair and lost herself in the moment.

It wasn't until Simone put more pressure on her shoulders that Astrid realized the inverted position may not be as comfortable for her. Wrenching her lips away, she whispered against her mouth.

"You want to come down here?"

"Hmmmm," Simone murmured. Her hands slid from Astrid's shoulders to her breasts where she stopped to tease her nipples through the fabric of Claire's Washington Ballet T-shirt.

"Oh, God," Astrid let go of her face. "Come down here, now."

Reaching up, she pulled at Simone's shoulders drawing her body further through the trapdoor. Physics were not in their favor. Astrid was working out the location of the nearest hospital, when somehow, Simone flipped over and began to shimmy down Astrid's body like she was a tree.

"Okay, that works." Astrid braced her hands on the outer frame of the trapdoor to stabilize her position on the bed. Simone's mouth was on her breast and she groaned. "That's not fair."

"But it's fun," Simone murmured, now at her stomach and moving south. Astrid's knees grew weak as she felt teeth sink into the waist band of her briefs. The fact that she didn't fall was attributable to the strength of her kayak-toned arms and Simone's agility. Ballerinas were notoriously gifted athletes and often quite fearless. Coty's favorite hobby was bungee jumping. Once he learned the trapdoor was functional, he'd want to install a fireman's pole.

In the end, Simone landed in a giggling handstand on the bed, the tops of her feet hooked on Astrid's shoulders, briefs in her mouth.

"That was awesome." Astrid laughed and struggled to keep her feet. Simone's handstand allowed Astrid delicious access to her pussy, the smell of which filled Astrid with wild need.

Gravity had rendered the loose-fitting shortie pajama pants useless. Astrid nudged them aside.

Simone hissed her pleasure and Astrid marveled at what she was about to do. She felt like they were staging a position from a French post card. Leaving one hand braced against the ceiling, she wrapped the other securely around Simone's waist, holding her upright. "This okay?"

"Yes." Simone whimpered, but still tried to make a joke. "Ladies and gentlemen, we are Cirque du Ceiling," she proclaimed and pushed her pussy up into Astrid's face.

Astrid dove in. Dragging her tongue from Simone's clit through her slit and back again, she made her scream.

"Oh, God, don't stop." Simone bucked her hips and Astrid didn't disappoint her.

Now braced securely, with one hand on the ceiling, and the other holding Simone steady in the handstand, Astrid was confident she could finish the job without falling. Simone tasted so good, and she was close to coming. Communicating her need with rolling hips and small moans, Simone led Astrid's tongue in an intimate dance. Astrid had never felt so connected to another person, powerful yet vulnerable in a way that frightened her.

When Simone began shaking Astrid gripped her more firmly and went in harder with her tongue.

"I'm going to come," Simone announced and then followed through on the promise, punctuating it with a low piercing scream.

Astrid lapped at every drop of moisture, glorifying in the communion of their bodies. The restaurant issue seemed so small when Simone's pussy was so close. Astrid wanted more. She tested Simone's clit with the tip of her tongue and was met with a whimper.

"I can't. I'm sorry. My arms are jelly."

"Don't apologize." Astrid laughed. "Let's get down on the bed."

"Okay." Simone didn't argue.

Gently taking her fingertips off the ceiling, Astrid removed Simone's ankles from her shoulders and held her steady as she dropped from her hands to her forearms. By degrees, they descended safely to the mattress and collapsed giggling into each other's arms.

"Glad you could drop in," Astrid said, gently kissing her lips. Flushed with arousal and adrenaline she covered Simone's body with her own.

"I was jealous of the cat," Simone said. Astrid couldn't see her eyes but knew by the tone in her voice they were dancing. "I was on the floor for one hour listening to you two make love."

"Stalker," Astrid teased, and kissed her nose. "We have laws in this country against that."

"Punish me?" Simone said, and pushed her thigh between Astrid's legs. "Please?"

The pressure felt amazing against Astrid's center. She was so turned on, so ready to let go. She kissed Simone slow and deep, reveling in the feeling of her wet mouth, the salty taste of her orgasm, of skin on skin. She began rocking and Simone matched the rhythm moving her hips sensually beneath her. Before the moment grew more heated, Astrid broke away. There were things she needed to say before she let go completely.

"Where are you going?" Simone whispered. She reached up to cup Astrid's face but then moved away from her and sat up on the bed. "What's wrong?"

"I want to talk to you about something," Astrid said, and pulled a blanket to cover her chest. Simone grabbed playfully at the fabric but Astrid held firm. "I'm serious."

"Okay," Simone said, and lay back on the mattress. "What's the matter?"

"I'm confused about something that happened yesterday." Eartha seemed to know Astrid was nervous and jumped on the mattress to lend support.

"Is it about Hannah?" Simone asked softly, and Astrid shook her head.

"Yes and no. I don't care that you slept with her."

"You don't?" Simone sounded disappointed.

"Well, of course I care," Astrid huffed. She'd just managed to banish the images of Simone and Hannah from her mind. "But

I'm not upset about that," she shrugged. "It happened before we met as adults, so it's got nothing to do with me. My feelings are hurt because I didn't know you owned the restaurant." She swallowed hard. "I felt like a complete dumbass when you told Hannah and Camille."

"Don't say unkind things about your beautiful ass."

"Can you stop joking for a minute?"

"Promise not to insult your ass again, and I'll stop joking."

"Simone, please?"

"My mother bought the restaurant last month."

Astrid was confused. Was Simone lying to her again? "I thought you said your uncle owned it."

"Giovanni is Mother's puppet."

"What? I don't understand."

Simone leaned back against the headboard. "Last month, I made the mistake of telling my mother about my new job."

"Why was that a mistake?"

"Because she is very rich and very controlling. We've been fighting my whole life."

"That sounds rough."

"It was much worse when I was younger. She wanted everything to be her way so I did things just to make her angry."

"Like what?" Astrid was curious.

"So many things," Simone smirked. "One time I dyed my hair blue just before my grandmother's birthday party."

Astrid slid her fingers into Simone's glorious curls. "I bet it looked beautiful."

"Mother did not think so," Simone laughed. "But what made her most furious is when I changed my name."

"Wait, your real name isn't Simone?" Astrid sat up straighter in the bed. This was indeed a night for revelations.

"I was christened Simona. Simone is the masculine version of the name. I changed it before we came to the USA."

Astrid was impressed. "Weren't you like twelve when you moved here? How did you pull that off?"

"I put Simone on all the ballet and school forms without telling her. It was just one tiny letter and she didn't notice.

There was nothing she could do to fix it. By the time we arrived in this country everyone was already calling me Simone."

"No way," Astrid laughed.

"It's true. I won that battle but the war has never stopped."

"I'm sorry." Astrid stroked her thigh.

"It's not an easy relationship," Simone shook her head. "After I completed culinary school, she tried to set me up with a café. When I took a job at a friend's restaurant instead, she got angry and refused to eat there for a year. One of the reasons I wanted to move back to DC was to get away from her."

"But then she bought the restaurant?"

Simone nodded. "I was so angry when I found out. I almost didn't come. There is no way I can work for my mother."

"What happened?"

"Everyone is still angry. My father was desperate to give me the restaurant to make amends."

"Do you want it?"

"Yes, but it was something I wanted to earn. Mother took that away from me. My uncle signed it over to me today. My father has agreed to be my silent partner. It is not possible for my mother to be silent."

"Why didn't you tell me about all this?"

"Because, I was embarrassed about what my mother did."

"Why did you share it with Hannah?'

Simone sighed. "I've been wondering that all day myself."

"And?"

"I think I was showing off." Simone sat forward. "I'm sorry. Part of me wanted to impress Hannah."

"Which part?" Astrid asked, pointedly. Because this was the real question. Her own reaction to Tara's advances had confirmed to Astrid what she'd already suspected: she'd fallen in love with Simone. If Simone wasn't on the same page, Astrid needed to close the book and return it the library.

"It was my huge Galliano ego that wanted to impress her," Simone admitted. "She's so rich and successful, I guess I needed to be too. I'm pathetic."

Sliding her legs from the bed, she began searching around the mattress for her pajamas.

"Where are you going?" Astrid reached for her wrist.

Simone glanced at the trapdoor. "Don't you want me to go?"

"Not unless you're going to get some fabulous, new sex toy I don't know about." She pulled Simone into her lap.

Simone curled into a ball and ducked her head beneath Astrid's chin. "You're not mad?"

Astrid stroked her back. "My feelings were hurt, but I get it. Hannah is a celebrity. Who wouldn't want to impress her? It just means that you're human."

"A pathetic and insecure human," Simone said derisively. "My parents have always bought me everything. No one ever takes me seriously."

"That's not true." Astrid tilted her chin up so she could see her eyes. "Don't forget, I saw you dance. Money can get you lessons but it doesn't buy talent or discipline and you had both."

"Thank you for saying that."

"It's true. And aren't you a graduate of Le Cordon Bleu? Their acceptance rate is only thirty-four percent."

"Really?"

"I'm a reporter. I looked it up."

Simone looked pleased. "I still have a trust fund but I'm trying to live within my means until I make it on my own, I don't want any part of their money. That's why I'm living here."

Astrid kissed her tenderly. "I think that's really impressive. I think you are really impressive."

"Thank you for saying that. You make me happy." Simone returned the kiss with passion and then drew back shyly. "Is that okay? Are we okay?"

"Just be straight with me?"

"I don't ever want to be straight with you." Simone joked.

"Ha ha," Astrid kissed her.

Simone grew serious. "Next time you're angry, please, don't shut me out. I was worried you didn't want to see me again."

"That's never going to happen."

The brown eyes locked onto hers. "Promise me?"

Astrid lowered her to the bed. "I promise."

CHAPTER EIGHTEEN

Big Brother

"Get that nasty shit out of here!" Astrid snapped a wet dish-towel at Coty's thigh where it landed with a satisfying thwack.

"Ouch!" he screamed, and leapt at least three feet into the air.

"Drama king," Claire teased her boyfriend, as Astrid opened the cabinet to search for the cast iron skillet.

"I am not the king, I'm Prince Charming," Coty reminded the sisters, and struck a valiant pose from the ballet.

"Okay, drama prince, no Old Bay seasoning in the crab cakes," Astrid said. Placing the pan on the range, she went in search of the panko. "We don't need your cheat-ass, fish-house recipes, *thankyouverymuch*."

"Preach!" Claire yelled, and Coty pulled a sad face.

"My grandmother used Old Bay," he said, and held the yellow spice box perilously close to the four prepared patties resting on the counter. Astrid had given Simone the promised tutorial earlier in the day. It was important to make crab cakes a few hours in advance because they held-up better in the frying process if refrigerated first. Astrid still had to roll the patties in panko before transferring them to the cast iron skillet. It was a delicate procedure as the crab meat was held together with only trace amounts of the other ingredients. Properly made, crab cakes were a one-man show. The mayo, breadcrumbs, sauteed shallots and pepper could not even be considered supporting players but were relegated to the orchestra. Old Bay seasoning was not allowed in the theater.

Coty didn't agree. "Crab cakes aren't the same without Old Bay."

"No, because they taste good," Astrid explained, and made a dive for the box. Coty yanked it back but Claire snatched it from his hand and ran to the other room.

"Hey!" he yelled, running after her, but it was too late.

She'd thrown it out the window into a massive holly bush below in the backyard. No one said anything for a moment, and then they all burst out laughing.

"She threw my Old Bay seasoning out the window." Coty turned to Astrid, as if she hadn't just witnessed her big sister's total boss move.

"You're lucky it wasn't you," Astrid said, and playfully pointed her spatula at him. Letting go of her resentment for Coty had been the best decision she'd made in a long time. It had been like putting down a heavy rock she needn't have ever carried. Better still, Claire seemed thrilled with Astrid's change of attitude and kept shooting pleased looks across the kitchen that felt like beams of sunshine.

"He was raised in northern Maryland so he doesn't know any better," she said now, swatting her boyfriend on his perfectly toned ass.

Astrid nodded sympathetically. "That explains so much."

"I'm a heathen from Baltimore," Coty drawled, pronouncing it "Balmer" like a true native. Then grabbing Claire playfully around the waist, he dragged her giggling into the living room while Astrid carefully rolled the crab cakes in panko. Eartha Kitty was figure-eighting her ankles, keeping watch in case a miraculous morsel found its way to the floor. Astrid tossed her a piece and she pounced on it.

"You are the best kitty."

It was Coty and Claire's welcome-home dinner. The Washington National Ballet had returned to town the day before to cap their triumphant tour with a Saturday night performance at the Kennedy Center. The special evening was slated for family and friends and the Dibellos were turning out in force. The cute cousins were flying in from Long Island and Katrina was hosting a brunch the following day. Astrid had asked Simone to come as her date.

Tonight's dinner would be a decidedly more intimate affair. Though, to Astrid, it felt momentous. She was eager for Claire to witness her rapport with Simone. She wanted someone else to say the magic was true. As the one person who knew them both, Claire would have the best perspective on the dynamic. Initially, she'd been shocked to learn of Astrid's whirlwind romance with her old friend but had agreed to reserve judgement until she saw them together. Tonight would be the first test.

Things with Simone hadn't returned to normal after the night of Cirque du Ceiling—they'd become even better. Every day she gave Astrid a bigger piece of herself, shared a little more. Her anxiety that people only liked her for her money wasn't unlike what Astrid was experiencing following the nose job. They'd commiserated, they'd looked at apartments and they'd had sex, lots and lots of sex.

Astrid still didn't have a place to live, though it seemed clear she'd be spending a lot of time at Simone's. Most of the stuff relocated from Leigh's had already found its way to the attic apartment. It seemed logical. Simone didn't have many possessions and Astrid had nowhere to put hers. She didn't want to make the same mistake she'd made six months ago with Leigh, but the relationships were so different, the argument didn't feel relevant. There was no uncertainty regarding Astrid's feelings for Simone. They simply were. The not knowing Astrid had experienced with Leigh had been the knowing. The only thing Astrid wanted to discover about Simone, the only thing she wanted to know, was how she could spend more time with her.

A light footfall on the stairs announced her imminent presence and Astrid turned toward the door to hide her goofy smile. Just thinking about Simone made her happy. She wondered how Simone would greet her. Would she be demonstrative in front of Coty and Claire? When Astrid had left her an hour ago, Simone been completely vulnerable. Laid out naked on the bed, glowing from a recent orgasm, she'd begged Astrid to stay in bed and cuddle another half hour. Would she claim her now?

There was a knock on the door and Astrid felt her smile grow. She was here.

As Coty went to let her in, Claire came into the kitchen and rested her chin on Astrid's shoulder. "Stinky got it bad."

"Slinky ain't lying," Astrid replied, pleased at the validation of being called out. Claire's recognition that something was happening made it more real. Simone had become very important to Astrid. She wanted the relationship to work.

"You look really hot, by the way." Claire tugged at the hem of Astrid's navy blue USWNT soccer jersey. "Good call on the shorts. The pockets are doing huge favors for your ass."

"Thanks." Astrid felt her face flush. "Now shhhh." She stole a glance at the doorway where Coty was still greeting Simone. His tall frame obscured her smaller body but Astrid could hear her voice. Goose bumps pricked her arm.

"Your ass owes those pockets a bottle of wine."

"Oh my God, will you shut up? She'll hear you."

"Like we heard you this afternoon?"

"Claire!"

"You were loud," she said beaming, and did the eyebrow thing.

"Oh my God." Astrid cringed. "That's so embarrassing."

Claire nodded. "But also, kind of great." She squeezed Astrid's elbow. "Let's go say hi to your girlfriend."

Arm in arm, the sisters walked to the foyer where Coty was questioning Simone about the bark muttsvah. Astrid's blog had come out the day before and the comments section indicated that she'd struck exactly the right tone. So far no one had chastised her for being sacrilegious. The Outsiders were all adding stories of their own animal parties gone wrong or asking questions about where to get rawhide Torah portions. Simone had lived it so could provide a first-person account to Coty. Gesturing wildly with her hands, she was describing the dog-mauled buffet when she noticed Astrid.

"Ciao, Bella." Her eyes grew a degree brighter and she stepped forward, in a now familiar motion, that Astrid recognized as a prelude to a kiss. She stopped short when she saw Claire.

"Claire, mi amore!" Bypassing Astrid, Simone kissed her sister instead.

"Simone!"

A stab of jealously punctured Astrid's buoyant mood. She felt it like a punch in the gut but forced a smile reminding herself that if it wasn't for Simone's friendship with Claire, Astrid wouldn't even know her. She wouldn't be here having dinner with her tonight, or a possible future.

"How've you been?" Claire released Simone from the hug but kept a hand on her forearm.

"Wonderful," Simone sparkled. "I'm so happy to be back in Washington." She rolled her eyes. "I am happy to be away from my mother."

"How is Queen Claudia?" Claire asked, laughing, and Astrid was further reminded of their history that didn't include her. Claire had once spent a week in Milan with Simone's family. She'd met the famous favorite grandmother. Nona had given Claire a Hermes scarf and was now dead. Nona would never give Astrid a scarf. She squeezed her hands until the tips of her fingernails dug into her palms. Where was this jealousy coming from? Simone and Claire had only ever been friends and Astrid didn't even wear scarves. There was nothing to worry about. All the same, she was happy when Claire removed her hand from Simone's arm.

"Claudia is still a royal bitch," Simone said. "But I'd rather not talk about her."

"No problem." Claire nodded. "I'm so glad you're here. You look amazing." She turned to Coty, grinning. "This is Simone."

"We just met," Coty said, good naturedly. Grinning in the doorway, blond hair flopping over his eyes, he reminded Astrid of a beautifully bred golden retriever. "She brought us some homemade body scrub." He handed Claire a plastic container that Astrid recognized as recycled from their Indian take-out two days before. Simone had ordered vindaloo and declared the spice ratio perfection.

"Is that the sugar-magnolia?" Claire's eyes grew wide with delight. "I can't believe you remembered!" She turned to Astrid. "Simone used to make this stuff in high school and keep it in her bathroom." She peeled open the lid. "Oh my God, it smells exactly the same."

"And it's edible," Astrid said, and then felt stupid. Searching for a way into the conversation she tripped up their walk down memory lane. There was a moment of awkward silence, and then Coty and Claire started to laugh.

"I'm always telling Claire that we don't keep enough snacks in the bathroom," Coty joked while Claire shook her head at Astrid.

"How dare you soil the magnolia scrub with your dirty mind?" She held the container protectively against her chest then rounded on Simone. "Are you corrupting my little sister?

Astrid expected Simone to make a joke. It was her way, and the easiest path out of the moment. But when she looked up, she saw that Simone looked serious.

"I love her."

"You do?" Both Claire's eyebrows shot involuntarily skyward and Simone nodded. She didn't look at Astrid but continued the conversation as if she weren't in the room.

"Yes, we've spent the last several weeks together," she explained, keeping her eyes fixed firmly on Claire. "Astrid is thoughtful and kind and she's very smart. I have learned so much from her." She shook her head sending the curls bouncing, adorably. "I haven't told her yet, but I think she knows."

Claire sighed deeply, reminding Astrid vaguely of their mother. "Don't you worry you might be moving a bit too fast?"

"I don't think I have much control over it," Simone told her. "I thought you should know that my intentions are honorable."

"Okay," Claire responded. "Break her heart and I'll kick your ass."

"That's fair." Simone turned shyly to Astrid and pretended to have just noticed her standing there. "Oh, ciao."

"Hi." Astrid felt her cheeks flame hotter but didn't break eye contact. Simone had just declared her love in front of Coty and Claire. She needed to know she was not alone.

Coty cleared his throat. "I'm going to find the Old Bay." He grabbed Claire's arm. "Come with?"

"Oh my God, yes." Claire didn't even get her shoes.

Astrid watched the door close behind them. She turned to find Simone had moved further into the apartment. Backlit by late afternoon sun streaming in from the open windows, her body appeared almost celestial.

"I love you, too." Astrid walked forward into the light.

They came together slowly, carefully, as if to not crush this new precious thing just hatched between them. Astrid held Simone's face in her hands and for a moment just stared into her eyes. The ever-present humor now held a tinge of vulnerability that mirrored how Astrid felt inside. When their lips met there was a rush of feeling that made Astrid feel weak. Clinging to Simone, she found support.

They kissed until the deadbolt turned, heralding the return of Claire and Coty. Astrid had no idea how much time had passed. Her mind was on another plain, spinning with adrenaline and hope. Simone had put words to the feelings, said them aloud. Pulling slowly away, Astrid met her eye and found the same intensity of feeling.

"You're amazing," she whispered, as the door opened behind them. She pecked Simone's lips again because she couldn't help it.

"You make me so happy," Simone replied, and squeezed her hand.

Astrid felt tears prick her eyes. "I think I need a moment."

Simone nodded. "Go in the bedroom. Take your time."

Claire and Coty were now back in the apartment, loudly greeting Eartha Kitty. Astrid walked into the bedroom and shut the door. Holy fuck. Simone loved her. She stepped to the window and looked out on the street. Part of her wanted to throw open the sash and escape into the day to be alone with the declaration.

Turning, she glanced in the mirror and confirmed what she already knew. Not quite tomato-red, her cheeks were the color of the pink, mealy things they passed off as tomatoes in the grocery store. She reached up and stroked the bridge of her nose. The numbness was completely gone as was the shock at her altered appearance. Okay, almost gone. Sometimes she looked in the mirror and still thought it was Claire. Though, more and more, she'd come to accept the reality. She was still the same Astrid on the inside, but the outside had changed. A knock on the door reminded her she did not have the luxury to ruminate. She took a longing last look out the window.

"Come in."

The door opened and Eartha Kitty ran in first, playing advance team. Greeting Astrid with a happy squeak, she leapt on the bed.

"Hey Eartha," Astrid leaned over to stroke her head, as Coty poked his head into the room.

"Sorry to intrude," he said, looking a little worried. "I just need a Band-Aid."

"Oh no. What happened?" Astrid asked with real concern. Claire and Coty had to be incredibly careful with their bodies. A bad cut on a hand or foot could easily jeopardize a performance. They only had one show left before the tour was over. Wrestling a holly bush for a box of Old Bay seasoning had probably not been the best idea four days out from the final curtain. "Are you okay?"

"It's nothing." Astrid was relieved to see no evidence of any real trauma.

"Who got hurt?"

"Me, it's nothing." he showed Astrid an angry scratch on his wrist. It didn't look too bad, but it was bleeding, and Astrid agreed he was smart to address it.

"Ouch. I guess the holly bush likes the Old Bay, too."

"The holly bush is really sharp," Coty quipped. He walked into the bathroom and Astrid heard the door on the medicine cabinet creak open.

"Did the Sleeping Beauty get pricked?" Astrid asked.

"Thankfully, no." Coty stepped out of the bathroom with a box of Band-Aids. "She stayed on the sidewalk to heckle me."

"That sounds like Claire."

"She may have shot a video."

"Probably." Astrid grinned at him. She watched him fumble with the Band-Aid for a few moments before taking it out of his hand. "Let me?"

Coty looked relieved. Standing back, he allowed Astrid to dress the cut. "Thanks, Stinky," he said, and then looked stricken. "I'm sorry. That's just what Claire calls you."

"That's okay."

"You sure?" He dipped his floppy head. "I don't have any siblings. I guess sometimes I like to pretend you're my little sister, too."

Astrid was incredulous. "But I've been such a bitch."

"Oh, well, I knew you'd come around," he said, with the confidence of the leading man he was.

"How could you possibly know that?" Astrid was indignant. "In case you hadn't noticed, the handsome prince thing doesn't work on me."

"I read your blog," he said, laughing away her jibe. "And you—" he poked a finger at her as if accusing her of some heinous crime, "—are a total sweetie pants."

"Sweetie pants?" Astrid nearly choked.

"Yep," he said, with utter certainty. "The way you write about nature? It makes me want to go outside." He reached down to stroke Eartha's head. "Your blog is the reason I got a cat."

"Really?"

"Absolutely. It was the piece about animals lowering your anxiety level."

Astrid nodded, remembering the story well. A nursing home had started allowing comfort animals and the results had been measurable in vital statistics. "That's so cool."

"I bet lots of people adopted animals after that story," he said. "I hope so, anyway. It really worked for me."

"Eartha Kitty is good people," Astrid said, deflecting the praise. "You got lucky with that cat."

"Claire's really special too." Coty looked her in the eye. "She's the best thing that's ever happened to me."

"As long as you know that."

"I do," he smiled, then pointing at the ceiling, gave Astrid two thumbs up. "Sounds like you're starting something pretty special of your own."

"Oh my God. I can't believe you guys heard us."

"Believe it," he said, sounding exactly like Claire.

"Is this what having a big brother is like?"

"Yes," he said. "We also take out the garbage, pick you up at the airport and don't let anyone take your lunch money."

"I accept," Astrid said.

CHAPTER NINETEEN

Jenga

The final performance of *The Sleeping Beauty* was a triumph. Center stage at the John F. Kennedy Center, Claire Dibello finally had her moment. Inhabiting the role she was born to play, she lifted the audience filled with her friends and family with every leaping twirl. Coty was splendid as her persevering Prince Charming. Agile and elegant, he danced beautifully alongside her until their final happily-ever-after brought the audience to its feet.

Astrid was swept away by the artistry of their performances encapsulated in the fairy-tale love story. She was glad that she hadn't seen the show while still in preview. They now performed the ballet with the mixture of joy and precision that only came from the muscle memory of practice. It was hard to fathom, but when the show began, Claire and Astrid had still been living in Mount Pleasant. Astrid had just met Leigh, and Simone was only a fantasy. Had it really only been a year?

Presently, Simone was directing Astrid and two of the Long Island cousins to set up the food for the celebratory brunch.

Valerie and Adrienne had taken the train in yesterday from Manhattan and were sleeping on the giant futon in Katrina and Jerry's basement. The two extra upstairs bedrooms were taken by their parents and great Uncle Stevie, who'd surprised everyone by driving down from Queens in an ancient Lincoln Town Car.

Simone had put together the de facto staff an hour ago when the catering van had arrived early and Katrina and Jerry were out with a client. Commercial real estate sales stopped for no one, certainly not for two frazzled looking caterers who'd only been paid for a drop-and-go. Simone had saved the day. Pouring everyone a Bloody Mary from the premade pitchers ordered for the party, she'd turned it all into a giggle fest. What might have been a chore had been seamless fun and everything looked beautiful. There was only one thing missing.

"Where are the utensils? Has anyone seen the cutlery?" Simone asked the group at large. Hands on hips, she stood next to a row of silver chafing dishes on the highest tier of the deck. As teenagers this had been Astrid and Claire's favorite sunning perch, the place where they'd famously once turned their blond hair orange with a nefarious online product. Katrina had dragged Claire to a salon for immediate correction, while Astrid had refused to go, swum in a chlorine-contaminated creek and turned hers an even deeper shade. It had stayed that way until Halloween when she'd dyed it black to be Wednesday Adams.

"I was just wondering the same thing," Adrienne said, coming to stand next to Astrid. Though closer in age to Claire, Adrienne had always been Astrid's favorite cousin. She worked for a prestigious midtown publishing house editing the type of novels sold in airports. Astrid kept Adrienne on speed dial for grammar questions and matters of the heart though she hadn't confided in her about Leigh.

So far, Adrienne hadn't warmed to Simone. Astrid wondered if Adrienne thought they were moving too fast. At dinner last night they'd made jokes about moving in together but that was only because Astrid still hadn't found a place to live. Perhaps that's why she was being uncharacteristically frosty to Simone.

Astrid looked around for any items they might have missed. "Do you think the caterers forgot to bring the utensils?"

"It's possible." Simone nodded. "I catered a wedding one time and the chef completely forgot to make the salads." She threw her hands dramatically in the air. "He had no excuse, none." The brown eyes grew wide as if she was surprised by her own story.

"What happened?" asked Valerie. Adrienne's older sister was a mother of two and lived on the upper east side of Manhattan with her investment-banker husband. She'd had the nose job and looked vaguely like Winona Ryder

"No one noticed," Simone said, laughing. "People don't care so much about salads," she shrugged. "Forget the wine and you have a problem," she said, sipping her Bloody Mary.

"Forks are kind of necessary," Adrienne said.

"Oh, I agree." Simone nodded and Astrid felt bad for her. She was working so hard to make Adrienne like her, and for some reason her normally placid cousin had her claws out.

"I don't see cutlery listed." Adrienne scanned the caterers punch-list with her editor's eye. "Maybe it wasn't ordered?"

"Mom's going to be pissed," Astrid said.

"Could we use the stuff in your kitchen?" Adrienne suggested. "Not Aunt Katrina's good silver, obviously, but the everyday stuff?

"I was just wondering the same thing." Simone gave her a conspiring smile that Adrienne didn't return.

She shook her head. "It still won't be enough. Even if we don't differentiate between the dinner and the salad forks. Fifty people got invitations and I heard Aunt Katrina invite half the audience last night."

"The ballet was amazing." Valerie clasped her hands to her chest. "I was so proud of Claire. She's worked so hard coming back from all those injuries. To see her dancing the lead was so satisfying." She closed her eyes, remembering.

Adrienne nodded. "Claire does work hard. The summer she lived with us she got up at four every morning and went for a run before taking the train into the city for ballet classes. She made so much noise. I used to throw stuffed animals at her."

"Oh my God, those unicorns." Astrid laughed, remembering Adrienne's infamous collection. "How many did you have?"

"Twenty-seven," Valerie said, with sisterly disdain. "Adrienne thought if she just kept buying unicorns, she wouldn't have to tell Mom and Dad she was gay."

"It worked, didn't it?"

"I told them you were gay!"

"Yes, but what started the conversation?"

Valerie rolled her eyes. "The goddamn unicorns, fine. Can we get back to the forks? What about plastic? There's decent stuff out there."

"No," Simone said, emphatically. "No, forking plastic utensils."

Valerie and Astrid cracked up but Adrienne only nodded. "I actually feel the same," she said, as if surprised to agree with Simone on anything. *What the hell was going on?*

"There's a set of flatware somewhere in the basement with my storage." Astrid frowned, trying to picture which box she'd packed the stainless. "If I can find them."

"That might be enough." Simone was encouraging.

"I'll help you look," Adrienne offered quickly. "I need to charge my phone anyway."

"Great." Simone smiled at her as if she hadn't been throwing more shade on her than the giant sycamore that dominated the back yard. "Valerie and I will get Katrina's kitchen utensils and we'll be all set. Everything else is finished."

"And it looks great." Astrid kissed her cheek. "Thank you for making it beautiful."

"I'll meet you in the basement," Adrienne said loudly over her shoulder and Simone's eyes widened a fraction. It was her first acknowledgement of any weirdness but she didn't comment.

"And I'll start in the kitchen." Valerie disappeared leaving Astrid and Simone alone.

"I'm so happy for Claire." Simone smiled.

"Me too." Astrid twisted their fingers together. "I'm sorry Adrienne isn't being nice. I don't know what's the matter with her."

"Not everyone likes me." Simone shrugged.

Astrid frowned. Simone was hilarious and beautiful. Everywhere they went, people fell at her feet. Doormen and old ladies, little children and dogs all loved Simone on sight. Why would Adrienne, gay as a rainbow-colored pair of Converse high tops, be immune?

"I don't see how that's possible. Did you meet her in high school?"

Simone shook her head, and the curls bounced around her face. "No, I remember Claire lived with her cousins in New York after graduation. I tried out for the New York City ballet too, but didn't make it."

"Oh, I'm so sorry," Astrid's heart broke for the eighteen-year-old Simone. She was so poised and confident it was sometimes easy to forget she'd once had the same aspirations as Claire. "That must have been really hard."

"It was the end of my dream," Simone said, wistfully. "But it's okay, I'm really happy with my life, now. I love being a chef and I'm excited about the restaurant." She gave Astrid a beatific smile. "And I'm happy for Claire."

"Me too," Astrid said. She took the opportunity to plant a chaste kiss on her lips. "I love you."

"I love you, too."

"See you back here in a minute?"

"One forking minute," Simone joked, and sashayed into the kitchen.

Astrid descended to the lower tier of her parent's deck, twice as wide as the higher one. Here, Simone had set up the bar. Bottles of Champagne, chilling in stainless-steel tubs and the pre-sampled pitchers of Bloody Marys sat waiting for guests who, given the open-house nature of the event, might appear at any moment. The lower deck was called the launching pad because it was the best spot to shoot fireworks over the river on the Fourth of July or any other occasion Jerry thought warranted pyrotechnics. Last year, on Claire's birthday, Coty had brought a box of Roman candles from West Virginia, further endearing himself to the patriarch, and they'd lit up the September sky like Bastille Day on the Seine.

Astrid walked down to the yard and the large flagstone patio that backed up to the bank dropping down to the river. The views were better on the decks but here there was space to move. Katrina had insisted on a marquee for today's occasion. Astrid had not seen the point, as the forecast was for sun, but there was no arguing with the finished product. Circular, with a vaulted top and sides that had been gathered and drawn back like elegant curtains, the tent was gorgeous. It looked like it belonged in a sheik's caravan. The whole backyard looked beautiful. Everywhere Astrid looked was understated elegance. It was almost hard to believe this was the same patio Jerry iced down each winter and turned into a skating rink.

Because the house rested on the crest of a palisade, a large part of the basement wasn't subterranean. In proper realtor speak it was called an English basement, which Astrid found ironic as it meant the apartment got more sunshine not less. Astrid walked into the large room where Adrienne and Valerie were sleeping. Once the recreation room, then Jerry's workshop, the space had undergone more makeovers than Katrina. Astrid had even lived here briefly after college. Currently, it was serving as a home gym but a huge, ancient futon couch also made it purposeful as a fourth bedroom in a pinch. The storage area, where Astrid's belongings sat alongside the seasonal decorations, family ephemera and stuff on deck for Goodwill, was through a door to the left in the former laundry room. Jerry, who liked to keep up with market amenities, had moved the washer and dryer upstairs to the second floor years ago, freeing more storage space, but it was back at capacity. Astrid knew where her stuff was but she might need to play a little basement-Jenga to access it.

When Astrid entered the room, Adrienne was rummaging in a suitcase. Tall and blond, but with broader shoulders, Adrienne was sometimes mistaken as Astrid and Claire's third sister. Astrid had no difficulty talking to her like one.

"What's going on with you? Why don't you like Simone?"

"It's not that I don't like her," Adrienne said, and Astrid appreciated her lack of pretense. At least she wasn't pretending there wasn't a problem.

"What is it then? Why are you being crabby?"

"I don't trust her," Adrienne replied and somehow managed to look angry and empathic at the same time.

"Why not?" Astrid asked. "I know our relationship is moving fast, but Simone makes me so happy. I've never felt this way before." She put a hand over her heart.

"I can see that," Adrienne said, and her expression softened. "I want you to be happy, I do. I just worry you may be a little vulnerable right now." She tapped the end of her nose.

"So, this is about my nose?"

"In a way."

"Well, I'm okay about that," Astrid said. She wondered if it was Adrienne who might have a problem with the surgery. She now had the distinction of being the sole Dibello granddaughter remaining in the *Cosa Nose-tra*. "Being with Simone is actually easier than being with most people because she doesn't give me weird looks. I barely knew her when I was younger. She was Claire's friend."

Adrienne sighed. "Yes, I know that."

"What do you know?" Astrid pushed her. "Why are you being so cryptic?'

"I'm pretty sure Simone was in love with Claire," Adrienne blurted, and then held out her hands helplessly. "I don't think it was reciprocated. I *know* it wasn't reciprocated, but your girlfriend used to be in love with your sister."

Astrid felt a chill run down her spine and then questions started coming out of her mouth as fast as they entered her mind. "What are you talking about? How do you know this? Who told you?" And finally, "Did Claire know?"

"Claire knew." Adrienne sat down heavily on the futon. "She even showed me some of Simone's letters."

"There were letters?" Astrid felt like she watching a lost episode of a favorite TV show where the heroine gets a pie in her face. "When was this?"

"The summer after high school, when Claire lived with us in New York. She got letters every week from Simone."

Astrid didn't want to believe it. "That's not so shocking. They were good friends."

"These were not friend letters," Adrienne insisted.

"You said Claire showed them to you. Did you ever read them?"

"No, not really."

"Then how do you know they were love letters?" Astrid said and tried to block out the image of Simone embracing Claire, the greeting she'd used, *mi amore*.

"The stationary was pink and smelled like perfume."

"Is that all?" Astrid said, with more confidence than she felt. "I'm not sure if you've noticed but Simone is a bit of a femme."

"Okay, Claire told me." Adrienne laid down the last card. "She wanted to know the best way to let down a lesbian with a straight-girl crush. She figured I might have insight."

"What did you tell her?"

"I told her to freeze her out, stop writing."

"You did not."

"Nothing sends a message better than no contact. It's a surefire way to end things for a straight girl. Messages can't be misconstrued if there are no messages."

"So, Claire just stopped writing her? But that's so mean." For the second time in an hour, Astrid's heart went out to teenaged Simone.

"They're still friends. So, it came out okay."

"So, then why don't you trust Simone now?" Astrid had to ask the question. She thought she knew what Adrienne would say but she wanted to hear the words out loud.

"Um, well," Adrienne stammered, clearly uncomfortable. "It's just you look an awful lot like her now. Claire, I mean."

"And you think that's why Simone's into me. Because I look like my sister."

"The thought has crossed my mind," Adrienne said, and then doubled back. "Maybe I'm just bugging out about the nose job. I mean, you look really different, so much like Claire. I'm sorry. I should have kept my mouth shut."

"Like that was going to happen." Astrid kicked her foot. "I thought you were going to punch Simone on the patio."

"I feel protective of you. I don't want to see you get hurt."

"I appreciate that." Astrid didn't know what to make of the new intelligence but she appreciated the heads up. Adrienne only wanted what was best for her. Also, it made no sense to kill the messenger when there was still the potential for more information. "It all happened a long time ago," she feigned nonchalance. "Claire was stunning at eighteen. Of course Simone fell in love with her."

"I shouldn't have said anything."

"I asked you, remember?"

"Because I was acting like a bitch."

"Yes, you were. Can you stop that now, please?"

CHAPTER TWENTY

Astrid Inside/Out

Astrid made it halfway through brunch before doubt began to take over. Simone had once been in love with Claire. The information filtered into her consciousness like a tiny drip of water on a laptop. Slowly it corrupted her internal systems. In the abstract, Simone's past feelings for Claire should have no bearing on what was happening now between Simone and her. Their love, though precariously new, was between two adult women. It was reciprocal and it was physical, insanely, deliciously physical. Simone had merely written Claire letters, dry, flat things that could blow away in the wind. According to Adrienne, the sentiments had been unrequited and Simone had likely had her heart broken. It had happened a decade ago and had nothing to do with Astrid. But what should be nothing was starting to feel like everything.

Looking down from the higher deck, Astrid watched Simone charm Uncle Stevie on the lower patio and wondered what was real. The vivacious woman who proclaimed to love her had half the brunch guests falling at her feet. During the toasts, she'd told a story Astrid had never heard before about attempting to corrupt Claire with cigarettes. She'd not succeeded and Claire had tricked her into attending a lecture on lung cancer at Georgetown hospital. She'd had everyone at the brunch laughing. The anecdote, though hilarious, had only further eroded Astrid's confidence. If she'd never heard a simple story before, what else didn't she know?

"Your new girlfriend is certainly the life of the party," a voice said behind her.

Astrid glanced over her shoulder and saw Tara come out of the kitchen. Beautifully dressed in a fitted A-line skirt and embroidered silk blouse, she was a walking billboard for her exclusive boutique. "Are you having fun watching her little show? I'd forgotten how entertaining she can be."

"Hi, Tara." Astrid forced a smile. *Great.* Last night, the fanfare of the ballet had allowed her to avoid a confrontation about Simone but several withering looks had put Astrid on notice. It would only be a matter of time and opportunity before Holy Tara demanded her due. And here she was.

"Why didn't you tell me you'd been seeing Simone?"

Astrid didn't have to look up to know the blue eyes were flashing. "I'm sorry about that. Did you get the wine off the couch?"

Tara groaned. "The couch and my clothes are fine, thank God, but Noodle still has a few bad spots."

"I stained Noodle?" Astrid was horrified to know she'd compromised the sweet little dog but filed away the story idea for a possible blog post.

"Yes." Tara pursed her lips and Astrid caught a glimpse of what she might look like in ten years. "I didn't know she'd been splashed until the next day. The stains had time to set overnight. I'll get it out or the groomer will."

"I've no doubt," Astrid said, "I'm really sorry that happened."

"There's no point crying over spilled Cab." Tara glared at her. "I want to know why you didn't tell me you were seeing Simone." Astrid looked down to the patio where Simone was giggling with Coty and Claire. "According to Miles, you're already at U-Haul status."

Astrid smiled despite the circumstances. "That was Simone being silly. Like you said, she's the life of the party."

"Why didn't you say anything the other night?"

"Because I wasn't sure what was going on with us yet," Astrid said honestly and then because Tara looked so upset, she gave her a little more. "I knew I had feelings for her but we'd had a misunderstanding and I was a little confused."

Tara's eyes gleamed at the mention of a fight. "What happened, did she lie to you?"

"No. What? That's none of your business." Astrid reacted defensively. Revisiting the lie of omission regarding the restaurant ownership would only cast a further pall on Astrid's drastically dimming mood.

"She did. She lied to you. I can tell."

"I didn't want to talk to you about Simone because I know you'd never been a big fan."

"What does that mean?"

"You were jealous." Astrid pushed back, refusing to be bullied. "Simone and Claire's friendship revolved around ballet and you weren't a part of that. It bugged you."

"I was never jealous of ballet," Tara spat. "Simone was in love with Claire. She was obsessed with her. I was being protective of my friend. Just like I'm trying to protect you now."

"Thank you," Astrid said, and struggled to maintain her composure. "But I don't need your protection."

"Just make sure she likes you for yourself," Tara said. Tapping the end of her nose she drove the point of her dagger home.

"Enjoying yourselves, girls?" Katrina walked out of the kitchen, saving Astrid the trouble of forming a response. This was a good thing for Tara because Astrid's impulse was to toss her over the deck. She took the opportunity to make her escape instead.

"Yes, I was just telling Tara that I need to mix more drinks." She pointed to the nearly empty pitchers of Bloody Marys on the tier below.

"Thanks so much, sweetie." Katrina gave Astrid a gentle smile. "See you down there in a minute? I'd like to take some family pictures, if that's okay."

"Sure, Mom," Astrid said, and fled. She would have agreed to naked karaoke to get away from the conversation with Tara. She felt the blue eyes on her back but didn't turn around for fear of giving herself away. Tara's last blow had landed. Where Adrienne had only hinted at the truth, Tara had spoken the words out loud. They both thought Simone only liked Astrid because she looked like Claire.

Bypassing the bar level, Astrid walked straight down to the patio and across the backyard to the path leading to the steep hill and the river. If anyone saw her go, they didn't call out to her. Fortunately, Jerry maintained the path all year round so Astrid didn't have to fight briars or poison ivy that flanked her on either side of the trail. But the hill was steep, and her sandals more fashion than function, so she slipped a few times and cut her hand on the descent.

She jogged down the familiar slope to Lock 6 of the C&O Canal. A short path through the woods and she'd found the emergency canoe Bob kept hidden between some fallen trees and pushed it out on the riverbank. There was a paddle tucked inside, and Astrid was careful launching the boat into the channel across from the island.

Once on the other side, she dragged the canoe up the beach, and into the cover of the trees. Leaving the paddle inside the boat, she went to find Bob.

Twenty minutes later, she was dangling over the Potomac in her familiar hammock, Django tucked safely under her arm. She breathed deeply, waited to feel better and then waited some more. Leaving the party had definitely been the right move. Astrid hadn't been able to think properly with all the new information swirling around in her head. The double whammy of Adrienne's well-meaning speech and Tara's diatribe had knocked her flat. Laying out the facts in her mind as if she was researching an article, Astrid tried to make sense of it all.

From her own experience, Astrid knew high school crushes could be very intense and completely one-sided. She didn't love the idea that Simone once might have had feelings for Claire, but she wished Simone had told her herself. How was

Astrid supposed to move past this obstacle if she didn't know it existed? She wanted so much to believe what was happening between her and Simone was real. But how could she be certain of anything when she never got the whole truth? If this was going to be problem moving forward, maybe she and Simone shouldn't be moving forward at all.

Django squeaked as if he'd heard Astrid's thoughts. Then he struggled to free himself from the crook of her arm.

"Where you going, buddy? Hold on." Astrid sat up, and the cat leapt from the hammock into the linden tree. "You'd rather be up there?"

"He's making room for me."

"What are you doing here?" Turning her head, Astrid looked down into the warm brown eyes of the woman she loved.

"Isn't this the afterparty?" Simone joked, and looked around at the treehouse.

"How did you find me? No one knows about this place." Astrid sat up fully in the hammock and kicked a leg out to balance on a branch.

"Claire told me." Simone started to climb the tree. The closer she got the sillier Astrid began to feel for running away.

"Why did you leave?" The brown eyes were now brimming with concern. "Is everything okay?" She perched on the branch just below Astrid looking up through the branches. "Is that a hammock?"

"Come up here and I'll show you," Astrid said, and felt her arms start to ache in anticipation of holding her. Why had she run away without first having a conversation?

Simone easily made the climb into the hammock. The loose, linen jumpsuit that hung so elegantly on her frame was excellent tree climbing clothes. When Astrid lay back down, Simone was now nestled by her side. The displaced Django kept a watchful eye from the branch above.

"I need you to tell me what's going on." Simone slid an arm beneath Astrid and pulled her in closer. "But first, I need you to tell me that this cat will not eat me."

Astrid snorted. "Django's very friendly."

"He belongs to your friend?"

"They belong to each other."

Simone seemed to like the answer. She was quiet for a moment and Astrid allowed herself to pretend that the party conversations had never happened, that they'd just woken up that morning and gone for a paddle.

"What did Adrienne tell you?"

But she had to face it. "She told me about pink, perfumed letters," Astrid whispered. Tears choked her throat, thickening her voice. "She said you might have been in love with Claire. It's okay, though. It was a long time ago. I'm just still processing it, that's why I needed to get away."

"I should have told you."

Astrid didn't argue. "Yeah, that would have been better." She sniffed. "Tell me now?"

"Nothing ever happened between us," Simone started and Astrid felt instant relief. "Claire didn't even know I had a crush on her until after I'd gone back to Italy."

"Tara seemed to know."

"Tara is a jealous bitch. I saw her talking to you on the upper deck. What did she say?" Simone sat up abruptly in the hammock and almost knocked them out of the tree.

"Watch out!" Astrid grabbed a branch to steady them. "I don't want us to fall."

"I fell for you a long time ago," Simone said, without a hint of a joke. She climbed carefully out of the hammock and braced her body upright against the tree. "Now, please, tell me what Tara said."

Astrid missed her presence but knew it was safer to have the conversation even keel. They needed to talk this out. "She said you were obsessed with Claire."

"Tara is an asshole bitch."

"Is it true?"

"No. I did have a crush on your sister," she conceded, blushing at the admission. "I haven't told you about it because you're so sensitive about the resemblance. I didn't want you to get the wrong idea."

"What idea is that?" Astrid pushed her. Simone had gone right to the heart of the affair. Now open on the table, it was time for resuscitation or autopsy.

"The idea that I'm only attracted to you because you look like Claire? I hate that you think that."

"Don't you?"

Simone's eyes flashed. "Lie down."

"What?"

"Lie down in the hammock," she commanded. "I'm going to tell the writer a story."

Astrid did as she was bid. She was so far gone on this woman. She hoped it was possible to navigate the road in front of them because the return trip to normal would be hell. Better to report out the story before booking her solo ticket home.

"I was never really in love with your sister," Simone started. "I was in love with ballet. My whole life I dreamed of being the perfect ballerina. It was a way to prove I was someone that didn't involve my family's money. When I didn't get into the New York Company I was crushed. We were also moving home after eight years in this country so I was dealing with that loss, too. It all got mixed up in my head. Claire was so nice. She let me down gently and wrote me a letter to explain to me what I was feeling."

"She wrote you back?"

"Yes."

"I didn't know that." Why was Astrid surprised? The reason there were no lingering hurt feelings between the friends was because tidy Claire had cleared things up a decade ago. "Adrienne told me she'd advised Claire to stonewall you."

"Claire didn't listen to her." Simone was indignant. "She was very kind to me. Because of her letter I was able to move on. That's why we are still friends today. Your sister is a very brave person and a good friend."

"She is," Astrid agreed. "And beautiful too."

"Claire is stunning."

"And I look just like her. The first time you saw me, you thought I was her. There is no getting away from that. I don't know how I'll ever be able to trust that you love me just for me. Part of me will always wonder that I'm the consolation prize."

"Tell me where this happened," Simone demanded.

Astrid was incredulous. "Are you denying that you mistook me for my sister?"

"I'm not debating if it happened. I'm asking you where it happened." The brown eyes flashed.

"You know where it happened." Astrid was nearly shouting now. Django chirped angrily but ran for cover. "It happened right here, on this beach."

"And why was I here?" Simone demanded, as if the answer could possibly explain the reason why it was okay for her think Astrid was her sister.

Astrid thought back to the sultry day and could only remember Simone's yellow sports bra and eating pawpaws from her fingers. That was it. Simone had been there to collect fruit for a cake.

"Pawpaws," Astrid said. "What's that got to do with anything?"

"I read your blog," Simone said, simply.

"I know you do." Astrid was confused. Simone was not shy about how much she enjoyed Astrid's writing and had even contributed bon mots on occasion.

"No, I mean, I always read it. I'm an Outsider. I was actually the first one."

Astrid was stunned. "How is that even possible? I don't understand."

Simone looked impatient. She let out a dramatic sigh. "How long have you been blogging?"

Astrid didn't have to think to know the answer. It was part of the bio that appeared on her website. *Outside Astrid* had started her next to last year of high school, the same year Claire had left to join the New York City Ballet. To combat her loneliness, Astrid had poured herself into the new hobby like the job it eventually became.

"In high school, when Claire went to dance in New York. I was missing her pretty bad. Writing helped. I guess that's the same time you were writing to her," she said, and something shifted into place.

"And maybe stalking her family a little bit." Simone smiled.

"You've really been reading *Outside Astrid* since high school?" The minute the words were out of her mouth Astrid knew they were correct. It explained so much. Both flattered and flabbergasted, it was moments before she could speak. "Why didn't you tell me?"

"I wanted to, believe me," Simone said. "But after our first misunderstanding over things I hadn't told you, I was afraid you might shut me out again. I didn't want to chance it when things were going so well." She looked pointedly around the tree house. "You have a habit of running away."

"I'm sorry," Astrid said. She rubbed her nose. "I've watched people respond to Claire's beauty all my life. When they started giving me the same treatment after the nose job it made me question what was real. I can't believe you've been reading me since high school."

Simone beamed and the light began to dance in her eyes. "Haven't you noticed that I always copy your gear choices?"

"We do have a lot of the same stuff. I thought it was a coincidence."

"I buy all the things on your dream gear list. I read your product tests before I buy anything. My friends do, too."

"You tell your friends about me?"

"Sure."

Astrid thought of Simone's car and kayak and knew what she was saying was true. Why hadn't she figured it out earlier? "That's really cool, I had no idea."

"It was the reason I was on the climb with Hannah."

"Because I blogged about their trip?" Astrid said, remembering the piece well.

"Yes. My family has a house in the Dolomites, so I went climbing that weekend and Hannah picked me up in a bar."

"That's my fault?" Astrid was smiling now, too. She longed for Simone to climb back into the hammock but there seemed to be something else on her mind.

"No. What's your fault is making assumptions about what I find attractive."

"But you were in love with Claire."

"Not because of her pretty American face." Simone grew agitated. "I was drawn to Claire for her courage and her kindness."

"Really?"

"Yes. Your American aesthetic is so boring, everyone has to look the same. Answer a question for me? Do you think I prefer your new nose or the old one?"

"The new one," Astrid answered immediately and Simone shook her head.

"Wrong. I prefer the old nose."

"What? You do?" Astrid didn't believe her.

"If was allowed to choose, I'd pick the nose with the most character. Just like I've chosen the woman with the most character. Plus, I am Italian and like the Roman nose better. But it doesn't matter because I love you, Astrid, inside and out. Anyone who thinks of you as a consolation prize is not thinking at all."

"Will you please get back in the hammock?"

"Promise to never run away again."

"I promise."

Simone settled in once more against Astrid's side. "Are you okay?" she asked, kissing her lips tenderly.

"I am now," Astrid said, and smiled into her mouth as fireworks exploded somewhere behind them. Claire's celebration event might be coming to a close. This one was just beginning.

EPILOGUE

An adolescent, orange tabby skittered around the corner, chasing a lacrosse ball from the hallway into the kitchen. A gift from Bob, who'd recycled it from the river, the ball was the cat's current nemesis and not to be trusted unsupervised.

"Get that ball, Pawpy, kill it," Astrid encouraged while Simone chopped onions next to the sink. Holding a slice of bread between her teeth, she wasn't able to comment but opinion brimmed in her eyes.

"Thanks for doing all this. I really appreciate it." Astrid gestured to the fresh seafood Simone had brought home from the wharf and then leaned in to nibble the bread in her mouth.

"Hmmmm," Simone hummed and tilted back her head to give Astrid better access. It was Sunday afternoon, her one day off from the restaurant, and she was making paella for Astrid's family.

"We could have gone out somewhere, you know?"

"Out?" Simone spit the bread dramatically onto the counter and pointed the knife playfully at Astrid. "You want to take your parents out to eat somewhere else besides my kitchen? Where? Tell me, please. Where are we going to take them?"

Astrid laughed. "You're so cute when you're pretending to be a homicidal maniac."

Simone shrugged. "You only think I'm kidding. Take your family to another restaurant and see what happens."

"I wouldn't dare," Astrid said. She picked up the discarded piece of bread and took a thoughtful bite. "This really tastes like onion."

"It's my favorite trick I learned in culinary school." Simone smiled. "The bread keeps the fumes out of your eyes and then you get to eat it."

"Genius," Astrid agreed and inhaled deeply. The apple pies Simone had made earlier in the day were cooling on the counter. They would eat one for dessert and the other would go home with Jerry and Katrina who'd returned the day before from a month-long cruise to Alaska. They'd promised to bring Astrid and Simone Russian vodka and stories of dog-sledding. Coty and Claire were bringing flowers and wine. After nearly a year, they all knew better than to bring food when Simone was cooking. It just worked better this way as Simone felt the same way about potlucks as she did about buffets. When she invited you to dinner, it was like an artist inviting you to a show. It was not expected you bring your own canvases.

"Can I do anything to help?" Astrid looked around the spacious kitchen but saw no apparent chore.

As always, Simone had everything under control. She was undoubtably more at ease in Bob's Georgetown kitchen than Astrid who, after nearly a year in residence, was still getting her bearings. She still couldn't believe she lived here. It was all due to Simone, whose first visit on Snake Island had not been her last. Finding common ground with Bob through indigenous food, they'd become true friends. When Simone mentioned Astrid needed a place to live, he'd offered the extra bedroom in his Georgetown apartment calculating her rent against the hours she'd spent helping him clear trash on the river. The deal was too good to pass up. Bob's parents, who owned the building and ran their map shop at street level, were thrilled to have someone in the space. After sampling Simone's pesto, they were much less obvious about showing their disappointment that Astrid wasn't in a May-December relationship with their son.

This was fortunate, as Astrid's devotion to Simone had only grown with time. They weren't officially living together yet but spent every night wrapped around each other like ribbons on a Maypole. Last month they'd adopted a cat. Pawpaw, as he was known on his vet registration, was also sometimes called Pawpy or Peanut or Sir Edmund J. Pawsifer, depending on who was talking. Not quite a diplo-cat, he was a lover nevertheless and traveled back and forth from Simone's Dupont Circle apartment to Bob's in a Versace pet carrier. To everyone's delight Pawpaw had become running buddies with Eartha Kitty who visited through the trap door via a retractable ladder Coty had purchased to facilitate the relationship.

"Rub my neck?" Simone asked sweetly.

"Sure." Astrid nodded. She was much more confident in her command of Simone's body than of Bob's kitchen. Sliding her hands up her back she stopped at the column of her neck and pushed her thumbs into the flesh.

"Don't be gentle," Simone commanded and leaned into Astrid's touch.

"I've got you." Manipulating the tendons with her fingertips, Astrid sought to ease the tension of the past week. Under Simone's guidance, unUsual DC had become a darling of the slow food world. She thrived in the dual role of owner and chef, but it was grueling work. The menu depended on whatever was local and in season, necessitating sunrise trips to the market each morning. Astrid likened Simone's efforts to a huntress and sometimes called her Diana after the Roman goddess.

"That feels amazing," Simone said, and Astrid felt her body begin to relax.

Long, glowing reviews had bred long waiting lists for reservations. Simone didn't like this, so added menu service at the bar to accommodate walk-ins. Locals had to show a driver's license to get a seat. The idea was as successful as the restaurant. When someone else in the Outsiders had learned of Astrid's connection, the group began having monthly dinners there. So far, Astrid had declined their invitation to speak but had joined them several times and now looked forward to the get-togethers. Simone loved being part of the group and gave them free appetizers and wine at cost.

Questions of whether Simone's attraction to Astrid was tied to Simone's past attraction to Claire had been put to rest. Her claim that she'd been reading Astrid for ten years was not an exaggeration, and proven time and again when she revealed random knowledge from past blogs.

Astrid ached to slide her hands around to the front of Simone's body and initiate more intimate caresses but there wasn't time. Her family was due any minute and they no longer tolerated public displays of affection. After granting Astrid and Simone a six-month grace period when they literally couldn't keep their hands off each other, Jerry had politely taken Astrid aside and told her to cool it. Astrid couldn't imagine the amount of embarrassment her father had had to overcome to initiate the conversation. She also couldn't imagine having it again.

She kissed Simone's neck. "Promise me we can finish this later."

"I promise." Simone reached her hand back and grabbed Astrid's fingers. Pulling it over her shoulder she laid it on her heart. "I love you."

"I love you, too."

Simone turned in her arms and pressed their lips together in a languid kiss. "And I love the word later."

"You do?"

"Think about it." Simone thumped her skull in the now familiar joke. "It has lay, right there as the first syllable."

"Oh, right. Lay-ter, excellent word," Astrid agreed.

She'd never been so happy and it was all due to the woman in her arms. The moment she'd seen her on the back porch, more than a decade ago, her entire world had changed.

Now Simone changed her every waking moment. Astrid hadn't been aware of how much she was missing before she'd come into her life. Now, she couldn't imagine life without her. Fortunately, she didn't have to.

Bella Books, Inc.

Women. Books. Even Better Together.

P.O. Box 10543
Tallahassee, FL 32302

Phone: 800-729-4992
www.bellabooks.com